REDIRECT

J. B. MILLHOLLIN

Copyright © 2018 J. B. Millhollin
All rights reserved
First Edition

Fulton Books, Inc.
Meadville, PA

First originally published by Fulton Books 2018

ISBN 978-1-63338-795-9 (Paperback)
ISBN 978-1-63338-796-6 (Digital)

Printed in the United States of America

PROLOGUE

July 14, 2006
Nashville, Tennessee

He had only the use of the light from a small voltage desk lamp to complete the task for which he was present. But now, as he took a moment to scrutinize the room, he noticed a sliver of white originating from a streetlight. It entered the room through a small gap between two horizontal slats in the window blinds where they had failed to completely close. That was definitely something he should have noticed. His penchant for detail had always been one of his best qualities. Next time, he would be more careful. Next time, he would check the blinds, if there were any, making certain they performed as they were supposed to when closed—keeping secret that which occurred behind them.

It was 3:15 a.m.—time to leave. It was time to wipe everything clean, put his clothes on, and get out.

But he hesitated—it was all so perfect. The scene played out exactly as he had envisioned. Months of planning had resulted in absolute perfection.

He sat in the middle of her bed, naked, cross-legged, watching her sleep. Well, she wasn't really sleeping, although looking at her from the breasts up, you could never tell. Her eyes were shut, and she had that peaceful look on her face most people normally did while they slept. For all intents and purposes, again, at least from her breasts up, she appeared to be sleeping. But the wound in her stomach, caused by his knife, and the stream of blood below the wound could draw one to the conclusion that a normal usage of the term "sleeping" would have been inappropriate concerning her current condition.

He had played it smart from the beginning. He cracked a smile remembering the care he took to make sure they were seen together by a minimum number of people while he courted her. He had told her to tell no one they were an "item" because his family had other ideas for their wealthy son, and she wasn't part of the overall plan.

How simple it was to feed her that line—how quickly she swallowed it hook, line and sinker. It *could* have been true. He made it so believable anyone would have accepted it. After all, that was the business of which he would shorty be involved—lying for a living— he *better* be good at it.

Investigating her—where she went, who she went there with, what time her classes commenced—was easy. She suspected nothing. When he met her, it was always at a different location, away from the lights of Broadway Street in downtown Nashville. He didn't want people remembering them as a couple because they had seen them together so many times.

When it became apparent sex with her was in their immediate future, he staked out her house, many nights, many days. He needed to determine whether there was a chance of anyone seeing him enter her house, and if there was, what options might be available to avoid that particular problem.

He had finally concluded the best way to circumvent detection when arriving and departing from her home for the last time was to have her take him there in her car. It would then, once finished, be an easy walk to his apartment. They would need to arrive at her house on a weeknight, sometime after 11:00 p.m. Her neighborhood was significantly overloaded with early sleepers. There was never a light burning in any house on the block after 10:00 p.m.

So tonight, after telling her his car was in the shop for repairs, she picked him up, and they went to a small but quiet bar in Bellevue, a suburb of Nashville. A couple of hours later, she agreed it was time to consummate their relationship. He suggested they use her home for that purpose. She asked about a motel, but he told her he would prefer the privacy of her home, to which she ultimately agreed. He smiled as he remembered observing the various houses throughout the neighborhood while she drove in her driveway—not a light on anywhere.

The sex while she was alive was good, but the sex after he had murdered her was *incredible*. It was easy for him to become aroused—not based on being in bed, naked with her while she was still breathing—but based on what he knew would follow.

What had they called his "problem"? He didn't view it as a problem, but there had been those that had. He remembered the appropriate term was necrophilia. That's what the doctors said he had. He made the mistake of showing an interest in the dead. Once his parents figured it out, he had been seen by many doctors while in high school while his parents determined whether or not his "disease" was curable.

He, however, had concluded it wasn't a "condition." He figured it was just normal for some people to find that a lack of rejection, a lack of resistance, which he found in anything dead, was preferable to the chaos he endured with the living. He worshipped the control.

Now, before him, he found a perfect example of nonresistance, of a lack of rejection—so peaceful, so quiet, no mistakes, no back talk, nothing but peace.

He hated to leave. This was his shrine. He wouldn't be in this position again for a while—certainly not until the craziness surrounding her murder had died down.

As he thought about the police investigation, he remembered early tomorrow morning he would once again need to discuss his alibi with his friend. He would tell the police, if they asked, that they were both together well into the early morning hours. It was going to cost plenty to convince this friend to be his alibi. But he had the money, at least his family did, and they provided him with it on a regular basis.

Money took the place of the family having to deal with him. He had that figured out long ago. Once the payment was made, he would wait until the investigation died down and then bury his friend, along with the alibi he had provided, someplace where the body would never be found. There was no logical reason to allow that loose end to hang around for the rest of his life.

It was time to move on. He had no idea when he would once again have this opportunity. It was imperative he remain as detailed with his next opportunity, whenever it occurred, as he had been with this one.

He stood and picked her up off the bed, sitting her in a chair. He then carefully reinserted the knife, which he had withdrawn while having sex, in precisely the same location where he had stabbed her. It was necessary it be reintroduced into her body at the precise location the knife was located when she died. He then positioned her head to make sure she was looking directly at the knife. He opened her eyes. He took both of her hands and locked them around the handle of the knife, as if she were committing suicide—as if she, like him, had basically just had enough of all this life had to offer. Once he finished staging her, he backed away and observed, in the partial darkness, the scene he had created. Complete perfection.

He dressed and then took the small cloth he had brought for a singular purpose and rubbed it over everything he had touched. Once finished, he picked up a small baggy containing the condoms he had used and put them in his jacket pocket.

He then walked through the front door and into the clean, crisp air of an early summer morning. It smelled fresh, the beginning of a new day—a perfect ending to a perfect evening. He would need to do this again. It was everything he had hoped it would be, *and just a little more*.

1

Outskirts of Nashville, Tennessee
September 20, 2016

He lay in the grass, actually the weeds, waiting for something, anything, to happen. Barrett Armstrong, all six feet, two inches of his muscular frame, had been in these very weeds since 4:00 a.m. Good thing it was early fall, and not midwinter. It was chilly enough lying here as it was, let alone dealing with the cold at that time of year. Midwinter would have been a deal breaker. They would have needed to figure their issues out some other way.

He remembered their initial contact. Mrs. Rose had walked in his office door for the first time, about three months ago. She was concerned her husband was screwing around on her. They had been married less than a year, but she just had a feeling. Didn't matter to Barrett whether it was "just a feeling" or she knew it for a fact. The fee was the same, and she was willing to pay whatever he asked.

The reason he remembered the day was because it was also the ninth anniversary of the opening of his first and only private investigator's office. She came in late in the afternoon, and he had to finally tell her he needed to leave—that he had a scheduled event to attend. Even though that was just the first time he met her, he immediately understood why a man who might be with her on a regular basis might actually want to leave her—to get away from her and seek other company. She said more words in the hour he had been with her than were in any standard dictionary now in print. He could only get a word in by literally stopping her, which he didn't hesitate to do as the conversation wore on.

Barrett had a solution to end her incessant chatter, but there was no solution for not getting paid. He finally stopped her in mid-sentence to discuss his fee before subjecting himself, once again, to the constant flow of crap that continued to spew from her mouth. In the end, money talked, and he took her on. Now he realized he had made a serious mistake, as the bug bites started to itch. He could feel them crawling up his legs. He would beat the shit out of them as they did, but he also had to be careful—he was only about one hundred yards from the Rose home and he couldn't take a chance of being detected.

She had told him where they lived and how to get there without going up their lane—how he could walk across a pasture and reach the point he needed to reach in order to watch what went on after she left. Of course, the goddamn route he had to walk took him through two gullies and over five barbed wire fences, all of which he had to navigate while it was still dark and while using a minimum of light from a small flashlight—again, he couldn't take a chance of being noticed. She told him how to get there right before she told him how good-looking he was, how muscular he was, how she loved his curly black hair, how blue his eyes were. He chased her from the office right after she paid him his retainer. As he later reviewed his conversation with her, especially that portion of the conversation concerning his physical attributes, he actually wondered who was screwing around on whom.

She told her husband she had a business meeting in Chicago that would last the next couple of days. In fact, she was staying in a small hotel near the outskirts of Nashville. She figured if her husband was doing what she thought he was doing, he wouldn't miss one minute being with the "bitch" the entire couple of days she said she would be gone.

So here he lay, in the grass, up to his ass in bugs, waiting for something to happen. He just hoped it happened soon. He wasn't sure how much more of these bugs he could take—and, of course, there was also the obvious possibility of snakes.

He had been there almost four hours and had seen nothing. He wanted to get up and run back the way he came but...

A car had just driven down the long lane leading up to their ten-million-dollar home tucked near the back of an acreage. It sure as hell wasn't the car his client had driven when she met with him. Mrs. Rose had shown him a picture of the woman she was concerned about, and as whoever it was snaked those long legs out of the car door, it was either the woman in the picture or her identical twin. He watched as Mr. Rose opened the door. He greeted her with an embrace and a kiss. They both walked inside, and as they did, he watched as Mr. Rose grabbed her ass, and she laughed. This was definitely the woman Mrs. Rose expected to show up, and she wasn't there to bake him some cookies.

He pulled out his cell and punched in her number.

"Mrs. Rose, she just showed up. You were right. I'm sorry, but you were right. Whatta you want me to do?" A few hours later, he waited in a small bar near downtown Nashville for the woman he had been dating for the last six months. Janet Thompson had been an every-weekend squeeze longer than many marriages, although he wasn't sure where it was all going.

He liked her—no, he *cared* for her, but it certainly wasn't to the point where they were making plans for the future. She had raised the question once or twice, but he had always sidestepped it, and they had moved on to other more important issues—at least issues that were more important to him.

Janet had surprised him when she left a message about meeting here tonight. They saw little of each other during the week—the nature of his job precluded that from happening with very few exceptions.

He stood, took her hand, and kissed her once she arrived at the table.

"You want something to drink?"

"No."

He watched her, trying to read what appeared to be an unusually unhappy demeanor, but she said nothing.

"Okay, you called this meeting, whatta we doing? What's going on?"

He reached across the table to take her hand—she pulled away. He said nothing. Finally, she broke their mutual silence. "Are we seeing each other exclusively or not? Where's this all headed?"

"Yes, I'm not seeing anyone else. And I guess I still don't know where this is all headed. Why? What's going on?"

"Goddamn it, be honest with me. Is this headed somewhere or are we just screwing each other for fun?"

"Well…"

"Don't get funny with me, Barrett. This is not the time, not the time at all."

"Well, I guess we're seeing each other exclusively."

"That's exactly what I thought until one of my friends told me she saw you with someone else downtown the other night."

He looked at her a minute, without saying a word. Finally, he said, "Damn, I knew we should have gone somewhere other than downtown. It was just that one time. I've not been with anyone else other than her, and that night it was only… for… business."

She stood. "You're really a bad liar, Barrett. You know, I've felt from day one this was going nowhere—that you had a small problem with commitment. I'm done. I got better things to do than waste my time with someone who isn't nearly as committed to me as I am to him."

"It was *once*. And it went nowhere. I'm here, I'm with you. What more do you want?"

"I want one hell of a lot more from you than you're ever willing to give me."

She turned and walked out the door, leaving him alone, thinking how quickly the conversation had all gone bad. Not the first relationship that went to hell, and probably not the last. He signaled the bartender to bring him another.

So that's how his day would end. Bit to living hell by the bugs while he lay in the weeds and losing his girl because of one insignificant fling. Tomorrow would be a better day, for sure.

As he took a drink, he thought about tomorrow. Then he reconsidered his assessment. His first appointment in the morning was with Mrs. Rose. He needed to get out of this rut. Maybe another beer or two would do it. He ordered another, although far from finishing the one he had just ordered. All in all, one hell of a day and certainly one he would just as soon forget.

2

C harles Whitmore, assistant district attorney for Davidson County, had never been in a situation like this before. He had been with the district attorney's office for almost ten years, but this had never happened. From the time he took a position with them, he had always had competent secretaries, well trained and knowledgeable in the legal field. But yesterday, that had all changed.

He had no one now, absolutely no one. His secretary had walked out without giving notice. She was the only secretary he had. As he sat in his chair and looked out the window over the city of Nashville, he was, at least for now, the one that would need to type his own letters, his own pleadings, and take care of those people who walked in the front office to see him. This could get ugly real fast.

If he was still married, if he was still enduring the hell he had gone through while married to *her*, she could have come to the office, for a few days anyway, and handled the secretarial work until they just couldn't stand to be with each other one more minute. Those few days might have been long enough to find someone new. But the marriage had ended a year ago. Parenthetically, no matter how difficult conditions in the office might have become without a legal secretary, enduring the nightmare, which would have best described the time his former wife would have worked with him, would have been much worse.

If that unemployed son of his had any typing skills, he could perhaps entice him to help, but snorting coke and typing at the same time would no doubt be more than he could handle. He thought back on all those times he had tried to get him to voluntarily enter a rehab center. Once or twice, he even said he would. But in the end, he always backed out, and at twenty years of age, he didn't figure *forcing* him to go would result in a positive conclusion for either of them.

Charles needed to concentrate on the problem at hand. He had left his door to the reception area open so he would be aware when someone walked in. Until this issue was resolved, he would personally have to deal with every person that walked in the door, which would include salesmen, distraught victims, and other undesirables.

Maybe he shouldn't have treated his last secretary so badly, but she was clearly incompetent. Maybe he could have trained her more thoroughly. She was only with him a few months before she left. She walked out crying. That was probably a sign that the office would soon receive a claim for unemployment. He would have to deal with that once he got the notice. She was incompetent, *period.* She would not qualify for unemployment if she was incompetent and simply could not do her job. He would do whatever he needed to do to make sure she didn't qualify.

The only bright spot in all this was that one of his associates had heard of someone, a friend of his, that was available. She told him she wasn't happy at the firm she was with and had given them notice a couple of weeks ago. He had called her, and she was to arrive for an interview, at any minute. If she was even close to acceptable, he would hire her on the spot. If she wasn't qualified... well, if she wasn't... He heard the door to the hallway open.

He figured that was her. He stood up, all five feet ten inches of his slightly overweight body, shoved the knot of his tie back up to where it belonged, and pulled on his suit coat, which had become about two sizes too small as his weight had increased.

She stood in the outer office, looking around for someone to communicate with. She was strikingly beautiful. Tall, thin, short black hair, dressed to kill.

"Are you Layla Adams?"

She turned to face the voice. "I am. You must be Mr. Whitmore?"

"Yes. Please come in."

Single file, they walked in his office, and he sat down, behind his desk. She continued to stand until he said, "Please, please have a seat."

He prayed her abilities matched her beauty. If it did, he was home free.

"Layla—do you go by Layla?"

"Yes, I do."

"Layla, I understand you're working for a law firm now, is that correct?"

"Yes, it is. And before you ask, I'm just tired of working there. I've been there eight years, and I just wanna move on—get into another area of law. No particular reason. They've been good to me, but it's my own personal choice to move on, and that's what I'm going to do."

"What type of work did you do with them?"

"Mostly criminal pleadings. That was my area of concentration."

He took a deep breath—just what he was looking for.

"So would it be fair to say you're very familiar with pleadings and the procedures used in the criminal process?'

"Yes."

"Are you familiar with the salary available for this type of job?"

"When I called to set up an appointment, I asked what the range was for the job. They told me and then said, because of my experience, they would probably be able to increase my starting pay. That's fine with me. I was fine with the conversation I had with them about salary when I talked to them."

"Any issue with the hours you would need to work?"

"No."

"You have children, Layla? Do you have any family issues that would preclude you from working on any particular day or days?"

"I'm not married, and never have been. I live not far away, so driving to and from here shouldn't create an issue."

"When can you start?"

"Tomorrow. My two-week notice I gave my employer ends today. They already have someone to replace me, so I could be here tomorrow morning if you wish."

The rest of the conversation consisted of a miniscule amount of useless personal information from both of them. Charles had already made up his mind to hire her, regardless of any additional information she might have to offer.

As they finished their conversation, the door to the front office opened and someone walked in. He could hear the individual take a chair in the outer office. He excused himself to see if he could take care of them in a brief few seconds, then return to the interview with Layla.

"Michael," he whispered. "What are you doing here? I thought you had a job interview today."

Michael looked around, then whispered, "Yeah, well, that kinda went out the window. My darn alarm clock didn't go off. Dad, why are we whispering?"

"I have someone in my office that really doesn't need to hear our conversation, that's why. Slept through it again, didn't you?"

He said nothing as Charles turned and walked back in his office.

"Layla, I think I know all I need to know. Can you be here in the morning, 'round eight?"

She stood, smiled, held out her hand and said, "Thank you. I'll see you then." He shook her hand, then followed her, watching as she walked out the door. She was a beautiful woman with a figure to match. Not that that made a difference here, in this office, but who knew what might happen in the future—between two consenting adults.

As he watched her walk out the door, Michael said, "Dad, who was that? I don't think I've seen her 'round here before."

"You haven't. You will now though. She just became my new secretary. Come on back." He walked in his office, with Michael in close attendance. "What're you doing here? I'll be home for lunch in an hour."

Michael said, "You know her well? You know her before today?"

"No, never met her prior to today. Now, again, what're you doing here?"

"Well… a… you got any money? I'm really broke."

"You have any job interviews lined up? You quit school, you're twenty years old, you're broke, and you're still living with your father. Most kids your age with all those issues would find a job and their own place to live—you know, like so many of your *other* high school classmates have already done. You have any intention of doing any of those things?"

"Sure. I sure do, man. But right now, I'm just a little broke. I'll call that guy back and tell him that due to an unforeseen event, I missed the interview. I'm sure he'll set up another one for me. Now, you got any extra money? I think I already asked you that."

Charles reached around and pulled out his billfold. "I've got about forty bucks, and that's it. I have no more cash on me. Is that enough?"

"Sure, Dad, sure. That'll do. I'll repay you, I really will." He reached out and took the money. "That woman gonna work in the outer office there, is she?"

"Yeah, why?"

"She married?"

"No, why? You interested in her? Better get yourself a damn job first, Michael. I'm not sure she'd take a second look unless you're workin'. Oh, and by the way, there's a little age difference. She's thirty-five years old. That too could be a problem."

"No, it wasn't me I was thinkin' of. You like her?"

"Don't even know her. Now, I got a little work to do yet today. I'll see you at home tonight."

Michael stood and walked out the door without another word. Charles knew how badly his son needed help. He needed support from his ex-wife as concerned convincing Michael he needed treatment, but she wasn't interested in any respect. Michael wouldn't go unless she at least helped convince him. The only time Charles talked him into getting some help, Michael, once released, told him if he ever put him somewhere like that again, he would commit suicide. Charles needed to talk to another expert in that field, again. He was afraid if he didn't get help soon...

Now where was that Cameron file... Holy shit, he needed a secretary.

3

A week had passed since Layla had started her new job. Charles could not have been happier with her work. She was not only good with the people as they walked in the front door, but as of yet, he had also found no aspect of her daily desk work to be unacceptable.

"Charles, your appointment is here."

"Send him in."

Jeff Wiley had been a cop for over thirty years, nine of those years in Nashville. He had recently been promoted to precinct commander covering the Bellevue area, and for good reason. He had, at some point in his career, been involved in every area of law enforcement. In addition, he was street smart, and the officers respected him. His only flaw seemed to be that he could be easily swayed—not in an illegal way, but just easily swayed. Charles would test that trait again this morning. Once seated, once the menial chatter concerning their personal lives had been discussed, they turned to one of the specific reasons for his appointment.

"Jeff, do you know the officer that's involved with that trial coming up next week concerning a fourth offense drunk driver—what's his name?" Charles took a quick look at his file. "The defendant's name is Thomas Arthur, and his trial comes up next week. You know about the case?"

"I don't know much about the facts. I know the case is pretty high profile. I know the man's insane when he's drunk. That's about all I've really heard."

Charles said, "We need to get him off the street—it's that simple."

"Well, then good luck."

"No, there's more to it than that."

"I don't understand."

"Have you discussed the case with the officer, King I think his name might be? Let me look. Yes, that's his name, Zach King. You discussed the case with him at all?"

"No, why?"

"Of course, I'm not trying the case, but I talked to the assistant DA that handles those types of cases. Now, as I understand it, apparently the officer lost sight of the guy. He saw the car being driven erratically, but as I understand the facts, he then lost sight of the car. When he finally located it a few minutes later, the defendant was walking away from a line of cars, drinking a beer and going into his apartment house. The defendant said he wasn't driving when the officer first saw him. He said he had allowed someone else to use the vehicle. But this officer needs to testify he *saw* him drive, and he followed him all the way home, where he watched as he got out of the car and walked into his apartment house. You know as well as I, the guy was driving and driving *drunk*. We need the officer to confirm it."

"But, Charles, what the hell can I do? He has to testify as to what he really saw that night. No doubt in my mind he won't do nothin' but tell the truth."

"Our office typed up the information against the guy setting forth his testimony, which indicated he *saw* the guy driving all the way to his apartment building. King knew what we used as his testimony at the time and said nothing. He needs to man up and testify the 'right way'—help us put this guy away once and for all."

Jeff looked away for just a moment, then said, "All right. I'll tell him what you said. You're right, we do need to get this guy off the streets. He's gonna kill someone before long."

"My thoughts exactly. Can we talk about one more thing before you leave?"

"Sure."

"Michael tells me he was busted the other night on a possession charge. Marijuana, I guess. You know anything about it?"

"I just heard that earlier this morning."

"Well, I talked to the prosecutor that's been assigned the case. It's just simple possession. He told me if it was okay with the officer, he would recommend a small fine and let it go. It occurred in your precinct. You okay with that?"

He hesitated. Finally, he said, "I guess so, but you know, Charles, Michael needs help. He's got a problem."

"I know that. You're not telling me anything I don't know, and I'm working on it. But it's gonna take a little time and putting him behind bars isn't gonna help. Can you just mention to the officer that a fine is enough? If you can, and he's good with that, I'll tell the prosecutor in charge, and we'll finish it up."

"Yes, I guess I'm all right with that, but you need to get some help for him, before he hurts someone, including himself."

"I agree, and believe me, I'm working on it."

Charles watched as the assistant DA finished his opening statement in the case of *State of Tennessee vs. Thomas Arthur*. The defendant sat beside his attorney. His demeanor reeked of self-confidence along with a large dose of superiority and arrogance mixed in.

The judge took a brief break, and once the participants were all back in their seats, the State called the officer to take the stand as his first witness.

"Please state your name and occupation."

"Zack King, officer with the Nashville Police Department."

"Can you tell us, were you on duty the night of September 15 at around 11:00 p.m.?"

"Yes, I was."

"What were you doing?"

"Just patrolling the area near downtown Bellevue."

"Tell us what happened at about that time."

"Well, a vehicle on one of the side streets pulled out in front of me and took off at a high rate of speed."

"What'd you do?"

"I went after him."

"What'd you observe concerning the vehicle?"

"It was swerving all over the road and driving way in excess of the speed limit. If the streets hadn't been empty that night, he could have easily had an accident that could have harmed other people."

"Were you able to follow him?"

"Yes."

"Where did you end up?"

"We ended up at an apartment building on the west side of town."

"When you arrived there, was he still in his vehicle?"

"Yes."

"What was he doing?"

"He was just exiting his vehicle and walking into his apartment building with beer in hand."

"Okay, now let me ask you this. Were you actually able to observe the driver when you first noticed the vehicle being driven in a reckless manner?"

"Yes."

"Can you point him out if he's in the courtroom?"

He pointed toward the defendant. "That's him sitting next to his attorney."

"Was anyone with him?"

"No"

"Were you able to keep track of the vehicle until it came to a stop?"

"Yes. I followed him the whole way. There was never a time he was out of my sight."

"And you were able to observe the individual who exited the vehicle and walked into the apartment building?"

"Yes."

"Is he in the courtroom today?"

"Yes."

"Please point him out."

Again, the witness pointed to the defendant. "That's him next to his attorney."

Charles looked over at the jury and noticed they were all taking notes on the pads provided by the court attendant.

"Now, you said you followed him into the building, correct?"

"Yes."

"Again, is that person the same person you had seen just seconds before, leaving his vehicle in front of his apartment house?"

"Yes, that's him next to his attorney."

"Never any doubt about who the driver was from beginning to end?"

The officer looked down for a moment before he said, "Absolutely not. He's the same one I saw from beginning to end."

The assistant DA then asked him a number of foundational questions that were necessary because the defendant had resisted taking a test for determining his state of sobriety or intoxication.

The trial lasted the rest of the day. Charles was in his office when he received a call indicating the jury had returned a verdict of guilty as charged. Clearly, his conference with the precinct commander had had its desired effect. Jeff was a good man, just easily swayed.

The only other issue stemming out of that conversation with Jeff the other day that needed to be considered was the portion concerning his son—his drug-addicted son. He had received a phone call from the precinct commander, indicating that a small fine concerning the charge of possession filed against his son was acceptable with the officer.

Unfortunately, Charles knew it might be acceptable with the officer and would take care of the smaller issue of possession, but the larger problem, the issue of his addiction still remained. He had been able to help him out of a small problem this time. But he felt it was only a matter of time before something else, something much more serious, would eventually happen, unless he could get him into treatment, and finally end the control drugs had over most every aspect of his son's life.

4

Michael Whitmore sat within the silence of a large, well-furnished living room, slowly darkening as late afternoon turned into early evening. He needed to think. It was hard to think when he was so easily distracted. As a result, he made no effort to turn on a light or the big-screen television or rock radio piped throughout this room and every other room in the house.

As he looked at the expensive furniture surrounding him, he figured his father had, indeed, been lucky. Even though he enjoyed a large salary, the woman he married had more money than she knew what to do with. His father had married well.

Most everything in the house that qualified as a luxury, or a quasiluxury, had been acquired by her. The money she brought into the marriage had proven a tremendous benefit to both he and his father, as long as she continued to provide it.

But the divorce had stopped the flow to his father, and now, even money to *him* had dwindled until it was almost nonexistent. Oh, every once in a while, she would provide a little, maybe for his birthday, or maybe for Christmas, but other than that, it was up to his dad, or he remained broke.

Even though he still suffered from a slight haze left over from last night, he could still review all the jobs he had tried to hold onto, because there were only three. Michael hadn't lasted a week at any one of them. Now today, he had to endure his latest job-related issue when he had missed his appointment and the job had been given to someone else who *had* been on time *and* who was well qualified.

That was a major problem too. What *was* he qualified for? He had no education beyond high school. He had tapped all his dad's friends for a possible position, but the drugs had always won out. One way or the other, drugs had always found a way to trump a new job. Prior to tapping his father's friends, he had gone through his mother's friends. As he sat, now in complete darkness, and considered his next move in the job market, he concluded most likely his job prospects were virtually nonexistent.

He had so few possessions left to sell. Most everything available for sale had been sold to support his habit. Those items he still had, he absolutely needed for his day-to-day existence. He wondered why she hadn't called yet. She always called by now. Michael had concluded his dad was his only hope. He had put on a good show for his father, who truly believed he wanted a job, but that was a complete ruse. Why work when he didn't need to? When he really needed money, he would simply ask his dad. When his father didn't provide enough, he would find something in the house to pawn. That had worked time after time, and although he was somewhat concerned his father might start noticing, as of yet, he hadn't noticed anything. Until he did. Michael wasn't going to worry about it. He tried dialing her number... went to voice mail.

Charles was the key. He was an easy touch because his father just simply didn't want to bother with him. It was easier to give him money than deal with him. He started to pace. The one thing he didn't want to happen was some woman interfering with the flow of money. That would really change everything. He didn't need another person for his father to spend money on. *He* needed it. There was only so much to go around. So far, since his divorce, there had been no one in his father's life but him and that's the way it had to remain. He would do what he could to make sure the supply of money he needed to feed his habit continued to flow. Even if his old man kicked off, there would be life insurance and, most likely, a pension. All that would come to him—if there wasn't a damn woman involved! That was the key and would remain an important issue from here on. The phone finally rang. He answered it immediately.

"Where you been, Annie? I've been waiting for you to call for an hour. You're never this late."

"What the hell's the difference *when* I call as long as I *call*? What time you pickin' me up?"

Michael said, "Maybe in a half hour or so. Does that work for you?"

"Oh no, I've got so much on my fuckin' schedule I just don't know if I can make it tonight. Don't be so stupid. *Sure*, that works for me. You got any weed?"

"I got a little. You got any money?"

"I took some out of my mom's purse when I went over to see her this morning. I don't know whether it's gonna be enough though. What about you—you got any weed left?"

"Very little. You smoked everything I had last night and I spent the last penny I had on it. We're gonna have to use the money you have, to buy what we need tonight."

"I have *not* got enough money for both of us Michael. Didn't you just hear me, 'cause I just said that. So, if you don't got no money, you probably just better stay home."

He thought for a moment. "I might be able to find something to hock around here. I can go downstairs and see what I can find."

"Then you'll be here in 'bout a half hour?"

"Sure will. I'll find something to sell or hock—we'll go have a good time."

She hesitated. "Well… okay, that's fine, but don't include in your 'good time' doing to me what you done to me last night. That's not happenin' again for a while. You're pretty mean when you're high, and you ain't climbin' aboard me again when you're like that. Besides that, if we need to sell something first, then make a buy, there's no time for that tonight. And I'm tellin' you without any question, *that's not happening again if you're high*. So put that in your pipe and smoke it, mister, 'cause I ain't kiddin'."

"Whatever. Maybe the time to do that is before we smoke. Whatta you think 'bout that? Does that suit you better?"

"Maybe. We could try that, but not tonight. I'm too damn sore. Just find something to hock. We'll go to that old warehouse and meet the rest of the group there. That's the most private place we have."

"See you in a half hour." He terminated the call. As soon as the call ended, he started looking around the living room for something to hock. He could find nothing there that would go unnoticed. Michael walked down the steps to the basement. It had not been finished when they first moved in, and all the arguments, which ultimately led to his parent's divorce, by then were in full swing. Finishing the basement was out of the question. They just turned it into a storage area for whatever they didn't use on the main floor.

He walked toward the far wall of the basement and noticed a throw rug over some type of object in the far corner. Michael pulled it off, and there sat an old clock, one he knew had belonged to his great-grandmother on his mother's side. He had no idea why she hadn't taken it with her when she left. Certainly, now, his dad wouldn't miss it. If his mother asked, both he and his dad would tell her they had no idea where it was. Perfect. He picked it up and carried it outside, placing it in the back seat of his old brown Chevy. The back window was still cracked all the way across. He needed to have his old man fix that. It got cold in the car during winter even though they lived in Tennessee.

Michael slid into the driver's seat as he remembered his dad mentioned he had to work late. As a result, he knew there was no need to worry about him driving in their driveway while he was driving out and noticing the clock in the back seat. Now, though, as he processed his father's comment, he wondered if "working late" had something going to do with that new secretary. He would need to monitor that. He didn't need a stepmom interfering with his source of funds.

5

She lowered the microphone. As short as she was, the move was just part of her normal pretestimony preparation. Every time she testified, whoever had testified before her was taller. Didn't matter whether it was man or woman, old or young—they were all taller than she was.

"State your name for the record."

"Kris Thompson."

"Occupation?"

"Private Investigator."

"How long and who with?"

"Going on five years, and I work alone."

She couldn't help but notice how quickly Charles Whitmore, the prosecutor, got to the point. There was clearly no fooling around with him. She had noticed the same thing both times he had prepped her. His approach certainly was no different today.

"What type of investigating do you do?"

"Pretty much whatever I'm hired for, but I specialize in corporate work, particularly in the theft of trade secrets and information of that nature. I also specialize in background checks of people that have been hired or are about to be hired. I work for a number of corporations."

"Is one of those corporations Mossman Electronics?"

"Yes."

"What have you done for them in the past?"

"Mostly just background checks of potential new employees. Especially if something unusual turns up after their initial investigation, which they normally do themselves. On occasion, I do other types of investigating for them, which was the situation in this case."

"This particular time, who was your contact person within the corporation?"

"The owner, Mr. Mossman."

"Can you tell us why he contacted you?"

"Well, he said——"

"Objection, hearsay."

"Overruled. Foundational. Is he here, Mr. Whitmore? Is Mr. Mossman here to testify?"

"He is, Your Honor."

"Continue with your testimony."

"He felt there was perhaps an issue with corporate secrets leaving the corporation. They had a problem with that a year or so ago, but let it pass. It wasn't that big a deal. But after it happened again, they felt there was a problem with one individual, that it wasn't systemic, and they wanted me to investigate that one individual."

"And is that one individual the defendant in this case?"

"Yes."

"Did they want you to investigate him and determine if he was selling trade secrets that belonged to Mossman Industries?"

"Yes."

"What did you do?"

"I first did my own background check on him. Then I started following him. I followed him for weeks."

"What did you determine, if anything?"

"I determined that he was meeting with people from two other industries and appeared to me to be dealing with them. What they were doing I didn't know for sure at the time, but I knew what they were doing out in the middle of a field at 2:00 a.m. was most likely not legal, nor appropriate."

"How often did that happen?"

"He met with people from one company twice and people from another company three times. I took pictures all five times—at least the best I could, during the middle of a night out in the middle of a dark field."

"What'd you do then?"

"I went to Mr. Mossman and showed him what I had."

"What happened next?"

"Well, as I say, I turned everything over to him, and my part of this, of the theft and sale of trade secrets, was over. I could tell you what happened after that, but it would only be information which came from others, so…"

"So… it would be hearsay."

She smiled. "Yes."

"We have the 'others' here to testify concerning those issues anyway, so that's not a problem. Did you ever have occasion to come in contact with the defendant again?"

"After I turned everything over to Mr. Mossman?"

"Yes."

"Yes, I did."

"What happened?"

"Well, I was driving up I-24 just outside of Nashville, going to see a client with offices just north of town. I noticed a vehicle coming from behind me at a high rate of speed, but since that happens in Nashville all the time, I, at first, thought nothing about it."

"Go on."

"As he approached, I thought the driver looked familiar. He pulled alongside, and I could see then it was the defendant."

"What happened?"

"He slowed down and rammed the side of my vehicle. When that didn't have the desired effect, in that he wasn't able to push me off the road, he pulled away, and then came at me again, hitting me harder this time."

"In your opinion, what was he trying to do?"

"As I just said, he was clearly trying to run me off the road."

"How did it all end?"

"After the second time, and as he pulled away to try again, I pulled out my pistol, rolled down my window, and fired a warning shot over the top of his car."

"Then?"

"He pulled back, and I never saw him again."

"Any doubt who the driver was?"

"None. He's seated there by his attorney."

"You pressed charges?"

She smiled. "No. He's got more than enough on his plate with the charges in this case. If he gets off of this charge with no jail time, I'll file then. I'll just wait and see what happens here."

Cross-examination by the defendant's attorney was mostly counterproductive, which she expected. He was not well schooled in trial practice, as was evident based on the lack of objections during her testimony. Kris was done by noon, which she had anticipated. Earlier that morning, she had arranged to meet her friend Art Jones at a local coffee shop on the east side in Nashville. He was always early. She was always late. But he would, without fail, wait for her, no matter how late she arrived. This time it would only be a matter of a few minutes.

Art said, "Late as usual."

"And I suppose you were early as usual."

He had a cup of coffee, and she passed right by, on the way to the counter to get hers. As she sat, he said, "You want some lunch? I ate earlier, but I'll sit with you while you eat."

"No, I just got out of court. I wanna wait a bit before I eat anything." She couldn't help but notice, again, how good-looking, how handsome he was. But she had been there, done that—he wasn't available to *any* woman, and she had been told that more than once.

"So how'd court go today?"

"Good. The jury should find him guilty, which is what he deserves. I probably should file charges too. As you know, the prick tried to kill me."

He smirked. "Were you able to pull the microphone down far enough to match up with your mouth? By the way, I think you're shrinking, or maybe I'm growing, not sure which."

"I'm not shrinking and you're not growing. End of that line of discussion."

"How did last night go?"

"You mean with Harry?"

"You know what I mean. *Yes, with Harry.*"

"Oh, fine. We had a good time, but I don't know that I wanna go out with him again. He's just so macho, so dominant. I'm just not sure I like that."

"Don't give me that bullshit. That's exactly what you like. Sounds like a good matchup to me. You know, you've not said much about that one guy—I think Andrew was his name. You saw him for a long time. What the hell happened to him?"

She hesitated. "You were right. He wasn't for me."

"What happened?"

"He wanted more than I had to offer."

"Oh, come on. I suppose you let sex get in the way? You need to get up to speed here, missy. It's not a big deal. You gonna remain a virgin the rest of your life?"

"Move on, Art. It had nothing to do with sex. He wanted a wife. He wanted a commitment. I'm just not ready for that. He still calls me. Drives me nuts. I just am *not* ready to commit."

"Based on what you had already told me, I knew that was going to happen with him. I knew that from day one. You need to listen to me. I got all the instincts, baby, I got the feelin'. I know 'bout these things. Just ask me."

"I know one thing. You're full of shit up to your eyebrows. That's one thing I do know."

He laughed. "So Andrew ended up in the Kris junkyard like all the rest?"

She wrinkled her nose and squinted at him. "You know you're not near as funny as you think you are."

"I don't understand why you don't get it, Kris. You have a killer body, for a woman. You're damn good-looking. You have everything a man would want except for this attitude. You got this bad attitude. You're always right. You're always smarter than everyone you date. You just don't get it." He sat back and took a deep breath. "Now I feel much better. I've been waiting to say that for a long time."

She looked into her coffee cup, then looked up at Art and smiled. "You're right. I know you're right. But the right man just hasn't knocked on my door yet. That's the problem. I just haven't met him. And until I do, my attitude is just gonna have to do."

"Well, honey, I hope when the right one does come along, you damn well recognize him. I, of course, will be there to help you figure that all out, when he does come along. And *when* he does, you better by god, be ready to open that door y'all are talking 'bout and let him in, because knowing you like I do, you ain't a gonna find many that qualify in your lifetime. No, sirree, you just ain't gonna find many that qualify based upon your standards, and that, sweetheart, is a fact!"

6

"Your son is here."

"Didn't say what he wanted, did he?"

"No."

"Send him in."

The door opened. Michael Whitmore walked in as if he just purchased the room and had arrived to take possession.

"Hi, Michael. You got any interviews today?"

"Yes, I do," he said as he took a chair in front of his father's desk.

"Great. Where at?"

"Well, I have one at that smoke shop down on Lincoln. You know which one I mean?"

"Not really, I guess. Who owns it?"

"Heck, I don't know. I just saw they had a job opening, I called, and they set me up for this afternoon. I have not a clue who might own the place. I'm just hoping this one works out. As you know, I need money to get along. But as usual, today I'm broke."

"And I suppose that means what it normally means—you need me to provide you with some cash."

"I sure do. I'd really appreciate it if you could loan me a little just to tide me over."

"When is the interview?" he asked as he reached for his billfold.

"'Bout an hour."

"You going dressed like that?"

"What's wrong with... no, I'm gonna run home and change. Wouldn't want anyone seeing me like this. Not with my dad being an attorney and all."

"I don't know about that, but I would think you'd have enough pride in yourself that you wouldn't want anyone seeing you like that. You look like you just walked out of a garbage dump."

He reached for the sixty dollars his father handed him and said, "You know, that's just what I was thinkin'."

"Have you seen your mother lately?"

"I was over there last week."

"She have any thoughts about where you might get a job?"

"She said she was late for something. I saw her for all of about five minutes, and she took off. Left before I did."

"You ask her for money to tide you over?"

"No." He smiled. "Just couldn't take rejection from her again. I wasn't going to give her the satisfaction."

Charles laughed as he said, "I have to admit, rejection comes easy for her."

"I guess it's pretty clear you two weren't made for each other."

"That's an understatement. It's just too bad it took us so long to figure that out. Let me know how the job interview goes."

"I take it you're done with me... ready to discharge me, Captain?" He stood and saluted.

"Don't be silly. I would have discharged you long ago like your mother has us both, if that's really what I wanted to do. I love you, son, and I've told you that enough times you should know it by now."

He turned to leave. "I can't take all this mush. I'll see you tonight."

"I may be a little late, but I'll see you when I get home."

Michael stopped and turned. "Why, what's going on?"

He smiled. "I got a date."

"Who with? No, let me guess. Is it with what's her name out front?"

"Sure is."

He turned to walk out the door. "You two be careful. Wouldn't want a little half brother hangin' round the house." He slammed the door behind him.

They asked for and were given a table, upstairs, where they could look down on the patrons as they walked in the front door and upon those already seated downstairs for dinner. Charles had decided to take Layla to Margot, a small restaurant in east Nashville, where he had, on numerous occasions, eaten in the past. He had never had a bad meal there. She, on the other hand, had never been there. Over a glass of pinot noir, the choice of both, he said, "I was surprised you decided to have supper with me."

"To be perfectly honest, I'm really not sure it was a smart decision on my part. You're my boss. I just don't know if this was a good decision—for either of us, actually."

"It's a first for me. I've *never* gone out with a secretary of mine—ever. In fact, I haven't gone out with anyone since my divorce. I just haven't been ready. I'm not real sure I am now, so you're kind of my guinea… pig—Oops, see, I'm not used to this. Sorry. I didn't mean that the way it came out."

She laughed. "Forget it. I understand what you're trying to say. What happened between you and your wife?"

"Well, she came from a whole different life. She had money. I didn't. She had friends who were involved in high society. I didn't. That part of her finally persuaded the part of her that loved me that I wasn't enough, I wasn't important, I wasn't high society, at least not the kind she wanted."

"And apparently Michael wasn't her 'type' either?"

"No. He was too earthy, too common for her."

"So how is life now—with just you and Michael?"

"Oh, it's fine. Michael has a problem that needs to be 'fixed.' I have tried to help him, but he needs treatment. I'm still working on it, but it's a challenge. He doesn't have a job. He's not in school. All that extra free time doesn't help with his problem either."

"I get a feeling he doesn't much care for me," she replied as she emptied the last of her wine.

"You know, I'm not sure who he cares for anymore. Actually, sometimes I worry that if he got really upset, he might try to harm me. But, he *is* my son, and I'll do whatever it is that needs to be done to get him the help he needs. He has no one else but me—he's my responsibility, my son, and I'll do what I can to get him through this bad spell in his life."

The waiter came back for their order. They told him to wait a bit while they perused the menu. He returned a few minutes later, at which time Charles ordered the duck, and she, the special of the night, which was grouper in a mild crème sauce. Eventually, the conversation took a turn, and she became the subject of discussion.

"So you just got tired of working for the other firm? Was that the truth? Somehow, that was a little hard to believe. Not that I thought you were misleading me, but I just figured there was more to it than you wanted to tell me. I really didn't care. I already knew about your abilities through my own sources, the salary was all right with you, and you were ready to go to work. That was enough for me."

She put her fork down, took a drink of wine, looked at him for a long couple of seconds, and said, "You're right. That really wasn't why I wanted out of there. I was just getting damn tired of being chased all over the office. It was never ending. I was single, I was available, and it just never ended. Guys I would never in a million years be attracted to felt they were God's gift to women, to me, and wanted to date me. I got sick of that, day in and day out. It really wasn't worth what they were paying me. I was going somewhere else, whether you hired me or not."

"I would think that would get old. Ever been married?"

"Once. For about two weeks." She took another drink and said, "I've had a couple of long-term relationships since then and, in fact, just got out of one, but I don't seem to be the marrying kind I guess. That really doesn't bother me, but unfortunately, that does appear to be my fate. Date a guy, break up, date a guy, break up—and on it goes. I seem to be doomed in the relationship world."

He finished his duck, and as he finished the last of his second glass of Pinot, he said, "You aren't doomed. You just haven't met the right guy. It's just that simple. By the way, the right guy is probably not the one sitting across from you either, but I can tell you one thing, you're a fun date. You're easy to be around, very attractive, and at least so far, a great employee. You got the whole package as far as

I'm concerned." He reached across the table placing his hand over hers, which was wrapped around the bottom of her wine goblet.

She pulled it away. "You haven't known me long enough to know who I am in any respect. Give me a little time. I just got out of one relationship and out of a firm full of sex-crazed fools. Give me time to get my breath... please."

He smiled. "I understand completely. I'll give you all the time you want. Let me know when you're ready. I'll be around when you are."

They small-talked their way through another glass of wine and a shared dessert. It had reached 9:00 p.m. when he drove her to her car. He thought about kissing her good night, but found himself unwillingly reconsidering, when she quickly slid out of the front seat, telling him she would see him in the morning, then closing the car door.

As he drove home, he concluded she would be a hard nut to crack—but well worth the effort. She was everything he wanted. He would not give up on her until she gave in or told him to give up.

7

Kris woke with a start and sat straight up in bed. The amount of light coming through her blinds told her it was way later than she normally arose. She was late. She worked alone—there was no one to open the office door but her. She needed to get her ass out of bed, and to the office as quickly as her short little legs would allow that to happen.

She removed her pajamas while on her way to the bathroom. She finished her shower in half the time she normally took, and as she toweled off, she felt thankful for her short, pixie haircut, which required no maintenance. She learned long ago, she had no time for insignificant issues like hair management. She had it cut short, and as she looked in the mirror, she concluded it was the right thing to do—little care, looked pretty good. She would not—Her cell phone rang, quickly terminating her hair assessment. She looked at the caller's name… *Andrew*! Not again! He had called her a couple of times last week, wanting to renew their relationship. She had told him then, as she would again, and again, they were not compatible. She didn't answer, and the call went to voice mail.

Kris put on her bra and panties as she stood in front of the closet, trying to figure out what clothes might work best for the activities she had planned for the day. She stopped to review her abbreviated body in the mirror. She was too short. What the hell could she do about that? Absolutely nothing. She had an athletic body. She didn't have a lot of fat, but she was just so short. Should she lose a little weight? Probably, but her excess fat was marginal. Everything appeared in proportion—breasts, hips, thighs—but she was too short. What could she do to improve what she had to work with and—The phone rang once again, and again, it was Andrew. She failed to answer, and again, the call went to voice mail.

She finished dressing, then walked into the kitchen to find something to eat before she drove to the office. Again, the phone, and again, it was him. She needed to end this before he started calling her while she was working.

"Morning, Andrew. Whatta ya need?"

"We need to talk."

"No, we don't."

"Oh, I think we do."

"What about?" she asked as she shoveled the corner of a pop tart in her mouth and walked through the front door.

"I don't wanna lose you. I wanna try one more time."

She started her car, as she said, "Well, I don't think that's a good idea. Tell you what. If I get a minute during the day, I'll try to call you back. I'm running a little late."

He hesitated. "You're never going to call me again, are you?"

"Nope, I'm not. We're done. Have a good day." She terminated the call. Why beat around the bush? No sense trying to work something out she already knew, deep in her heart, was never going to work.

As she approached her office, she noticed a limo parked across the street. She noticed it because limos didn't frequent this part of town on a regular basis. She parked her vehicle and opened the front door of her office. As usual, they weren't standing in line to get in. But, on the other hand, she was thankful—her practice had grown substantially during the past five years. Until last week, she had not hired a secretary. She just really didn't feel she needed one. But she had finally decided it was time. The office was just becoming way too busy. Her new secretary would start in a couple of weeks.

As she checked her calendar, she heard someone walk in her front door. Since she had no other appointments until later in the morning, she walked out to greet whoever it was, figuring she could see them now, if they wished.

"Good morning, can I help you?" He was tall, good-looking, and dressed to kill.

"You have time to see me, like now?"

"Sure, sure, come in."

He walked in, and as he sat, he said, "My name is Chad McNamara. You might have heard of me. I'm in the music business." He hesitated, clearly waiting for a response—waiting for her to acknowledge she had heard of him. She hadn't, which is why she sat quietly, waiting for him to continue.

When she didn't respond, he cleared his throat and said, "I my need your services. I'm going through a nasty divorce. Extended visitation is an issue. As a result, who I might be seeing outside the marriage has become an issue. Is everything we say confidential?"

"Yes, of course."

"Okay, so without admitting or denying I'm seeing anyone, my wife is absolutely certain I am, although she has no proof whatsoever."

"Is she seeing someone else?"

"Yes. And I already have all the details concerning her relationships, which were many."

"If you have the information you need about her, what do you need me for?"

"Because I think I'm being followed. I can't tie down who it is or even whether, for sure, I *am* being followed, but I know her well. She's in a bind, and I have little doubt she's got someone tailing me."

Kris sat back in her chair, waiting for the punch line. He said nothing. Finally, she said, "So what is it you need from me?"

"I wanna know who it is that's following me—where his office is and what his name is." He sat forward in his chair and said, "Once I know, I'll take it from there. He needs to understand I'll never be caught in a compromising situation with a woman or man while this divorce is going on." He sat back. "Of course, in addition to that, I just don't want anyone following me. I have a business that thrives on privacy, and I don't want some dumb fuck following my every move. I have an employee or two that could handle dissuading him from following me, if you know what I mean, but they don't have the time nor the skills to follow me around all day trying to figure out who the individual might be that's doing the following. I need someone to figure that out for me first. Then I can take it from there. By the way, you come highly recommended."

"Well, that's good to hear. I'd be available to help you if you wish. I would, however, require a sizeable retainer for that, but…"

"Here's your retainer. I assume it will be sufficient." He shoved a check across the desk.

She quickly looked at all those numbers on the check, swallowed hard, and said, "Certainly, that will be sufficient. I'll start right away."

"Here's my card. Call me when you know something."

She had been following Mr. McNamara for five days, nothing to close, just far enough away so she could take in the whole picture—what happened when he pulled away from a curb, when he left his home in the morning, when he left work at night. She had seen the same vehicle pull away just a few minutes after he pulled away on multiple occasions.

Late one afternoon, when she, once again, saw the same vehicle drive away after Mr. McNamara had driven away first, she decided to follow whoever it was just to see where it might lead. The vehicle proceeded straight to a small office building in south Nashville, and a young, good-looking man exited his vehicle walking into an office. The sign above the door indicated it was occupied by a private investigator by the name of Barrett Armstrong.

She parked and walked through the front door, where his secretary was just shutting down her computer, ready to leave for the day.

"Hi. My name's Kris Thompson. I'm a private investigator, and I need to see Mr. Armstrong."

"We're about to close for the day. Can I set you up for a time tomorrow?"

"No, no, I need to see him now." His door was open, so she walked in his office, contrary to the verbal warnings she continued to receive from his secretary.

"Mr. Armstrong, my name is Kris Thompson. I'm also a private investigator, and I need to see you for about two minutes involving a case you're involved in." Barrett's secretary had hold of Kris's arm and was attempting to pull her out his office door.

"Wait, wait, Joyce. Let her stay. What's this all about, Miz Thompson?"

She sat as she said, "Let me get right to the point."

He smiled. "Okay, why don't you do that?"

"You have a client by the name of Mrs. McNamara. You're following her current husband, Chad McNamara. You need to stop. He's come to see me. He knows someone is following him, and he knows why. He indicated to me, there was no way in hell you were ever going to catch him in a compromising situation with anyone, and that you might as well stop trying."

Barrett clasped his hands together and put them behind his head as he leaned back in this chair. "Really? Well, you can tell him it's not me."

"Yes, it is. I know it is because I've been following you while you've been following him. I have no idea how he determined someone was following him, but you might wanna be a little more careful in the future. Now, I'll tell you this for your own good. This guy appears to me he could be dangerous. I recommend you follow my advice and stop. Tell your client you were unable to find him with anyone else, collect your fee, and move on."

"Oh, really… that's what you'd do?"

"Look, I don't know you from shit. But I respect the fact that you and I are in the same business. He wants your name. I'm not going to give it to him because I have a feeling you would hear from him, or his friends. But I'm telling you you're never going to get anything on him, and I really believe he's someone you don't wanna mess with. Just take my advice."

He thought for a moment, as he assessed his position. "Well, I suppose if he *knows* he's being tailed, which he obviously does, I'm not going to uncover much, that's for sure. I'll probably stop. I wasn't coming up with anything anyway. How long you been in the business?"

"Five years."

"I've never heard of you."

"You will." She stood. "I need to go. Thanks for seeing me. Be careful."

"Hey, wait a minute. You wanna get a drink? The day's over. I got time if you do."

She walked out the door, and once in her vehicle, she called Mr. McNamara's office and told his secretary to have him stop by in the morning.

"Good morning, Mr. McNamara."

"What'd you find out?"

"I figured out who it was. I talked to the person, and they decided to stop tailing you. It's taken care of."

"Who was it?"

"Doesn't matter, it's taken care of. That's what you wanted, that's what I got done." She pushed a check across the desk. "I deposited your check in my trust account, took my fees out, and this is an office check to you for the balance. As you can see, you still have plenty left over."

He leaned on her desk. "But part of our deal was that you were to provide his name. You haven't done what you said you would do."

She stood and leaned on the desk, face-to-face with her client. "I never said I would provide you with a name. I got stopped what you wanted stopped. If you think for one minute I'm giving you the person's name so you can send someone to rough them up, you're mistaken. They were just doing their job, and now the job's over. If there's nothing else I can do for you, have a good day."

She had no idea how he would respond, but she really didn't care. That was how it was going to be handled—end of story.

He said nothing for a long fifteen seconds, then started to smile. "Okay. You got spunk, I'll give that to you. Thanks for what you did. Thanks for getting them off my back." He started to walk away, and as he did, he turned and said, "I assume you'll be available if I need some assistance in the future?"

"Depends on what you want done, Mr. McNamara. It just depends on what you want done." She sat down, as he walked out the door.

In her haste to get to work this morning, she forgot to put on deodorant. After her conversation with him, she would definitely need to go home and take care of that particular problem, which had surfaced while she was standing nose to nose with him. Before he walked in, she had no idea how he was going to take what she had to say. She was not going to rat out another private investigator under any circumstances, and especially one that was as good-looking as this Barrett Armstrong was. She might have to call him one of these days and just take him up on that drink. Even though Armstrong had made a mistake and let his guard down concerning the Chad McNamara case, it appeared he might be someone she wanted to get to know, both professionally and personally.

8

As Michael walked in the door, Charles said, "Where were you last night?"

"Oh, I just stayed with a friend. It got to be pretty late, and I didn't wanna fall asleep coming home."

"Who were you with?"

"Like I said, some of my friends."

Charles was having a cup of coffee prior to driving to work. He was obviously concentrating on the articles in the newspaper he was reading, and not his son's response to the questions he asked.

Michael had reasoned if he walked in after Charles left for work, he would avoid the questions he knew would follow if he were still home. Unfortunately, he had mistimed his return.

"You 'bout ready to get that back window in your car fixed?"

Michael grabbed a sweet roll that had been in the cupboard for a couple of days, hoping it was still good, along with a cup of coffee. The sweet roll had hardened, but still appeared edible.

"Oh, I suppose. Who should I call?"

"Let me figure that out. You paid the premium on the insurance policy, didn't you? You're insured, right?"

"Sure did. I'm all covered. You sure insurance covers the window?"

"I'll have to check your policy. I'm thinking probably the deductible is too high. Dig out your policy, and I'll take a look."

"Okay."

Of course, first of all, Michael didn't even know he had a policy, and second, he hadn't paid a premium forever. It would definitely be a while before they returned to the subject, at least if he had anything to say about it.

Charles stood, put on his suit coat, and said, "How'd the interview go?"

"Good. It went good."

"Have you heard back from anyone yet?"

"No, it's only been a couple of days. I figure maybe I'll hear in a day or two."

The truth of the matter was that there had been no interview and there was certainly no possibility of a job.

"How did everything go the other day with that secretary, Joan, or whatever her name is?"

"You mean Layla, my secretary?"

"Exactly. How did that all go for you?"

"It went fine. We had a good time. We went to Margot to eat. It was a nice evening."

"You two have something going on, do you?"

"No, not yet. I like her. She's a good soul, but we have nothing going on as might concern a romantic relationship if that's what you mean. At least, not yet."

Michael noticed a significant change in his demeanor as he talked about her. "You think this could turn into something permanent?"

Charles was walking toward the door and turned as he answered, "Oh, I don't know. Why?"

"I just wondered. I was just wondering where it was all headed, that's all."

Charles stopped as he reached the door. "You know, even if it does turn into something, or even if eventually I should find someone else, that will never affect our relationship, Michael. You know that, don't you?"

"Sure, sure, I understand. See you tonight."

Charles waved and walked out the door. As he got in his car, Michael said, sarcastically, "Won't affect our relationship *my ass*."

Michael sat around most of the day watching gameshows and a little porn, until it was time to meet up with Annie. She had a small apartment in south Nashville and worked during the days as a waitress. She made barely enough to make ends meet. Michael knew it took both their combined resources, what he could get from Charles and what she made at her day job, to provide enough income to support them both and to feed their drug addiction.

Prior to the time he knew Charles would arrive home from work, he drove to her apartment and waited for her to get off work. She walked in at five thirty, and as she did, she said, "You been here all day?"

He stood, walked up to her, kissed her, and said, "No, I just got here. How'd the day go for you?"

She dropped into the other chair in her living area that Michael wasn't sitting in and said, "Oh just fuckin' swell. I made at least thirty dollars in tips, and adding that to my salary, I must have hit at least fifty or fifty-five bucks for the day. How 'bout you? How'd you do today?"

"Pretty good actually. I hocked an old shotgun Dad had lying round in the basement. Picked up one hundred dollars for it. We got anything around here, or should I go make a buy?"

"I got nothin'. And if you're going, you better get goin', because I'm beat. I'm goin' to bed early tonight. I need to be at work by six thirty tomorrow morning, and I'll never make it if I'm up 'til midnight tonight."

Michael left, and when he returned, he had made a buy—just enough to get both of them where they wanted to go. He would stay the night and go home when she went to work. While she changed into something more comfortable for the evening, he said, "You know, I have a feelin' there's more to my dad's relationship with that fuckin' secretary of his than he's telling me."

She pulled an old sweatshirt over her head and said, "Whatta ya mean?"

"I know they went out that one time I told you 'bout. I don't think they've been out again, but I talked to him about it this morning, and I just get the feelin' something's going on."

She sat down and said, "You think they're involved already?"

"I don't know. If they aren't yet, it looks to me like that's where it's headed. He told me this morning not to worry 'bout him becoming involved with anyone else—that it would never change our relationship, but I'm not so sure. You know as well as I do that once a man's dick comes into play, things can change quickly."

"You worried?"

"A little, yes."

"Ya know, you could just get a job. That might take care of the problem."

"Oh, I will, someday. If it becomes really necessary, and I have no other option, that's what I'll do. But for right now, I'll live off him as long as I can. And if something happens to him down the road, I may never need a job. Right now, things are just fine the way they are, but if he starts up with this Layla, I'm afraid we could be looking at a big change."

"So what are our options?"

"I don't know. Maybe something should happen to Layla. You know, not something real bad, but just a little bad. Bad enough so she's unable to work, for a while, or forever, I don't know. Whatta ya think?"

She smiled. "That works for me. Whatta you got in mind."

"Let me talk to Dad a little more in the next few days and see if I can get a grip on what's going on between them. If I think something's still going on, I'll try to learn a little more about her and her schedule. We can take it from there. Whatta ya think?"

She smiled. "I think anything that keeps food on the table, and drugs in our pocket, is enough of a life for me, that's what I think."

"Well, then, since using our brains is out of the way for the night, why don't you just slip off that sweatshirt, drop those jeans, and start the night off right."

She stood, pulled her sweatshirt off, displaying her braless breasts, and dropped her jeans as she moved toward him. *"Nothin'...* like a man with a brain and a few drugs. Now, lose those pants, buddy."

9

Barrett dreaded his appointment this morning. He had thought about it most of yesterday afternoon, and it remained on his mind as he tried to fall asleep last night. He hated lawyers—at least most of them. He figured at least 90 percent of those he knew were loud, overbearing, and contentious. He hadn't met the one he had an appointment with this morning, but he had no reason to believe this one was any different from the rest of the bunch that were part of the 90 percent he had already met.

Unfortunately, he had done some investigating for the wrong client. Well, she wasn't really the wrong client, but the case turned out to be the "wrong" case for him to have become involved. He just didn't know it when he took her retainer.

His appointment was at 9:00 a.m. and he showed up right on time, at least as concerned *his* schedule—he actually sauntered in the attorney's door at *nine thirty.* As he walked in, the first thing that greeted him was an incredibly beautiful woman. He started to change his way of thinking—maybe the stars were aligned just right, maybe this was fate, maybe his client was, in fact, the *right* client and not the *wrong* one.

"Good morning, may I help you?"

Barrett smiled. "I think so. I was to be here at nine, but I'm running a little behind."

"Let's see, you're obviously Mr. Whitmore's 9:00 a.m. appointment, but you're over a half hour late? That most likely won't sit well with him. You'll need to take a chair. I'll tell him you're here."

He looked quickly to see if she had a ring on while she contacted Whitmore. She didn't, which was what he had hoped for.

As she waited to hear from Charles, she said, "Mr. Armstrong, have a seat, please. I really don't know how long it will be before I can get you in. He's on a conference call, which was to start *after* you left, not before you arrived."

He picked up a magazine and appeared to be reading it, but he looked over the top of the magazine at her much more than he read the print. As she continued to work, he said, "How long you worked here?"

She stopped typing, turned to him, and said, "Oh, I guess I've been here about a month now. Why? Any particular reason or just small talk?"

He lowered the magazine, smiled, and said, "Small talk. I didn't mean to bother you."

"Oh, you aren't. I'll tell you when you're bothering me." She returned to her typing.

He thought for a moment then said, "Where'd you work before?"

Again, she turned toward him and said, "For another law firm here in town."

As she started to return to her typing, he said, "I'm a private investigator. Have been for years. Don't suppose you've heard of me?"

"No, sorry, I haven't."

"You like your job?"

Slowly she turned toward him, and said, *"Now* you're bothering me. Sorry, once or twice was okay, but I have work to complete yet this morning."

He turned a dull shade of red and said, "I'm so sorry. It won't happen again... at least, not soon it won't happen again. Can't guarantee what the future... might... Sorry, I'll stop."

She picked up her intercom phone, then looked up at him and said, "Mr. Whitmore will see you now."

He stood and continued to stare at her. "Do... I go in... that door?"

She smiled. "Yes. That other door takes you into the hallway—you know, the one you just came in."

"Sure. Yup, you're right on that particular point. I'll just be going in this door now." He watched her as he moved toward the door. She went back to typing, but he watched her until he felt for and found the doorknob, turning it and walking into Whitmore's office.

Quickly, his attention moved from a woman of intense beauty to an overweight attorney, with hands on hips.

"Am I wrong or was your appointment at nine?"

"No, you're right. Sorry, had something come up. I hadn't intended on that happening. I assume you've been in a situation like that before, haven't you?" Barrett reached out to shake Whitmore's hand, which he really hoped he would take. When he did, Barrett squeezed it, not quite as hard as he could have, but close. About that time, he was thankful for all the weight training he had done in the past year. The look on Charles Whitmore's face was indeed priceless. He quickly freed his hand from Barrett's vicelike grip.

"You got a pretty good grip there, Mr. Armstrong. Let's see if you're as strong mentally as you are physically. Have a seat."

Trying not to sound as if he was mocking him, even though that was exactly what he was doing, Barrett said, "Sir, I wouldn't have a snowball's chance in hell of matching you mentally… no, sirree."

Charles sat back in his chair, obviously assessing the man he faced. Finally, he said, "Again, have a seat." As Barrett sat down, Charles said, "Okay, let's get right to it. You're a private investigator, correct?"

"Yes, sir. Have been for about ten years now. You need some work done? I can cut you a deal if you wish. Course I'd need a little something in return every once in a while, maybe a favor now and then—you know what I mean."

Charles thought for a moment, finally leaned forward, and said, "What the fuck are you talking about? Do you know why you're here? Did Layla tell you when she set up your appointment?"

"Who's Layla?" He was hoping it was the young lady out front, but he just wanted to make sure before he walked back out Whitmore's door and into the outer office.

"My secretary, Mr. Armstrong, my secretary. I don't know what difference her name makes to you, but did she tell you why I wanted to see you?"

"Let's see." He looked at the floor for a second, appearing deep in thought, before he said, "Oh, yes, maybe something about Mr. and Mrs. Portland? Is that it?"

"Yes, that's it. You know he shot her, killed her, not long ago, right after he beat the hell out of her. Did you know that?"

He looked away for a moment as he said, "Yes, I did hear that. Nice woman."

"Were you doing some work for her? I heard you were tailing him and might have taken some video of one of the times he beat her. Is that correct?"

"Can't go into that. That was between her and me, no one else."

"She's dead. Be a little hard for her to give her approval, now wouldn't it?"

Barrett leaned forward until he had both forearms resting on Charles desk. He said softly, "I will admit I did some work for her. She paid me. She was my client, not you. Whatever information I have belongs to her, or her kids. I'm not giving it to anyone else, unless of course it's subpoenaed. Then I'll give it up, but only because I have to. Don't get me wrong. I want that son of a bitchen husband of hers in jail just as bad as you do. But my records belong to my client or her heirs, and by god, that's the way it's gonna remain unless I'm forced to give them up."

"Gonna make this difficult, are you? Not a problem. I know you have relevant information now, and I'll go get a subpoena. Expect it real soon, Mr. Armstrong, real soon indeed. You can get out of here now. And by the way, you better honor the subpoena in a timely fashion, and not like you did being a half hour late today, or I'll have your sorry ass in jail. You understand?"

"Oh, I understand," he said as he stood. "You get me a subpoena. I'll get you your records. Now, sir, am I free to go?"

"As I already told you, get out."

Barrett walked out the door, slamming it as he left. Once in the outer office, he stopped in front of Layla's desk, looked at her, and said, "Nice man you work for. What a prick."

"Now, now, Mr. Armstrong," she said, as she stopped typing, and looked up. "He's not a bad guy. You must have just caught him at a bad time."

As he turned, he whispered under his breath, "Doubt it." He shut the door behind him, and as he reached the elevator, he remembered what he had forgotten. He turned and walked back into the outer office, stopped in front of her desk, and said, "Could we have a drink together sometime?"

She thought for a second and said, "Maybe, sometime. I'm not really free to do that now because I'm somewhat involved, but I don't think that's going to last long. Come back and see me in a couple of weeks. Maybe we can set something up."

"I'll be here two weeks from today, at this exact time. You can count on it."

She smiled as she said, "I have no doubt you're most *always* on time, Mr. Armstrong. I'm sure today was just an off day for you. See you then."

10

Barrett sat quietly, near the back of the courtroom, watching John Weatherly work his magic.

"Judge, we call the defendant, Sam Hanson, to the stand."

The defendant rose, walked toward the bench, and stood quietly while he was sworn in. He then walked to the witness chair as each juror watched his every move. John remained standing as he said, "State your name for the record."

"Sam Hanson."

"How old are you, Sam?"

"Twenty-four."

Barrett couldn't help but recall his late teens and early twenties. John was his best friend and the two of them ran around together even though they weren't in college at the same school—he attended Belmont; John attended Vanderbilt. During those years, there were many times the two of them found themselves in trouble—nothing of any consequence—just trouble. They seemed to wiggle out each time, but a couple of times, it was a close call. They had talked about those days many times since college, which now seemed like an eternity ago.

"Ever been in trouble with the law?"

Sam looked at the jury. "Once or twice. Nothing major. Just a traffic ticket here and there. Once I was charged with driving drunk, but that was dismissed. Other than that, I have no record."

"You employed?"

"Yes. I'm a roofer. Have been for years—since I was nineteen."

"You have family here in Nashville—you married?"

"Yes, all my family's here and I'm married. Got two kids."

Barrett thought about his relationship with Janet. He was still trying to sort it all out. He compared his social life now to when both John and he were in college. He quickly concluded it hadn't changed much for him. John got serious and married Maggie soon after he graduated. But for him, it was certainly a very different story. He never could commit. Maybe he just couldn't find the right girl. While John was having a couple of wonderful children, Barrett was still playing the field.

John sat as he said, "As you're well aware, you've been charged with the break-in that occurred a few months ago at the pharmacy on the south side of Nashville. You do it?"

"No."

"The eyewitness that testified said he saw you running from the building—that wasn't you?"

"Absolutely not."

"Where were you?"

"At home, with my wife and kids. I work long days during this time of year, right before winter. We try to take advantage of the good weather and finish up all the jobs we can. I was home that night, got to bed at a decent hour, and went to work on time the next day. Whoever that guy saw that night I wouldn't know, but I do know it *wasn't* me."

He met up with John at least once a week for lunch or supper. Today was their day for lunch. Unfortunately, he had heard stories from friends about John's home life, which weren't good. He quizzed him a couple of times, but each time, John would say, "Everything's fine. We have our problems just like every married couple does, but we love each other and..." He would always ramble on about how close they both were. Barrett thought the world of Maggie and of both kids. He had decided to believe everything was fine within the marriage until he saw a problem himself, or was told about specific issues in the marriage *by John.*

"You saw the video. Even though the intruder had a mask on, it sure looked like your general build. And he identified you as the one that took the mask off outside that pharmacy as you were getting ready to drive away. What do you say about that?"

"Do you know how many men in Nashville are built like me— many. I have no idea who the man was, but it wasn't me. It was dark. He just made a mistake that's all. It wasn't me."

"Is your wife going to testify today on your behalf?"

"Sure. She'll be up here right after I finish."

"Would she lie for you knowing how much the family needed you on the job? That's what the prosecution will assert, you know— that she's lying. Would she lie if she knew it was you, but needed the income you provide to keep food on the table? Would she do that for you?"

The defendant smiled. Sarcastically, he said, "You have to be kidding. Absolutely not. She don't lie for nobody. Nobody at all."

"You do drugs?"

"No. They test me at work. I couldn't get up on those roofs and do what I do if I were on drugs or booze. I can't take the chance of being on a roof and needing a hit during the day. No, I don't do drugs and don't drink that much either."

"Once again, I assume your wife will verify that?"

"Sure. Ask her when she gets up here."

"Prosecution may cross-examine."

The judge said, "Well, before he does that, let's take our noon recess. Jurors, remember the admonition I gave you earlier this morning. We'll be in recess until one fifteen."

They walked to a small coffee shop not far from the courthouse for lunch. Barrett knew they would need to wait in line, but the food was good, and to leave the area and drive somewhere else for lunch would have taken more time than standing in line.

Once seated, Barrett said, "How's the family, John? How's Barrett and Hanna?"

Once he had swallowed a huge bite of his Ruben sandwich, John smiled and said, "Good. They're both growing too fast. You need to stop over. Barrett's asked about his godfather more than once. It's been a while since he's seen you."

"I know, I know. I've just been so damn busy. How's Maggie?"

He hesitated, then said, "She's fine. I suppose you heard I left the house for a week or so. What I did was stupid, and I realized it later. Just one of those things. Everything's fine now."

Barrett sat back and looked at John as he said, "You're not screwing around on her, are you? You messin' with someone else?".

"Relax. No, I'm not. We're fine. Just a little misunderstanding, that's all."

Barrett returned to the rapid consumption of his roast beef on rye. "You know, if I found out you were messin' around, I'd do everything I could to support her, don't you? Wouldn't matter to me what the reason might be. I love her more than I do you, man."

John smiled. "And that comes from someone that dated three women at the same time while he was in college and *still* can't commit to one all these years later. Somehow, I got the feelin' we're both lacking a little something when it comes to relationships and the opposite sex."

"Not to change the subject, but do you know a prosecutor by the name of Charles Whitcome… Charles Winsome—"

"Whitmore? You talkin' 'bout old Charley Whitmore?"

"That's him. You know anything about him?"

"Yes, I do. Good prosecutor, but kind of a prick. He doesn't have many friends in the business or outside the practice. His son is a druggy. Why do you ask?"

"I bumped heads with him the other day. He wanted some information from me, which I refused to give him without a subpoena. Probably could have, but his attitude was awful, and I just wasn't going to accommodate him. But I may need you to help me before this is all over."

"Not a problem. We've bumped heads many times. He's tough but he's sure as hell beatable."

"You gonna get this roofer guy off?"

"I don't know. I thought he was pretty convincing today, didn't you?"

"I did. But of course, I haven't heard what they've got against him either. Is his wife going to be a good witness?"

"As good as it gets. Yes, she'll help in a big way."

"You always have the defendant take the stand?"

"Yes, unless the evidence against him is absolutely worthless, I won't even take the case unless the defendant is prepared to testify on his own behalf. The State has *always* got enough to prove its case, even if its marginal, or we wouldn't be there in the first place. So I want that defendant on the stand, to swear under oath he didn't do a damn thing. And it needs to be believable and consistent with the facts, or I won't take the case. It's just not worth it to me."

"Well, from what I understand, you're as successful at what you do as anyone in the city, so your approach must work."

"I can't handle representing these people in any other way. Either they need to be prepared to testify, or they need to go see someone else."

"We better go. By the time, we get back to the courtroom, it'll be time to start up again."

They walked back to the courthouse. Barrett remained to listen to the cross-examination of the defendant. He also hung around to watch the best friend he ever had work his magic, until the jury came back an hour later finding the defendant "not guilty" as charged.

11

Two weeks later to the day, Barrett Armstrong walked into the outer office of Charles Whitmore. Layla was working on paperwork with her back to the door. He stood patiently, waiting for her to turn around. When she finally did, he said, somewhat apprehensively, "Remember me?"

She smiled and said, "Now, how could I possibly forget a face like that."

"It's been two weeks—to the minute."

"Okay."

He looked down. "You don't remember, do you?"

"Remember what?"

"I told you I'd stop by in exactly two weeks, and maybe we could go out for supper and…"

"Stop." She started to smile. "Sure, I remember. When and where?"

"How 'bout day after tomorrow?"

"Can't then, but how 'bout tonight?"

"Great. Wanna meet me or can I pick you up?"

"Why don't you just pick me up outside the building?"

"What time?"

"About five forty-five or so? I'm working a little late tonight. Lord knows I've plenty to keep me busy."

"It's a deal. I'll make reservations."

He stopped in front of her office building at five forty-five, and she walked out right on time. They had reservations at Reflect, a small restaurant on Westend Avenue in Nashville. Their table was ready when they arrived.

As they sat, he said, "My good god, you're a beautiful woman. I'm sure you hear that all the time, but it's the truth."

She smiled as she said, "Whoa, you don't hold back, do you? Thank you. I guess I could say I've heard it a few times, but believe me, it never gets old—it's always nice to hear it again. Tell me about yourself, Barrett. I've learned a little about you as a result of a few unsolicited comments from my boss, but let me hear it from someone that's not already biased in somewhat of a negative way."

He laughed. "Good to know he feels the same about me as I do about him. I always hate to be on a different level with someone, you know—you liking him, he hating you. I'm glad to know we have a mutual problem."

"He didn't have many good things to say about you, I'm afraid."

"Well, I feel good in saying I don't care what he thought about me. By the way, he doesn't even know me. We had one conversation, and that's it. In response to your question..." He stopped in mid-sentence as the waiter arrived, and both ordered a glass of the house Merlot. "In response to your question, I was born and raised here, never been married, went to school at Belmont, and been an investigator for about ten years now."

"Why never married?"

"I just could never pull the trigger, I guess. I've dated some great girls, but just couldn't finish off the deal."

"You live here in town?"

"I do. I have a condo in east Nashville."

Layla said, "Do you work alone?"

"Yes. At least for now, although my business has grown so much I've thought about adding a partner."

"Business is that good?"

"Yes, it is. I'm sure that's contrary to the impression Mr. Whitmore conveyed to you about me. I assume he told you how difficult I was to deal with."

She laughed. "He made it clear you two didn't get along, I'll say that. How come you aren't in a relationship? You're a good-looking guy, good job, great personality. Seems a little strange to me you aren't already taken."

He hesitated. "To be honest, I just got out of one. Since that one ended, I've been a little reluctant to jump right back into the dating game. Besides that, after I met you, I held off calling anyone until I had a chance to be with you."

"Is the relationship you were in really over?"

The waiter interrupted the conversation. After they both ordered supper, he said, "Yes. To answer your question, yes, the relationship is over. We both tried, but it just didn't work. My fault I'm afraid, but looking back, I guess there were problems I wasn't aware of. I don't miss her. At least, I don't have that burning desire to patch things up. It's over and I've moved on pretty easily. What about you? You know, I could ask the same question about you. Why aren't you involved?"

"Oh, I have been, many times."

"That's not a surprise. But apparently, you haven't found the right one yet either."

"No, I haven't."

"How long have you been with Whitmore?"

"Only about a month."

"How's that going?"

She took a drink before responding. "Fine. It's going fine. I'm really not sure, though, how everything's going to work out. The work is good. I already had a considerable amount of experience in the legal field, so I was comfortable with that part of it from the beginning. But he asked me out about a week after I started working there. I didn't wanna turn him down so we had supper. Now, I'm afraid he might be expecting more of me as concerns our personal relationship. But that's just not going to happen. I haven't told him that yet, but I'm afraid I'm going to have to. I'm not sure how everything's going to work out after we have that conversation. I knew I shouldn't have gone out with him, but I didn't wanna piss him off the first week I was there."

Barrett smiled. "You know, there's a well-founded reason that's not supposed to happen. There's a reason women don't date their boss, and you, of all people, at your age and level of experience, should have known that."

She grimaced. "I know, I know. And unfortunately, I just got out of a similar situation like that with the job I had prior to going to work for him. But I didn't know him… I didn't know how he would react if I turned him down."

"So what about now? What happens next?"

"I'm going to tell him there's no sense in it going any further. The two of us are going nowhere as concerns our personal relationship, and that's that. I think he'll take it okay. He needs me now as a secretary more than a lover. I should be okay."

As they brought salads for each of them, he said, "So you aren't involved with anyone else right now?"

"No. I, like you, just ended a long-term relationship with a guy, and like you, I don't miss him much. I just haven't found the right person either. Not sure I ever will. I'm just pretty damn independent after living alone all these years."

"Speaking of living alone, where do you live? You in Nashville?"

"No. I'm living in a small home I purchased in Bellevue. I just don't like all the hustle and bustle—the fast pace of Nashville. I can drive home after work, drive down a quiet street, walk in my front door, and relax. Many nights I can sit out on my front porch and watch an occasional car drive by, maybe watch someone walking their dog, and totally relax—get away from the insane pace of life in Nashville. I love it there."

"No children?"

"No, but I'd like children. I just haven't found the right person I would wanna say was their father. I will. I just need a little more time."

"So when is your confrontation with Charles to take place? When are you going to 'let him down gently' as they say."

She laughed. "Tomorrow. He's asked me out a couple of times, and I've always had some kind of excuse. But that's over. I'll tell him tomorrow, and that hopefully will end that, once and for all."

Shortly thereafter, they brought the main course. While he consumed a steak, potatoes, and baby carrots, and she a large portion of rare tuna on a bed of grits, he said, "Are you ready to date after your experience with Charles and the end of that long-term relationship you told me about, or you just wanna relax and avoid the game for a while?"

She took a bite of tuna, wiped her lips with her napkin, and said, "It would obviously depend a lot on who the other individual might be."

"Let me put it this way. I've enjoyed our evening. I'd like to see you again. Once you remove Charles from your life, would you have time for me?"

She smiled. "You don't have to wait until I've taken care of Charles. Of course, I'd have time for you."

As they finished their meal, he arranged to pick her up day after tomorrow. He just happened to have tickets for a show at Bridgestone Arena, which had been provided by a former client. He let her off at her car later that evening.

As Barrett drove home, he was excited—this could very well be the beginning of something special. But then again, he thought the same thing when he first started dating Janet Thompson, and that relationship ended up in the shitter real quick.

12

This was without doubt the most boring conversation Barrett had ever sat through. He knew he needed to concentrate. The insurance company this man represented had provided him with a considerable amount of business during the past few years, but he hated to discuss *any* case with this particular representative. He had been in his office for over an hour and had reiterated, in his soft-spoken, wimpy sort of manner, the same set of facts time after time after...

"We don't know where he went. We really don't. And she's about to file a claim for his life insurance with us, but we're just sure he's alive, and that's why..."

"Okay, I get it. I understand. Leave your paperwork with my secretary out front. Let her make copies. Stop back later to pick up what you left here and I'll start looking right away."

"The guy is about six feet, three inches tall. He weighs about—"

"Isn't all that in your paperwork?"

"Well, yes... but—"

"Is there anything *else* that I should know that's *not* covered in those papers you have in your hand and on your lap and on the corner of my desk. Anything at all?"

"No, I guess there isn't, but..."

Barrett stood. "Nope, no 'buts' in this office. Thank you. I'll be in touch."

The rep stood, shoved everything into his briefcase, and stuck out his hand. "Well, okay, I'll just leave everything..."

Barrett shook his hand as he said, "That's right, you leave every-thing out front with her, and I'll get back to you."

Barrett came out from behind his desk and walked to the office door, opening it, then indicating the way out with a sweeping motion of his arm. He closed the door once the rep walked through, then returned to his desk and sat back down.

Barrett considered the many times he had been with Layla during the last month. Even though they hadn't been intimate, he just couldn't get her off his mind. He wanted to call her, to find out what her thoughts were about last night, but most of all just to hear her voice.

However, he hesitated to call her at the office. Today was the day. Today was the day Layla was going to tell her boss to lay off. He wasn't sure why she had waited so long—she was initially going to tell him weeks ago. But she had mentioned a couple of times lately she was having trouble reading him—that he seemed short, even with her. He had become more difficult to deal with when she told him, on multiple occasions, she was unavailable for supper. However, yesterday she had consented to have supper with him tonight, right after work. She would tell him then that they were done as concerned any type of romantic situation—that she was involved with someone else.

Barrett had told her, whatever she did, not to tell Charles who her relationship was with. Telling him to lay off would most likely have enough inner-office ramifications, without telling Charles he was the "other man." A knock on his closed office door interrupted his train of thought.

"What."

The door opened, and his secretary walked in as she said, "I got a couple of messages for you."

"That guy leave all his paperwork?"

"Yes. I'm copying it now."

"Good. Don't let him back in here with me for a while. I need to be at a point, mentally, where I can take him. Shit, he just goes on forever. Give him his originals when he comes back in. If he wants to see me, set him up at least a week from now, or tell him I'll call him. I can't handle him again this week."

She giggled, replied "Okay," and walked out. The second of the two messages was interesting. It was from Kris, that private investigator that had "schooled" him on being more careful.

"Morning, Kris, Barrett Armstrong. I see you called. We got a problem with Mr. McNamara again?"

"No, no, but I do have a question or two for you. How's your schedule for early afternoon?"

"Not good. In fact, I won't probably have any time until tomorrow. Does that work?"

Kris said, "No, not really. What about meeting you for a drink right after you close for the day?"

"That works for me. Maybe round five thirty? Where at?"

"What about that little bar in the Hanson hotel? That's not far for either of us."

"See you then."

After they had both ordered a beer, Barrett smiled and said, "Okay, what's the purpose of your meeting—why'd you call us all together?"

She smiled and said, "Really, it was no big deal, but I got a client that wanted me to investigate a guy that's missing. I told him I would. And to be honest, I've uncovered quite a bit of information on him. But now, I get this call from the DA's office. Apparently, they're looking for him too. He's…"

"Not to interrupt, but it wasn't from Whitmore's office was it?"

"How'd you know?"

He laughed. "I didn't. But I know him. He's a total prick. In fact, a girl I've been dating works for him."

She took a drink and sat back in the booth. "You're dating someone now? Last I talked to you, you weren't involved."

"Well, that's true, I wasn't. But I am now. Go on with your story."

She took another drink. "How serious is your relationship?"

J. B. MILLHOLLIN

"Oh, hell, I don't know. They all seem serious at first, don't they? We're just gonna see where it takes us—one day at a time. Now finish your frickin' story, Kris."

"Oh, sure, well anyway, he wants all my records. He just wants me to give them to him. I don't feel comfortable with doing that. I've talked to my client, and they don't wanna give them up either. You have this happen before? I mean, this guy is insistent. He says there could be severe consequences if I don't give the records to him."

Barrett leaned forward and said, "To me, you have three choices. First, just give them to him. Second, tell him you need a subpoena to testify before the grand jury, and you'll bring them all with you, or third, I got the name of a great friend that's a defense attorney. Go talk to him if it will make you feel more comfortable."

"That third option sounds best to me. What's his name?"

"John Weatherly. Tell him I sent you. That'll get you right in."

"That's exactly what I'll do." Again, she hesitated. "So you're really involved right now?"

"I am for the moment. Who knows about tomorrow, or even later tonight. My life just changes that quickly."

She laughed. He waited for her to continue. She was easy to read. She had something else on her mind. Finally, after a number of uneasy seconds had passed by, she said, "Do you have issues that come up in your business and are of such a nature that you wish you had someone to visit with—someone to help you figure out a solution? Does that happen to you much?"

"Oh sure, like probably once or twice a day."

"So do I."

"Okay, move on. What're you thinking?"

She leaned back and said, "You ever think about partnering up with anyone?"

He took a drink, before answering. "I have, yes. I've considered it, and in fact, I've been approached to do that very thing, but I've never made the move. Most of the time, it was with other guys I didn't think I wanted to deal with, but I've certainly considered it."

"Wanna consider it again?"

"I guess I could—with you?"

"Yes. My business continues to grow. I have questions every day that I would give anything to discuss with someone else, someone I could trust. And I have business that comes in I just can't handle—that I need to refer to another firm. It's just getting to be more than I can handle by myself, but I have a hell of a time turning away business. I really need a partner."

"Hmm. Let me think on it. You need an answer right away?"

"No. You're the first one I've approached. I'm getting along fine the way it is, but I think the income and the overall benefits of expanding would be incredible. Just think about it and let me know within the near future."

"I will."

Later that night, after each had gone their own way, he thought about her proposal concerning partnering up. The tone of the conversation had started in a fashion that had, at first, concerned him—obviously, she was interested in a personal relationship with him. But it had quickly turned to a business issue, and that had happened after knowing he was involved with another woman. The issues would need to be kept separate, but he was definitely interested in her proposal—certainly not as concerned a romantic interest, but as concerned the combining of both offices. It made good business sense and was, without question, a viable option at this point in both of their professional careers.

13

"Now, George, I'm telling you, even though you failed to perform the test and have already lost your license, if you testify at your trial, I still might be able to get you off the actual charge."

"How's that, Mr. Weatherly? I don't understand. I thought if you failed to take the test, as I did, you was just automatically guilty."

"Nope, George, that's not the way it works. You *do* lose your license, and the fact that you didn't submit to the test to determine if you were over the legal limit can be used against you, but the issue of whether you were actually driving while intoxicated is still in play."

John had been at this for almost an hour, trying to help George understand what the law was, as it applied to him. It had been difficult. George just wasn't smart enough to really get it after going through a plethora of issues the first time. Twice worked sometimes, and three times always worked. He would continue, but only because George had acquired money from somewhere or from someone to pay a handsome retainer, and that was what really mattered.

"So what am I gonna need to do to get out of this, to put this all behind me, as they say?"

"We need to try the case, unless they dismiss it, which they probably won't, and you need to testify you weren't drunk—that you never had enough to drink to get drunk. When they ask you why you didn't sign the form, you need to tell them you just didn't understand what it was. We're also going to need one or two witnesses. They need to testify that they were with you right before you got in your car, and you hadn't been drinking, at least not enough you could have been drunk. Can you line up a couple of witnesses that will say that?"

"Well, I think so. Give me that pen and a piece of paper."

John gave him both.

"Now, exactly what are they gonna need to say? Let me write it down so's I don't forget."

"They need to say you weren't drinking, at least to any extent, before you got in that car and drove away. Had maybe one beer, but that's it. And they need to be firm about it. They need to swear under oath, that you only had one. Can you find a couple of guys that will do that for you?"

He stood and gave the pen back to John, carefully folding the paper. He then shoved the piece of paper deep into the pants pocket of a pair of jeans that were hanging so low, a drop of another inch would have left him exposed.

"Yes, sir, I can do that. When you want me back here?"

"Set something up with my secretary for next week."

"I sure will, Mr. Weatherly, and thank you."

As he left, Grace, his secretary, walked in and said, "Barrett Armstrong called you. He wants you to call him back."

"Why the fuck didn't you put him through?"

"Sorry. I didn't think you wanted to be bothered."

"I've told you before to put Barrett through, and that's exactly what I meant. Good god, decent help is hard to find. Get him on the phone."

As he waited, he reflected upon how many secretaries he had gone through. But not one of them was exactly what he wanted. Grace had been with him only six months, and he was already starting to look around. His phone rang.

"Hey, buddy, what's up?"

"Hi, John. I just wanted to forewarn you. I talked to a fellow private investigator the other day and told her to contact you. Kris Thompson was her name. She—"

"Already heard from her. Just a minute." He put his hand over his phone. "Whatta ya want? Can't you see I'm on the phone?"

Grace said, "I can, but the district attorney's office is on the other line, and they say it's important. You wanna talk to them?"

"You know, I've told you ten times, nothing is important when it comes to them. I'll call them back."

"Sorry 'bout that, Barrett. It was my secretary concerning a call on the other line. I need new help. You wanna job—good pay, not-bad benefits, starting today?"

Barrett laughed. "If you weren't such an asshole, I might consider it. How many secretaries you been through? Did you talk to Kris?"

"I did. She came in and I just told her to tell them to give her a subpoena or a subpoena ducas tecum, and she'd provide the records. I told her not to give them the records under any other circumstances. I also told her if she needed help, to give me a call."

"Thank you. I appreciate your help."

"No problem. By the way, there was a shouting match going on when she was here. I'm sure she wondered what the hell was happening. He's a former client and the son of a bitch thinks I owe him some money, which I don't. The argument started in here, but continued to some extent, out in the reception area. She heard it all. Meant nothing to me, but I'm sure my clients that were waiting to see me had a few questions they never asked. Tell her not to worry about it... all is fine."

As he terminated Barrett's call, he noticed it was about time to shut the door and turn out the lights for the day. He remained apprehensive about going home. This morning, he had left the house in the middle of an argument with his wife, and he dreaded returning home to continue where they left off.

As he drove in his driveway, later that afternoon, he couldn't help but smile as he remembered how the two kids used to run out and greet him when they were younger. He grabbed his briefcase, and walked up the sidewalk through the door, and saw both of them sitting on the living room floor, transfixed by small animated creatures running across the screen of the television.

"Hi, you two. How was your day?"

Neither moved a muscle. Neither said a word. He turned and walked into the den, setting his briefcase down, which contained pleadings he would need to review later this evening. He walked into the kitchen where he found Maggie, leaning over the kitchen sink and apparently fixing supper.

"How was your day, Maggie?"

She turned her head just far enough he would know she was responding to him, said, "Fine," then went back to whatever she had been doing before he had interrupted her.

John walked back into the den. He poured himself a half glass of bourbon, grabbed what was still left of the morning paper, sat down, and put his feet up.

A few minutes later, Maggie walked in and sat down on the edge of the ottoman, as she said, "You and I have to finish the conversation, John."

"What's left to say? You told me how you felt. I explained how I felt. Isn't that enough?"

"No. You *have* to quit drinking so much. Can't you cut back a little, for the sake of both kids and for me?"

"I *have* cut back. And besides that, it can't really be that bad, can it?"

She looked away and, after a brief hesitation, said, "You're at your worst the more you drink. You haven't cut back at all. You're mean, John. And when we go out, you make sexist, degrading comments to other women, embarrassing me, embarrassing yourself. Now, I've told you I've had enough. I've said it before, but I mean it this time. If this continues, I'm out of here, and this time I'm not kidding."

He raised the paper, looking for a decent article to read, and said, "Okay, I understand. I'll do my best."

"Hope so, John, or we—myself and both children—are leaving." She got up, and as she turned to leave, she said, "Supper will be ready in about a half hour. Try not to get drunk before we eat."

As he sat by himself, he knew it was time for a change. Unfortunately, the kind of change he envisioned had nothing to do with the amount of alcohol he consumed. But what would that kind of change bring? Most likely alimony, child support, and of course, half of everything would go to her, all of which would create many more problems than he had now.

As he finished his first of what would most likely be multiple drinks during the course of the evening, he figured the best and clearly the cheapest way to stop all the turmoil would simply be to cut down his consumption. As he stood to pour himself another, he figured it would be worth a try. Maybe he would start cutting back tomorrow night—well, not tomorrow, but maybe the first of next week. That should certainly be soon enough to appease her.

14

He had endured a difficult day. However, it was well worth it knowing what waited for him once he could close those office doors. Charles had asked Layla out for supper a couple of weeks ago, and she had agreed to go, but not until tonight. For that he was excited. But getting through the rest of the day to the point he could enjoy his time with her would be like pulling teeth.

His first problem concerned the appointment he was now facing. Kris Thompson sat before him, waiting for an explanation as to why he needed the information she had. He had tried to explain on the telephone, but she wouldn't listen. He finally "invited" her to his office, so he could explain in detail why the information she had was so necessary.

He told her the man she was following had been seen with people that were under indictment for multiple criminal violations. He told her he assumed they were all in business together, but he had no proof, physical or otherwise. The truth of the matter was he simply had nothing to establish they were known associates. If Kris had been following him, then she most likely had information, perhaps pictures, establishing the relationship. He needed to know—he needed what she had.

Charles had used her as a witness in a prior hearing. She had done quite well and was easy to deal with. But today was a different situation altogether. Initially, he figured she would cooperate. But he had misread her. She had turned into a pain in the ass.

"You know, Mr. Whitmore, I have a responsibility to the people who hired me to keep their information confidential. After your initial call, I called my client. They told me the information they paid me to acquire goes to no one but them. What am I supposed to do? You tell me, what am I supposed to do?"

"Well, as far as I'm concerned, you're supposed to give me whatever you have concerning the man you're following. That's what *I* believe you're *supposed* to do. I tried calling the man that hired you, but he won't return my calls."

"Okay, let's just cut to the chase, Mr. Whitmore. I've sought legal advice concerning this matter. I've tried to figure—"

"Who'd you talk to?"

"John Weatherly."

Charles rolled his eyes. "Did you give him *all* the facts?"

"Well, really, Mr. Whitmore, there aren't many to give. I have a client I work for, and he doesn't want me to release my work product to anyone but his firm. It's really not complicated. It's really…"

He leaned forward in his chair and, in little more than a whisper, interrupted her as he said, "I'm going to get this guy, one way or the other, and when I do, I'll subpoena everything you have concerning this case. Between now and then, you better keep your nose clean. You don't wanna screw up here, Ms. Thompson… concerning anything… or I'll throw your ass in jail for virtually nothin'. You screw up, I'll make sure I'm the one who prosecutes you. Now do we understand each other?"

She hesitated. "Are you threatening me? Is that what you're doing here?"

"Guess maybe I am, yes… now I'm sure of it. I sure as hell am. Now you get your ass out of my office and don't you ever expect a favor from the Davidson County District Attorney's office—for anything!"

She stood, turned, and walked out his door, closing it quietly behind her.

Charles leaned back in his chair. Even though he knew she would be a hard sell, he figured he could get her to cave in. He hadn't anticipated she had already seen an attorney. Of course, it would have been better if she had gone to anyone other than John Weatherly. He was a good attorney, he knew the law, especially criminal law, and he had done his job correctly. She had no obligation to release the information.

"Charles, your son's on line 2."

He picked up and said, "Hey, what's going on?"

"Just got done with a job interview. Nothing firm yet, but it doesn't sound too bad. When you comin' home?"

It didn't take a genius to figure out why he needed to know when he would be home.

"Oh, I don't know. I've something going on this evening, so it'll probably be later than I normally am. Why?"

"I was going to... I figured I would start supper for us and just wanted to know when to expect you. Where're you goin' tonight?"

"I'm going out for supper. I'll probably be home around nine o'clock or so. You need money?"

"No, no, that's fine. Thanks. You going out *with* someone or is it just you?"

"No, I'm taking someone with me." Charles had decided to keep information involving his relationship with Layla, or any other woman, to himself. He noticed tension when he discussed that type of issue with Michael, and he had recently concluded, at least for now, it was best to keep this "relationship" information to himself.

"Who you goin' with—that secretary of yours, Layla? Is that who you're going out with?"

He hesitated. "Yes, it is. I'll just see you when I get home. I won't be late."

"Fine. I won't wait up." Michael terminated the call. He figured it was time to discuss the small issue that seemed to have developed between the two of them when he got home. The rest of the afternoon was spent with issues involving file after file, which he tried to figure out by himself, without the assistance of Layla. He felt the longer they remained away from each other during the day, the more interesting the conversation might be during the evening.

At exactly five, he walked out and said, "Let's shut this place down and go eat. I had nothing for lunch and I've been looking forward to being with you all day. Let's get outta here."

She smiled and said, "Sounds like a good idea."

Each took their own vehicle, meeting at Mitsi's, a small intimate café in east Nashville.

They each ordered a glass of wine and, while reviewing the menu, discussed the day's activities. The conversation was nonstop, but as the waiter brought a shared desert consisting of candied pistachio cake, drizzled with caramel, he said, "You driving home from here?"

"Yes. I've got a number of things I need to take care of tonight before I call it a day. In fact, I need to leave shortly so I can get started."

He hesitated. "You want some company?"

"Where? Where do I 'want some company'? You mean at my place?"

"Yes."

"Oh, I don't think so, but thanks for asking."

He put his fork down. "Okay, I need to know. Is this going anywhere or not? I've been putting off even looking at anyone but you since that first time we went out. Should I be dating others, or is this, you and I, going somewhere?"

She stopped eating and looked down for a moment. Finally, she looked up at him and said "I've been meaning to talk to you about that. I had the feeling you thought it might be a permanent situation between the two of us, but no, it's not. I've been putting off telling you that and figured tonight was the night. Don't get me wrong… I love my job… I love working for you, but as far as a personal relationship is concerned, I'm afraid that's not going to work out."

"Is it something I said, something I've done?"

"No. It's just I don't feel we're compatible, and to be honest, I don't feel comfortable working with you during the day and seeing you at night."

"So if I fired you, we could still see each other?"

She smiled. "No, that's not going to work either. I just don't have those kinds of feelings for you. You're a great boss, and I really do enjoy our working relationship, but I just don't want a *personal* relationship with you. I'm sorry, but I felt it was time you knew."

"Is there someone else?"

"Oh, that's maybe a small issue. It's too soon to say. But yes, I have been seeing someone else."

"Might I ask whom you're seeing?"

"No. It's not his fault. He has nothing to do with this. It's my issue and my issue alone."

He looked away, considering her comments and trying to figure out how to get out of this uncomfortable situation, which he had created, when she said, "I need to go. I'll pay for my share of supper." She started to fumble with her purse.

"No, no, you're not paying for anything. I enjoyed the meal, at least up until now, and I asked you out anyway. It's my responsibility. I'll just see you in the morning."

She reached over and placed her hand over his. "I'm sorry, I really am. I should have told you sooner, but it's taken until now to make sure I knew that you would understand—that there would be no issue with us working together during the day."

He smiled and said, "No, there'll be no problem with that issue. I need you right where you are on a daily basis. At this point, you're way too important to me as a secretary to lose you over a personal issue I might have."

She stood, smiled, and said, "Thanks. See you in the morning."

He watched her walk away. Certainly not the ending to the evening he had anticipated, but an appropriate ending to the day he had endured.

Charles arrived home near seven o'clock and found Michael eating a bowl of cereal.

He said, "Couldn't you find anything else to eat other than that?"

"I like cereal. I could eat it at darn near every meal. How'd your date go?"

He hesitated before he answered. He had concluded it was no one's business how his love life was going, and that included Michael. Besides, he was a little embarrassed over the way it had all ended. A lack of information concerning who he was and wasn't seeing wouldn't be a loss to Michael anyway.

"Good. It went good."

"I'm surprised you're home this early."

"It was just for dinner. We had dinner, she went home, I came home. That was that, at least for tonight."

Michael put his spoon down. "So this is now an ongoing relationship, is it?"

"I don't really know. We'll just have to see what happens. I need to go shower, and I've got some files to review before tomorrow. You need some money? You going out tonight?"

"Don't need any money. Yes, I'm going out. In fact, I'm leaving right now." He got up and as he walked out the door, he said, "Don't wait up."

He was just ready to tell Michael to put his dishes in the sink but, instead, watched him walk through the door. He picked up the dishes himself, put them in the sink, and walked toward his bedroom.

Charles concluded it was a fitting ending to a day from hell. He would shower, review files, and have a stiff drink. Maybe the drink would help him forget a day that was clearly forgettable from beginning to end.

15

Barrett had been with clients all day—some new, some old. His business was ever expanding, and he considered perhaps it might be time to start turning away potential clients. He knew if he tried to handle too many clients, some of them would not get the attention they deserved. That would eventually result in the movement of new business, but definitely in the wrong direction. Turning business away would be difficult to do, in light of the fact that during his early years, it was absolutely necessary for him to take on anyone and everyone that walked in the door. He would definitely need to develop a completely different mindset if he were to ever become comfortable turning away potential clients.

"Barrett, you have a call on line 1."

"New client?"

"No."

"Old one?"

"No."

"Layla?"

"Barrett, it's Kris. Now would you just take the call?"

"Sorry, sure, sure." His secretary had been with him from the start—probably with him too long—they knew each other way too well.

"Hi, Kris, what's up?"

"Hey, Barrett, I just wanted to tell you I met with Charles Whitmore, and you're right. He's a complete jerk."

Barrett smiled. "Told ya. Did you give him the records?"

"No. He didn't seem too happy I'd been to see Mr. Weatherly, and I can tell you Whitmore and I definitely aren't friends after my trip to his office. He told me to never ever ask for a favor from the district attorney's office. He isn't one to mince words. He was a real jerk."

"I agree. I've had all the contact with him I want."

"Oh, by the way, I saw a mutual friend of ours while I was sitting in John's reception area."

"Who's that?"

"Chad McNamara. I heard a lot of commotion going on in John's office while I was sitting out in the reception area. As it died down, Chad came out. I wasn't sure what they were arguing about, but they carried, at least part of it, right out into the reception area. McNamara was really unhappy about something. He didn't even acknowledge me. John said nothing about it, and I didn't ask."

"Maybe it had something to do with his divorce, who knows."

"I wasn't going to stop him and ask—he was really upset." She hesitated. "I was thinking—you wanna get together tonight, have a drink, maybe catch some supper, and talk about a partnership?"

"I would love to, but I can't tonight. Sorry, maybe sometime next week?"

"Sure, no problem. Got a hot date, do you?"

He noticed a different tone in her voice. She really sounded disappointed. "Not sure it's that hot, but I do already have plans. Let me call you the first of the week and make arrangements. Will that work?"

"Sure. Have fun tonight."

He waved as she walked in the front door. Layla had decided to meet him at Reflect rather than leaving her car at work and having him pick her up. She was right on time. He had only been there a few minutes, hesitating to leave the office when he did. With so much to do, he felt it might be difficult keeping his mind on her, knowing he should be dealing with all the files and all the phone messages that still remained unattended as he walked out the door. But as soon as she walked in, his thoughts of what he should be doing at the office quickly disappeared.

He stood as she approached the table. "You look great. How'd the day go?"

She sat as he helped her with her chair. "It went fine. Missed you. What's it been, almost a week now?"

He sat, and as he did, he said, "Yup. And I've missed you every one of those days. I almost called you a couple of days ago, to see if I could stop by the office, but I thought better of it when I quickly remembered who you worked for."

She smiled. Just as she was about to reply, the waiter came to take their drink order. Both ordered a glass of Pinot. "He's not been the easiest to get along with lately. Did I tell you we had a little talk?"

"About the two of you?"

"Yes."

Barrett said, "No. I knew you were going to, but we haven't had a chance to discuss what happened. By the way, I would rather we not be separated quite that long again. I really missed you."

"It was a long week for me too. Charles had asked me out for supper, on a number of occasions. I so dreaded telling him I wasn't interested in him. I had just put it off and put it off. But finally, I realized the problem wasn't going to go away by itself. I needed to take care of it, so I told him I'd have supper with him. While we were eating, I told him."

The waiter brought a couple of glasses of wine, while she continued. "He really took it pretty well. Better than I thought he would."

Barrett smiled. "Didn't have much choice, did he? I'm sure he needed you at the office, and I'm assuming he didn't want to adversely affect you continuing as his secretary."

"Even so, it was pretty uncomfortable. I told him I was seeing someone else."

"I hope you didn't tell him it was me."

"No. I wasn't going down that road with him. He was trying to process his rejection. I wasn't going to tell him who I had chosen to be with rather than him. He'll find out later anyway."

As they finished their glass of wine and discussed the day's activity, Barrett heard a familiar voice say, "Well, you just never know who you're going to run into anymore, do you?"

He turned as John Weatherly walked up behind him, putting his hand on Barrett's shoulder.

"Hi, John. Didn't even know you knew about this place. I've never seen you here before."

"This is the first time Maggie and I have been here. We just finished. Food was great. Would you mind introducing us?"

"No, of course not. Layla, this is my good friend, John Weatherly. John and I have known each other since we were in college. We've been the best of friends for years. John, this is Layla Adams. She's Charles Whitmore's secretary."

John extended his hand and said, "It's nice meeting you. I do offer my condolences for having to work with Charles, but I'm sure you can handle him."

She shook his hand and said, "He's a good boss. We get along well. What do you do, Mr. Weatherly?"

Barrett jumped in and said, "He's an attorney—specializes in criminal law. One of the best in Nashville. I've sent a number of people to him."

"I guess I haven't run across your name yet on any of the paperwork in Charles's office."

"I have about six or seven cases pending with the district attorney's office right now, but none with Charles. I think when I do, now knowing you work for him, I might just bring in the paperwork myself rather than mailing it. Might just hand-deliver it."

Layla smiled, as Barrett said, "If I hadn't seen that look on your face before, I wouldn't have to tell you that Layla and I are an item, John. You're married. Both those issues should preclude you from hand-delivering anything to her. Nice to see you. Now just mosey on back to your Maggie. Tell her hi. Bye, now."

John smiled and said, "Very nice meeting you, Layla. Watch this guy. He's always been pretty successful with the women. Dates them, bonds with them, breaks their hearts. Just keep that in mind."

"Get out of here, you jerk. Don't stop until you reach your table."

John smiled, gave both a half wave, and walked back to his table. The waiter was waiting to take their order, once John walked away.

"Sounds like you two have been friends a long time."

"We have. I'd trust him with my life. I've lost track of the number of times he's helped me out. It's not always been a matter of life and death, but just a number of little things—matters of which I just didn't know how to handle. Good guy—good family."

"I'll keep that in mind if I need someone."

Their food arrived shortly thereafter, and as they ate, they discussed their work, their prior love lives, and their future aspirations. As the plates were being removed from the table, she reached over and placed her hand over his as she said, "You drove here, didn't you?"

"I did."

"Wanna follow me home?"

"Didn't think you'd ever ask."

As he started to stand, she pulled him back down. "You know, if I hadn't had this issue of Charles hanging over my head, I would have invited you over long ago. I was so concerned about what his reaction might be, I didn't want to move any direction too quickly until I felt I had him under control. You understand, don't you?"

He smiled. "Certainly. I understand completely. I knew it was bothering you. I was willing to wait. Now, I'm really not interested in waiting much longer, so if you don't mind, let's get out of here."

It was almost 3:00 a.m. and he still hadn't fallen asleep. As tired as he would be the rest of the day, it would take effort to get through all the work he needed to complete, even if he fell asleep now. But it was well worth it. She was an amazing woman. She knew what to do to please a man like no woman he had ever been with. She was experienced, to say the least. His relationship with her had reached a new level. He had never been very good at relationships in the past once they reached this stage. Apparently, to hear her talk, she hadn't either. It appeared to him it would now be a case of the blind leading the blind. He cared for her, but did he care for her enough to marry her… to live the rest of his life with her?

Time to get some sleep. That question was way too involved, full of too many contradicting issues to be considered at this hour of the night. In addition, the resulting answer would also, most likely, lack some degree of objectivity while she was actually lying by his side. That decision would need to be made another day, when he wasn't with her, when he had had some sleep, and when there were far fewer issues to assess at work.

16

Barrett focused upon the restaurant door while drinking his cup of coffee, as he continued to consider the events of last night and watch for John. He had spent the evening with Layla. It had been an interesting evening to say the least—and far removed from those evenings he had spent with her the many weeks prior to last night.

John walked through the door, grabbed a cup of coffee, and as he approached the table, he said, "Morning. Glad you were able to get a table. This place is packed."

Barrett said, "Always is. Maybe you and I should get into this business—offer coffee, donuts, and other pastries, which you could bake at your law office prior to opening each morning. I could do the books."

John took a chair and said, "That's funny. And it really sounds like you too—I do the work, you do... let's see... you do very little."

Barrett laughed and said, "You busy today? What's your agenda for the day?"

"Got a couple of arraignments here at the courthouse and then a few appointments at the office. It's really not a very busy day for me."

"Does meeting here each week on Mondays still work for you? We can sure as hell change days if some other day would work better."

"No, today's fine. What'd you do last night? You out late?"

Barrett hesitated, then said, "No, not really. I was home early for a change. Layla and I went out for supper. I took her home, then just went on home alone. She was completing something at home that pertained to her work and needed the time, alone, to finish up."

He cocked his head and said, "You seem disturbed by that. No sleepover last night? Sorry, buddy, but sometimes that just happens. Can't get that action every day of the week, you know."

"No, no, I understand that, John, believe me, I understand. But I've come to the conclusion she's just a little different. She's not like anyone I've ever dated before."

"In a good way, bad way—whatta you mean 'different'?"

"She's just not like anyone I've ever met. When I first met her, she seemed warm, caring, interested in my life and, eventually, a possible life together. But I've been with her now for almost two months, and I can really feel a change. She's not who I thought she was." He smiled. "Of course, she's probably thinking the same thing about me, but we need to sit down before long and talk this out. I really care for Layla. Her uniqueness was, and is, appealing to me, but there's something that's not quite right between us, and I need to figure out what it is before we go much further."

"Did the change in her attitude come about right after you first had sex? Maybe you aren't enough of a man for her, ya think?"

"Smart ass. I've slept over at her house many times within the last month, but this problem has been getting progressively worse, especially the last couple of weeks. We need to iron it out. I don't wanna lose her."

"So how'd you leave things the last time you were with her?"

"Just a minute." Barrett walked up to the counter and warmed up his coffee, filling his cup from the container of hot coffee available to the patrons as needed. When he returned and as he was sitting, he said, "She told me she had things to do all week and would see me sometime next week. I finally talked her into going out Saturday night. I got reservations at Reflect, and I'm going to try to get that corner table, the one that's somewhat removed from the rest of the tables. Maybe over some good food and a drink or two, we can iron this all out."

"Well, I hope it all works out for you, but it sounds to me like she's dumpin' your ass—that's what it sounds like to me."

"Hope not. I don't wanna lose her." He looked away, took a drink of coffee, and said, "Let's change the subject. How's everything going with you? How was your weekend?"

"Just one more thought before we move on. You know, for you, this scenario isn't unusual. You've loved 'em and left 'em for as long as I've known you. This certainly isn't the first time this has happened."

"I realize that, John. I know that. But I really thought this time was different. I really cared… *care* for her. I just hope we can get this all figured out. Now, again, how'd your weekend go?"

John smiled and sat back. "Not bad. Worked most of the time. Spent a little time with the kids Sunday afternoon—as much as they could stand—but other than that, I didn't do much."

"Isn't that a little unusual for you? Normally, at least in the past, you would spend the weekend with the kids *and* Maggie. Was she gone somewhere?"

"No."

"You two having trouble again?"

He said nothing.

"Don't wanna talk about it?"

"Why talk about it? It's always something. It's either I drink too much, I work too much, I wanna screw too much, or something. Always something. Especially lately. This past week, she's harped at me about everything."

"You gonna try counseling? I know you've mentioned it once or twice, but to the best of my knowledge, you haven't gone yet. Is that in the cards?"

"Not yet, but I'm afraid it's coming. She talked about it again the other day. I really don't think it'll do much good. Right now, I don't think she much likes me."

Barrett smiled. "I can identify with that. You're an asshole. I've told you that forever. You better look into counseling if you wanna save your marriage. It sounds to me like it's coming down to that."

He smiled. "Maybe if you and Layla are done, I'll check her out, and just let Maggie go."

"You know, that's such a stupid statement on so many levels. First of all, hopefully, we're not done, and second, you better figure out what to do to save your marriage before you start looking around. By the way, you got someone else you're seeing? Is there another woman?"

"Hell no. I can't handle the one I have, let alone trying to handle another one. There's never been anyone but her. But I'm getting damn tired of the hoops I have to jump through to keep this marriage alive, I know that."

Later that afternoon, after Barrett had returned to the office, he reflected upon the totality of the conversation he had with John earlier. It sounded as if his marriage was indeed in trouble. He hated to see them going through these issues—he deeply cared for both of them. But he knew John. Even though they were good friends, he could be a little tough to be with, to be around, and he figured after as many years as they had been married, Maggie had most likely endured enough.

He dialed Layla's number. She answered. He wasn't sure she would. "Hey. We still on for Saturday?"

"Yes, we are."

"I'm looking forward to it, I know that."

She hesitated before she said, "Yes, so am I."

"Have you had a full day?"

"Yes, and it just goes on and on. Charles is a bastard today, and people won't quit walking through the front door."

"You wanna get a quick drink after work?"

"No, not tonight. Let's just plan on meeting Saturday at Reflect like we had planned."

"Okay. Are you sure you don't want me to pick you up?"

"No. I've got to be somewhere that afternoon, like I told you, and I'll just meet you there. I better go. Too much going on here."

"Okay. I'll plan on seeing you Saturday."

He heard her terminate the call. No "Goodbye," no "Okay" or "Sounds good." Nothing. He needed to quit worrying about John and his issues. He clearly had one of his own with Layla, which did not appear to be resolving itself on its own accord. Hopefully, with a glass of wine, and some good food, they would be able to settle whatever the hell it was that was bothering her. He was afraid if something didn't resolve itself soon, their relationship would be over virtually before it even got started—a quick conclusion he would never have guessed was possible only a short month ago.

17

They were parked in the parking lot of a small mom-and-pop operation north of Nashville. Annie had found it while driving around the outskirts of the city. They had been inside more than once, ostensibly for the purpose of purchasing a few items, but their true purpose was to determine the layout of the store and ascertain whether they had security cameras, which they didn't. Normally, at this time, there was only one clerk in the store, an old lady that apparently had nothing to do near the break of day but work the off hours of a broken-down general store far off the beaten path. They had watched her arrive the last four weeks at exactly the same time and noticed that the pattern of traffic this time of day was virtually nonexistent.

"You scared?"

Annie hesitated. "Hell yes—scared shitless. Never done this before."

Michael said, "We got this. We've planned it well. Besides that, we don't have much choice. We really need the money."

"You know, if you just had the balls, you could put the screws to that old man of yours. Then we wouldn't have to do this." She looked around. "This is what it's come to—this is what we're having to do because you can't put enough pressure on that old man of yours to keep us in money. I should just shut you off until you get everything figured out. That's what I should do. No more sex until you get this figured out, you prick."

"I'm sorry. I'll do better from now on. He'll come around. It's just that right now, it's not so good between him and me." He studied the storefront. "Now, let's focus. Can you just concentrate on what we're doing right now? Let me worry about my old man later today, tomorrow—let's just focus on the job we're about to do. You don't have a very big part you know. All you gotta do is keep me informed. I don't wanna be in there doing this when someone's walking in behind me."

"Goddammit, I *know* what I'm supposed to do. Now let's get this over with. Is your phone on, ready to go?"

"Yes. Just send a text if someone drives up—just like we practiced."

"Go, go, get going."

Michael got out. He shut the door, gave her a thumbs-up, then walked toward the front of the store. A few minutes later he burst through the store door and motioned for her to drive forward. She drove toward him, and before she could come to a stop, he had opened the door, jumped in, and slammed it behind him.

As she accelerated, she said, "Well, what happened? You kill her? How much did we get?"

"No, I didn't kill her," he said as he pulled his ski mask off his head. "I made her lie down on the floor after I took her phone and told her if she contacted anyone before she counted slowly to a hundred, I would find her, kill her and kill all her family."

"What'd she say?"

"She said, 'I don't have a family.'"

"Oh shit. That didn't work out, did it? What'd you say?"

"Well, I thought for a second and then I told her I knew that, and that I was just testing her. Then I told her I'd kill all her friends."

"Good thinkin'. What'd she do then?"

"She started counting." Michael pulled the money from his pocket.

"How much we get? Count it. Hurry."

"Just slow down. You're driving too fast. Stick to the plan and cut across the next gravel road and then south on 65. Just keep your eyes on the road and relax. It's over. We don't wanna get picked up for speedin' or end up in a ditch. Let me count this."

A few minutes later, as she turned onto I-65, he said, "We got three hundred forty-five dollars. That should last us a while."

She turned and smiled. "Great. That's more than I expected. Now, you little prick, you get started on that old man of yours. I don't wanna do this again. If I have to do this again, I'm shuttin' you off for two—no, *three* weeks. You'll get nothing for three weeks, and I ain't kiddin'. That old man of yours has got plenty. If he's spending it on that secretary of his, you better figure somethin' else out 'cause I'm not doin' this again. You understand?"

"Just relax. I'll get it figured out. I'll get it figured out."

Later that evening, he was watching TV when Charles walked through the door.

"You're getting home a little late, aren't you? You never get home after ten o'clock. Where you been?"

He dropped into a chair across from Michael and said, "Been workin'. I'm trying to get ready for a big case that starts next week. By the way, why aren't you working? You even trying to find a job or you just stop trying altogether?"

"I'm still looking, just can't find nothin'."

"You know, I'm not going to be around forever to finance you. Do you want me to start looking for you? You're gonna have to start doing something before long, Michael. What about going back to school? I'll help you get in somewhere."

Michael laughed. "I think my days in school are about over. But I'll tell you what. Let me look around this winter, and if I can't find anything I wanna do, I'll enroll somewhere starting next fall. Does that suit you?"

Charles smiled. "It's a deal."

"Now, where have you *really* been tonight?"

"Really, I've been working."

"Alone?"

"Yes, alone, why?"

"Doing what?"

"Getting ready for a trial, like I told you."

"Who with?"

"No one, now what the hell's going on? Why all the questions?"

"Layla, or whatever the hell her name is, wasn't with you?"

"No, and to be honest, it's none of your goddamn business if she was. Why all the interest in my love life, Michael? Do you have some strange idea that if I become involved with someone, it's going to change our relationship somehow? Because if you do, let me tell you right now, it won't. Nothing is going to change the fact you're my son and I love you. If I do become involved with Layla or anyone else, absolutely nothing will ever change our relationship, and that's the truth. Do you understand that?"

"It did with Mom. My relationship with her changed when she got involved with that idiot she's with now, that's for sure."

"You don't think your drug use might have affected your relationship? I don't think getting a new husband had anything to do with altering her relationship with you."

"Well, I do." He paused then went on. "So what's your situation with her—with Layla?"

Charles stood. "Okay, now while nothing is going to change between you and I, whether there's a woman involved or not, it's also true that I don't think I need to explain my personal life to you, ever. You don't explain yours to me, and I don't ask you to. I know you have something going on with a girl by the name of Annie, but I never get into that with you. Likewise, you shouldn't with me. It's literally none of your business, and it's going to stay that way—just like me staying out of your love life is going to stay that way. Does that make sense?"

Michael sat back in his chair, resigned to the fact that, first of all, his father *was* involved with her, and second, he was never going to discuss it with him.

"Okay, Dad, I get it. I understand. Glad we had this little talk. See you in the morning."

Charles smiled. "Great. Now are you out of money? I'll be glad to float you another loan if you need a little."

Michael smiled and said, "No, Dad, I'm fine. I don't wanna cut into what you might need in your ever-expanding social life—your life with Layla or whoever. I'm fine. I'll get by."

Charles took a deep breath, shrugged his shoulders, and said, "Whatever. See you in the morning."

He watched as his father walked up the steps. Once he was out of hearing distance, he pulled out his phone and punched Annie's number. "You awake?"

"Yeah, why?"

"Good. We need to talk. I got an idea or two I wanna toss around with you concerning my father's new love life. You still got some of that good stuff left?"

"A little."

"Okay, I'll see you in about fifteen." He stood, walked out the back door, and headed for his vehicle. Maybe it was time to take a little action. If his dad wasn't going to tell him what was going on, he figured he would just handle the issue himself. One way or the other, the flow of money from his father needed to continue, and if he needed to take matters into his own hands to resolve the problem, he was more than willing to do so.

18

Layla slowly opened her eyes. She was still tired. She had been out late, with Randall, her most recent addition to the list of names of men she was currently dating. She lay there for a moment, thinking about her time with him. He was a great guy, as were most of those guys she dated, but to conclude he was the *right* guy was a stretch.

She got out of bed and walked to the bathroom. She didn't have the luxury of taking her time to get ready for work. It was already after seven, and she needed to be there no later than eight o'clock. In fact, as much as there was going on today, she really needed to be there *before* eight o'clock. There would be no time for breakfast— makeup would be applied as quickly as possible.

Once she had done all she needed to do and had time to do, she hurried to her car. She would grab a cup of coffee at the diner near the office building and, hopefully, make it to her desk prior to eight o'clock. Charles would be waiting, as he always was on trial days, and on days when she had so much paperwork to prepare for him.

As she drove, she again considered last night. Randall was a good man, divorced, two children, with a successful business. He treated her with dignity and respect. He had more money than he knew what to do with. But he just wasn't right for her. In fact, she had concluded late last night, as she lie in bed, alone, no one was right for her. She was done with this dating game, at least for now. She was going to sit back, relax, and enjoy life without the interference of a man, *any* man.

She would need to pass her sentiments on to Barrett this coming Saturday night and hope he took it the right way. But if he didn't, it really didn't matter to her. This was the way it needed to be, at least for now, and he would need to accept her explanation and her conclusion—she would give him no choice.

Layla parked in the parking garage, where she always parked, and quickly moved toward the crosswalk. She stopped and reconsidered. Rather than going down to the intersection, she would cross here, in the middle of the block. Quicker, but always a little more dangerous because of the extensive traffic this time of morning. She waited until there was nothing coming either way, stepped off the curb, and squeezed her way between two cars. Seeing nothing either direction, she moved out into the street and started to cross. She reached the middle of the street, when out of nowhere, a vehicle pulled out of a parking spot about a half block away and, with the engine roaring, came directly at her. Layla heard the sound of the motor, looked up, saw the vehicle coming at her, and jumped out of the way, just as the vehicle flew past.

She quickly picked herself up and looked up the street just in time to see a dark brown vehicle, with what appeared to be a cracked rear window, quickly disappear around the corner and out of sight.

Layla had worn a light jacket having heard the weather forecast, knowing it would be chilly. Her contact with the ground had torn a hole in the elbow area. She stood there, continuing to look up the street, thinking how close she had been to her own demise.

Clearly, the driver of the vehicle had tried to hit her. There was no other logical conclusion. They had waited until she moved out into the street, and then done all they could do to hit her. She couldn't see the driver—she could, however, see there was only one occupant. She saw the color, and the rear window issue, both of which she would report to her friend, Jeff Wiley.

Layla walked in the office door and immediately sat down. She never even made it to her desk. Her knees were weak, and she felt dizzy. If the driver had been successful, that literally could have been her last breath. Who hated her that much? Maybe she was mistaken.

Maybe it was just a bad driver, high on something, or angry about something.

That wasn't how it appeared. It appeared whoever it was, waited, pulled out when she moved into the street from between parked vehicles, then accelerated on purpose, just missing her.

Charles walked out of his office while she was sitting in one of the chairs meant for the public. He smiled. "I think you've forgotten your role here. You're in the wrong chair. Must have been a tough night for you."

She stood and started toward her desk. "You're not gonna believe this, but someone just tried to run over me." She looked at the torn cloth where her elbow had just found an opening. "I tore this as I hit the ground."

She found the precinct commander's number and punched it in. Once his secretary had put her through, she put him on speaker and said, "Morning, Jeff. I'm still a little shaky, so bear with me, but I was almost run over outside the building this morning."

"You're kidding. What happened?"

"I was coming to work, and someone in a brown older-model car, with a badly cracked rear window, pulled out of a parking spot at a high rate of speed and just missed me."

"You're sure it was intentional?"

"Yes, no doubt in my mind."

"Okay, now you need to go to your local precinct and fill out a report. They're gonna need something in writing before it can be investigated. It's not in my precinct, so I can't really help you, but they can and will."

"Okay, I'll walk down there during my noon break."

"Do you have anyone in mind that might have done this?"

"No. I don't have an enemy in the world—at least no one that hates me enough to kill me. I have no idea who it was."

"Get the statement filled out. They'll take it from there."

Charles said, "Jeff, I wanna see you sometime later today or tomorrow when you have a second."

"It'll need to be tomorrow. I'll give Layla a call in the morning and set something up with you."

"Thanks, Jeff." Layla terminated the call, looked up at Charles, and said, "I'm afraid to walk to my car."

"I'll walk with you when you go home tonight. If you see anything else that seems a little suspicious, certainly call me or the police, but I'll be available if you need me, day or night. Don't hesitate to contact me. You going to be all right here at work today?"

"I'm fine. I'm just so confused about who might dislike me so much as to try something like that."

Her phone rang. It was Barrett. She looked up at Charles and said, "I need to take this. I'll be in as soon as I'm done."

He turned and walked back into his office, apparently understanding what she was telling him, because he closed the door behind him.

"Morning."

"Hi, Layla. How was your evening?"

"You don't own a brown piece of shit car, with a cracked rear window, do you?"

He laughed. "I own nothing brown. And I don't have a vehicle with a cracked rear window, so no on both counts. Why?"

"Someone tried to run over me this morning. Apparently, it wasn't you."

He hesitated. "You okay?"

"I'm fine. Tore my jacket, but I was lucky. They missed me by an inch."

"You're kidding me. Do you have any idea who it was?"

"None. I have to fill out a report at noon. I already verbally reported it. But it does worry me. I didn't think I had an enemy in the world. Apparently, I do."

"Do you want me to come over tonight and stay with you?"

"No. I don't know what time I'll get home. I'm going to see if Commander Wiley will run a car up and down my street a few times during the night just to make sure, but I'll be fine. I gotta go. I have a million things to do. I need to get at it. I've already lost time this morning because of whoever the idiot was that tried to run me down. I'll just see you Saturday." She terminated the call and opened one of the folders she needed to deal with before the morning ended. She started to type. Her fingers missed the appropriate keys. She sat back and only then noticed how badly her hands were shaking.

Layla decided, work or no work, she needed to just stop, have a cup of coffee, and calm down. The incident had clearly affected her more than she thought it had. She would sit and take a few deep breaths as she tried to figure out who might hate her enough to have taken such a risk, attempting to kill her, on a busy public street, at such a busy time. It had suddenly become quite apparent someone she knew *really* wanted her dead.

19

Charles hardly slept all night. After Layla's near-death experience, he had gone home early to speak to Michael. There was, after all, no doubt in his mind whose car that was and who was driving it. He had remained awake as long as he could will his eyes to remain open. Finally, somewhere around 3:00 a.m., he had fallen asleep in his chair in front of the TV, waiting for Michael to walk in the front door. That never happened. He woke up later than usual and hurried around to get to work on time.

Charles now waited for Layla to walk in the office door, hopefully unharmed. He would deal with his kid later. He just wanted to make sure nothing had occurred during the night, and that she was still in one piece. A little before 8:00 a.m., he heard the door open, and someone walk in. He walked out into the reception area where Layla was just turning on her computer and sitting down to begin the day's activities. He quietly breathed a sigh of relief.

"Morning. Any problems last night?"

She looked up, smiled, and said, "Morning to you. None whatsoever. Today I wonder if maybe the whole thing was just a fluke. Maybe the guy was high or upset or just lost control. I'm sorry now I even filed anything with the police."

"I thought about that last night too. I was thinking that's exactly what happened. I'm just glad to see you here this morning in one piece and ready to go. When you have time, grab that Jackson file for me, will you?"

"Sure thing."

He turned and walked back in his office. He was certain it was Michael driving that car, but his motivation remained unclear. Was it the relationship he had with Layla that was creating the problem? And if it was, *why* was that an issue? They had discussed the fact their relationship would never change if he did become involved. But Michael had referenced the problems he had with his mother when she had found someone else. That, combined with what could be a reduced ability to reason because of his drug usage, was the only scenario he could imagine that would create a strong-enough motive for him to try to kill Layla. He just needed to talk to Michael, but it was hard to talk when he wouldn't come home and wouldn't answer his cell.

"Layla, could you contact Jeff Wiley and remind him I need to see him, preferably sometime this morning?"

"Will do."

A few minutes later, she walked in his office and said, "Can you see Jeff now? He's ready to come now, if you have the time."

"I do."

A few minutes later, Commander Wiley walked in his office door with a number of files in hand.

"Morning, Charles."

"Have a seat, Jeff. Looks like we've got plenty to discuss."

"We do."

He just started to pull out one of the files when Charles stood and walked over to close his office door. As he returned to his desk, he said, "Before we get into the files, could we discuss Layla's situation first?"

"Sure, sure. By 'situation' I'm assuming you mean what happened yesterday morning?"

Charles said, "Yes. She went down and filled out a statement."

"Okay, good."

"Just between you and me, I had a long talk with her this morning about the incident. I think she's thinking maybe it was just a freak accident. Like maybe someone inadvertently hit the gas pedal or was upset about something and accidentally almost struck her. She really doesn't want to pursue it. Can you just stop by the local precinct office after you leave here and tell them to hold the complaint for a while? She doesn't really wanna use up police resources to push something that may just have been someone's silly mistake."

Jeff sat back and thought for a moment. "Has she had any other problems since yesterday?"

"No, none whatsoever. That's one of the reasons she just really wants to forget all of it and move on. Do you have a problem with that?"

"Not really, I guess… if you don't."

"Believe me, that's her decision, and that's what she wants to do. So let's put it in a dead file somewhere, and don't even think about investigating it any further unless you hear from one of us."

"Okay. I'll stop by there after I leave here, tell them I've talked to the district attorney's office and no one wants to pursue it. I'm sure they'll have no problem with that. They sure as hell have enough on their plate the way it is."

They then discussed upcoming trials for over an hour, until the last file was reviewed, at which time just as Jeff was walking out his office door into the reception area, Charles yelled out and asked Layla to come in. He didn't want them discussing the complaint in the reception area as the precinct commander left the office. As a result, they passed by each other, never speaking as they did, just as Charles had hoped would happen.

He tried calling Michael a number of times during the afternoon, but to no avail. The call would always go to voice mail. He would always ask him to call back, but the call never came. Near 5:00 p.m., he told Layla to close down, and he would walk her to her car as he walked to his. She resisted, but ever so slightly, and he did walk her to her car, which proved to be unremarkable.

Charles arrived home near five thirty and immediately placed another call to Michael. After again leaving a message, he checked around the house to see if anything was missing, or if there was any indication Michael had been there. Nothing had been touched since he left earlier that morning. As he sat down to have some supper, his cell rang. It was Michael.

"You tryin' to reach me. I see you called like forty times today, or some such number. Whatta ya need?"

"Where are you?"

"Stayin' with Annie a day or two. Where are you, man?"

It was clear he was high on something. Charles could tell this conversation was most likely going nowhere. "What have you been doing? How come you haven't been home?"

"Like I said, man, I'm just stayin' here with Annie for a day or two."

"When you coming home?"

"Oh, a day or two. Not really sure."

Charles heard someone in the background yell, "What the hell you doin', Michael? Let's go. Hurry up."

"Where you going?"

"Just out, man, just out. Gonna have a little fun. No big deal. I better go."

"Michael, before you go, let me ask you—where were you yesterday morning, early, say around 8:00 a.m.?"

"Probably still sleeping. Why?"

"You didn't happen to be driving near my office about then, did you?"

He hesitated. "Don't think so, man. I normally sleep in till later than that."

"You were there, weren't you? It was your car that tried to run over Layla. That was you, wasn't it?"

Again, the hesitation. "Hey, I don't know nothin' about what you're talkin' about." He laughed. "Why would I try to run over your secretary? I got no motication... no movitation... What would move me to do something like that?"

"Because you don't want me involved with her. You've made that pretty clear from the first time I went out with her. You don't want me having a relationship with her. Was that you or not?"

"No. Now, I gotta go. Talk to you later."

"Wait. Michael, you leave her alone. Don't you dare harm her. Do you understand? You need to come home... We need to talk..."

He heard Michael terminate the call. He put his phone down on the table and sat in silence trying to figure out what to do next. He needed to find some way to convince Michael they weren't involved in a relationship. He was afraid if he didn't, with Michael's obvious involvement in drugs, Layla's life was truly in danger.

He no longer felt like eating. He stood and walked into the living room, poured himself a drink, and then sat down, as he continued to process his options. Michael was a good boy. He just needed help. Charles concluded he would continue to try to locate him. In the meantime, he would prepare the paperwork necessary for an involuntary placement somewhere so Michael could get the help he needed. For now, there was little else he could do. He would watch out for Layla the best he could. She was safe as long as she was in his office. Hopefully, now that Michael knew his father had an idea he was the perpetrator, he would leave Layla alone. If Michael did come home, perhaps he could scare the living shit out of him and tell him they suspected him as the one that tried to run over Layla. Perhaps if he was aware the cops were looking at him, he would leave her alone. Maybe he should call and tell him that right now. He dialed Michael's cell—straight to voice mail. He took another drink. There was no more he could do tonight. He would prepare the paperwork tomorrow, and as soon as he found him, Michael would be put away until he dried out. He just prayed to God Layla remained safe until then.

20

Barrett had been waiting for her almost an hour. Layla told him she would meet him at six thirty, and he had arrived a half hour early. She was late, and she hadn't called, both troubling issues that had not surfaced through the course of the first few weeks of their relationship.

He had ordered a beer, and by the time she was to arrive, it was already gone. So he ordered another, hoping she got there before he was completely drunk and unable to carry on a rational conversation.

Fifteen minutes later, he watched as she walked in the door. He signaled to her, and she noticed him immediately. As she walked toward him, he noticed no spring in her step, no smile, and in addition, once she saw him, she failed to maintain any eye contact whatsoever. He had a feeling, as she sauntered toward him, this was not going to be an enjoyable evening.

About halfway to their table, she smiled and stopped to visit with someone. As he looked closer, he noticed Maggie and John had apparently come in and been seated at some point in time after he got there—he knew they weren't there when he initially arrived.

Once their short conversation ended, she continued her walk toward his table, and he rose as she arrived. He pulled her chair out for her as he said, "Hi. You look great. I saw you stop by John's table. I didn't even see them. You wanna invite them to join us?"

"No," she said as she sat down. "We need to talk alone."

He sat as he said, "Okay, what's going on? You wanna drink?"

"Yes. I need a glass of wine. Don't care what it is as long as it's red."

He beckoned to a waiter, who then asked if they were ready to order dinner. Barrett told him they weren't, ordered her a Merlot, then said, "Okay, now, what's going on?"

She looked down, only to look up once her glass arrived. He didn't push her. Obviously, what she had to say was important, at least to her, and he wanted it said on her time, in her words, and in her way. "We've been going out now, for what, about two or three months?"

"Yes, I guess that's about right."

Again, she hesitated. "You been seeing anyone else during that time?"

"No. Why, have you?"

"Yes."

"Who?"

"Doesn't matter. You never said anything about being exclusive. If that subject never came up on its own, until it became a specific issue of discussion for some reason or another, I wasn't going to *make* it an issue." She was quiet, taking a sip of wine. While still staring into her glass, she said, "I don't wanna see you anymore. At least, not the way we have been."

"Okay. Guess that's up to you. Was it something I said or did?"

"Not really. I'm just not interested in a long-term relationship, and I know that's what you want. Better we shut things down now rather than have one of us—you—fully committed, and the other—me—nowhere near committed."

"Is it this other guy you've been seeing?" He reached over and placed his hand on hers. "Is he the problem? Do you care for him?"

She pulled her hand away. "Not really. I'm just not interested in getting involved with anyone right now. I'm certain our relationship isn't headed anywhere, and I'm sorry about that, because I know how much you care for me. But we definitely don't feel the same way, and I just don't want to carry on this charade any longer."

"How long have you felt this way?"

"A few weeks now."

"Is there something I can do to change that would help? I mean, you're right, I really care for you. I've even thought about marriage. I really don't know what to say."

"There isn't anything to say. We just need to walk away."

Again, he reached for her hand, placing his over hers. She quickly pulled it away, as she said, in a voice loud enough for those near their table, to hear, "Quit. Don't do that."

Barrett looked around, smiling at those who turned in their direction, then looked at her quizzically, as he whispered, "Okay, okay, I'm sorry. I can't believe you feel so strongly about all this. I had no idea you felt this way. I thought we were getting along great." He hesitated, as he looked at the bottom of an empty beer glass. "I really thought we were good together." He looked up at her. "Where do we go from here?"

She smiled a condescending smile as she said, "*We* go nowhere from here. *We* are done. That's what I've been trying to tell you since I sat down."

"Okay, now wait. What about this? Could we just stay away from each other for a few days, or weeks? Would that help you think all this through?" Again, he tried to touch her hand.

This time, she pulled away, stood, and said, in a voice loud enough for most of the patrons to hear, "We are *done*. I've told you that for the last time. We are not spending a *little* time away from each other. We are spending *all* our time away from each other because we are done. Do you get it *now*? I don't wanna see you again."

He used his hands motioning in a downward direction, trying to get her to lower her voice, as he smiled politely to those surrounding his table. She leaned on the table with both hands, as she said softly, "I do *not* want to see you again, period."

"You got it. If that's what you want, I can accommodate you. Now, you wanna eat a little supper with me?"

She looked at him for a moment and shook her head. She then reached down, picked up her purse, walked past John, and out the door. There were still people looking at Barrett as she walked away. He just smiled, shrugged his shoulders, and cupped his hands around an empty glass. The waiter was walking by, and Barrett signaled he needed a fill-up, to which the waiter acknowledged. He was just thinking about leaving, when John walked over to his table.

As he sat down, he said, "Well, that was interesting. We hadn't planned on a little entertainment with our meal. She was obviously pretty upset. What the hell happened?"

"That's what's strange, I really don't know. She said she wanted to be with me on Saturday night, and I just figured it was to make future plans or something, but certainly not this. I told you something wasn't quite right with her."

He smiled. "Sure good-lookin' though."

"I just don't get it. I really thought everything was going okay with us."

"So do the two of you have any items that need to be divided up between you? Or is this the last time you'll ever see her?"

"Oh, I've got some stuff over at her house I need to get. I'll probably just wait a day or two, drive over, and pick it up then. But nothing else. Easiest breakup I ever went through. No tears, no arguing, no nothin'. It was all one-sided. She made it quite clear she didn't want anything to do with me."

"Certainly no doubt about that. Do you want me to see if I can pick up your stuff?"

Barrett looked at him, frowned, and said, "I'll pick it up myself. I'll use that as one last opportunity to make things right with us. You probably need to stay out of the middle of all this, for more reasons than one."

"Whatta ya mean?"

"You're my best friend, and I want it to stay that way. Stay out of the middle of this. Leave her alone. You're married, buddy. I've seen how you look at her, and believe me, from what I've seen, she's not someone a married man would ever wanna get involved with."

"Haven't messed around on Maggie yet and don't expect to. I just thought I would try to help, that's all."

"Never met anyone like her. She's a little scary. Best it ended this way I guess. I hate that it was so public, but it wasn't my choice."

"I would agree she's a strange woman. Now, why don't you get out of here? I'll pay for your beer. You've had enough trouble tonight. The least I can do is pay for the booze."

"Thanks." Barrett stood. "I'll keep you updated. I'll see her in a day or two and let you know how it all turns out. Based on my time with her, who knows—she may wanna get back together again. But I fuckin' guarantee *that's* not gonna happen, not as strange as she is."

"What if you go over to pick up your stuff, and she says, 'Come on in, let's mess around'? What happens then?"

Barrett stared at him and thought for a moment. "That's not gonna happen." Again, he hesitated. Then he smiled and said, "On second thought, I guess if that's what she said, I would probably just have to accommodate her—yup, that's what I'm thinkin'. I'd probably just have to accommodate her."

21

Barrett processed his rejection most of Sunday. He recon-
structed their relationship day by day, week by week, trying to
figure out where he had gone wrong. Nothing seemed to fit.
No singular event stood out during their time together that might
have created the attitude she exhibited on Saturday night. What the
hell had he done to deserve a total rejection? One thing was, however,
crystal clear—he was definitely in love with her.

He hadn't felt this range of emotion concerning a woman for
as long as he could remember. In the past, if one of his "women"
had walked away, he shrugged it off and moved on. This time, even
though it appeared to be his only option, it would not be easy. In
fact, he was going to give it one more try before he resigned himself
to the fact they were through.

He sat in his office Monday morning and watched as the growing tower of unreturned phone messages continued to rise. Joyce
walked through his office door and said, "Kris is on line 1 and wants
to talk. You wanna visit with her, or you wanna just continue to suf-
fer in silence?"

He had discussed his confrontation with Layla on Saturday
night with his secretary as soon as she walked through the office
door. She told him to move on. Most likely, good advice and advice
he would follow when and only when he was sure it was over—he
just hadn't quite reached that point.

"Tell her I'll call her back."

"Okay." She smiled. "By the way, let me know when you're out
of your little funk, will you? There's a few office issues we need to

discuss, but I hate to have your answers tainted by that lover rejection attitude you seem to have."

He looked at her and frowned. She turned and walked out his door, closing it behind her. Layla had sent him an email reminding him he still had some items at her home and that she had sacked them up for him. She would be glad to drop them off whenever it was appropriate. He hadn't acknowledged the email. He just figured tonight, about seven o'clock, when he knew she would be home from work, he would stop over and pick them up, unannounced, not giving her the opportunity to provide him with an excuse for not going to her home.

Later that afternoon, after he had moped through the day, Joyce brought in the remaining phone messages, which included another message from Kris. He just laid them all on top of the pile.

Barrett arrived at Layla's home just prior to 7:00 p.m. The lights were on, so he knew she was home from work. He got out of his vehicle, walked up to the front door, and knocked.

She opened the door, holding a sack. "Here's everything you had here. Again, I'm sorry."

"Wait, just wait a second. Can I come in? Let's go through this one more time. Maybe we can discuss the issues in a little more detail. Now that the shock has worn off, maybe we can come to a different conclusion—discuss it with a little more objectivity."

"Don't think so. I can guarantee we won't come to a different conclusion. Now here, take this. I'll see you around." She started to close the door. With one hand, he grabbed it and held it open. With the other, he grabbed her shoulder. She tried to pull away. He wouldn't let go. "Let go of me now. Let go of the door, you jerk."

"But, wait, can't..." She pulled away, grabbed the door, and yelled, "We're *done!* Period. I do not wanna see you again. Do you understand?" She shoved the sack against his stomach. He clutched the bag, as she slammed the screen door shut, then did the same with the inner door. He stood, speechless, now looking at nothing but a pair of closed doors.

Barrett looked away, stood quietly for a moment, then walked down the few steps to the sidewalk leading to his vehicle. As he did, he noticed the family living next door had just pulled into their driveway and started to exit their vehicle. They had witnessed the whole episode and stood, transfixed, looking at him as if they were watching a movie, or some made for TV series. He smiled, waved, and quickly got in his vehicle.

As he drove, he punched in John's number. When he answered, Barrett said, "Well, that went well. I just picked up my stuff at Layla's. Never even got in the door. I told you I'd follow up and keep you posted, but I don't have much to tell you. It was short and sweet. She's frickin' done, and I mean with a capital *D*."

"I'm sorry, Barrett, I really am. I know you cared for her, and I know you really thought this was the real deal. You gonna be okay?"

"Oh, hell yes, but this one is gonna take a little time. I'll be fine, but I'm not jumping back into anything for a while, I know that."

"Oh sure. I have no idea how many times I've heard you say that."

"I better go. I'll talk to you later this week."

He drove back to the office, confused and frustrated. That was not the way their meeting was supposed to go. He had it all figured out before he went to her home. But as he thought back through their relationship, there never was one aspect of her he had figured out *correctly* from day one and its conclusion was certainly no exception.

Upon arriving at the office, he looked at a mountain of phone messages. He started shuffling through each of them, looking at the words, but comprehending nothing. His mind wasn't on his work. There was no sense looking through these now and then looking through them again tomorrow, when perhaps he would be ready to comprehend what they said.

As he put them down, one fell out of the handful. It was from Kris. Her message indicated she had called twice and needed to talk to him.

As he sat there alone, continuing to assess his relationship with Layla, he concluded maybe it was time for a change in scenery. Maybe it was time to laugh a little, have a drink or two with someone who *did* like him, and think about something other than the relationship that had just been unilaterally terminated.

He looked at the note for a full five minutes before he returned her call. At first, the conversation was somewhat strained. After all, he was calling her a full three hours after the office doors of both their businesses had closed.

He said, "I realize it's long after the close of business, but do you wanna talk, maybe have a drink?"

"Sure. I'll need to look at my calendar, but I'm sure I'll be fine. What day?"

"Now."

"As in right now?"

"Yes."

"Okay, sure, I can do that. Where?"

"What about Tin Alley... maybe thirty minutes?"

"Works for me. See you then."

He terminated the call. Probably a mistake, but what the hell. Lately, his life seemed to be full of them—what was one more?

She was waiting when he arrived. "You're a beer drinker, right?" she said as he approached.

"I am."

"Hope that suits you. I ordered it when I ordered mine."

"Thanks," he said as he sat opposite her.

"What'd you wanna see me about?"

"I just wanted to once again discuss the possibility of combining our businesses. After talking to you about it the other day, it seemed the right thing to do. If you aren't interested, I wanna start looking elsewhere."

The discussion concerning a partnership continued through two beers and over a span of an hour. Finally, he said, "You know, I'm sorry, but I'm really tired. I should probably get going. Why don't we have John, you know, that attorney you went to the other day, draw us up some kind of partnership agreement? He handles those kinds of matters. As you can tell, I'm definitely interested, and I think it would be a good business move for both of us. I wanna look at your financials, and of course, I'll provide you mine, but I think we can make this work."

"So do I. Can I ask you something personal?"

"I guess." He smiled. "As long as it's not really, really personal."

"You know, I don't know you all that well—yet. But I do know you well enough to know something's wrong. You just seem a little off tonight. Am I wrong? I could be wrong, and if I am, I'm sorry, but you don't seem upbeat or quite as on top of things as you normally are."

He looked away before he said, "Well, I just got dumped by a woman I really cared for. That may be more than you wanna know, but you asked. I have no idea what the hell happened. She won't tell me. All I know is we're done."

"Mind if I ask who she was?"

"Guess not. It was Layla Adams, Charles Whitmore's secretary."

"Well, I don't know her, but I saw her when I went to Whitmore's office. Beautiful woman." She hesitated, before she said, "I'm sorry, Barrett, I really am. I know how that hurts. Do you wanna talk about it? I'll be glad to buy you a beer and sit here for a while and listen. I'm doing nothin', but going home and going to bed."

"No. Thanks, but no. It's my problem and I don't wanna burden you. Besides that, there's not much to talk about. She won't tell me why or what the problem is. Hard to discuss the issues when you don't know what the issues are."

A few minutes later, he was on his way home and again considered how strange his short-term relationship with Layla had been, literally from day one. But she had made her decision, and that decision was binding on him. There was nothing he could do about it. It would be hard to stop loving her, but from now on, he would try to keep her out of his thoughts the best he could. That might indeed prove difficult to do, but considering all his remaining options, he really had no choice.

22

Charles hadn't talked with Michael since his abbreviated call a week ago. He had tried calling him a few times, but to no avail. He hoped eventually he would come home. They could discuss the problem and then go from there. Obviously, there was little that could be done if he wouldn't communicate. Charles was concerned if Michael didn't, on some level, seek help for his problem, the days of talking everything out were numbered.

Today would indeed be a difficult day at the office. It was quiet now, during these early-morning moments before the phone began to ring. He sat with a cup of coffee, simply enjoying the peacefulness and going through all the testimony of witnesses that would testify during a trial starting tomorrow morning.

He had an hour before Layla arrived. With her arrival, the office would jump into its normal insane pace of action, and he would need to multitask as he always did. Right now, he needed to concentrate on each of the witness statements one more time, make sure his opening argument still sounded compelling, and his proposed instructions to the jury still seemed appropriate.

As he was finishing everything he needed to do, he heard the phone ring but remain unanswered. He quickly glanced at his watch and noticed it was eight fifteen. Time had really slipped away from him. He stood and walked into the reception area looking for Layla. It was not like her to be late—ever. Unfortunately, her timing for arriving late for the first time since she had been employed couldn't have been worse. He tried to call her, but the call went straight to voice mail. People started arriving. He finally put a small handwritten sign on Layla's desk, telling them to take a chair until someone could help them. Midmorning, when he called her for the third time and, once again, the call went to voice mail, he knew something wasn't right.

"Jeff, Charles. I need a favor."

"Okay, what's going on?"

"It's Layla. She hasn't shown up for work yet. It wouldn't concern me so much, but for that problem she had a couple of weeks ago. I've tried to call her, but the calls go straight to voice mail. I'm concerned. She's never been late since she came to work here."

"Whatta ya want me to do?"

"Could you send someone over to her house? Just have them make sure she's all right. I'm not upset she's late, so just have them tell her to get here when she can. My primary concern is her safety—I just wanna make sure she's okay."

"I can do that. I'll let you know when I hear back."

Charles terminated the call and set about trying to handle the people that walked in the front door *and* the people he already had in his office. His mind was on so many things, he had in fact forgotten why he was so busy in the first place, until his personal cell rang. Jeff Wiley was on the other end.

"Charles, I'm on my way to her house. There's a problem."

"Whatta you mean 'a problem.' What's wrong?"

"Just wait until I get there. Let me check this out myself first. I'll call you back as soon as I have some additional information."

"But, Jeff, what—" The call had been terminated, and he suddenly found himself talking to no one.

His efforts the rest of the morning were wasted. His mind was on Layla. Finally, at noon, he locked the front door and left a small sign indicating they would reopen at one o'clock. He pulled out his cell and dialed the commander.

"Jeff, what the hell's going on?"

"You better come on over, Charles. Layla's dead. I'm here at her house and there are cops everywhere trying to figure this all out. You best come on over. This isn't pretty."

"Be right there."

He immediately replaced the sign on the door with a new one indicating the office was closed because of an emergency and would reopen tomorrow morning at eight o'clock. His mind continued to try to comprehend and accept what he had just been told.

Upon arrival, he had a difficult time, even with his credentials, getting through the traffic stop. At the moment, everyone was prohibitated from traveling the street. He left his vehicle outside the perimeter and walked to her home.

After pulling on a pair of latex gloves and walking through the front door, he found Commander Wiley in the living area. "What the hell happened here, Jeff?"

"She was murdered. The officer walked up to her front door, knocked, no one came to the door, so he tried opening it. It wasn't locked so he walked in. He heard nothing and continued walking through the house until he came to her bedroom. He found her there. You'll need to see this. I can't adequately describe this to you. Come with me."

Charles followed the commander into a sunlit room, well decorated and full of charm. As he walked in and looked to his left, he noticed the bed. On the bed, propped up against the headboard, stark naked, her body facing the opposite wall, was the dead body of Layla. Her eyes were open, full of surprise, and her head was positioned in a downward angle. Her legs were spread, and there was a knife protruding from her midsection. The blood had dried. Her hands were both wrapped around the handle of the knife.

Charles backed up and simply said, "Dear God."

Jeff, who had followed Charles around the end of the bed, said, "In all my years in law enforcement, I've never seen anything like this."

As Charles continued to look around the room, he said, "Any indication who might have done this?"

"None. We're processing the room now, and we need to get out of here so they can continue."

As they walked around the end of the bed, he said, "Notice the top sheet is missing. We concluded, whoever did this figured it was most likely full of his DNA. He must have just pulled it off and taken it with him when he left."

"Any idea when it happened?"

"Obviously, sometime during the night. I'll have a better idea when they more carefully examine the body."

Charles took a deep breath before he said, "And again, you have no idea who might have done this?"

"We've talked briefly to the neighbors. No one saw anything last night, but they did indicate she apparently just ended a relationship. It didn't end well, I guess. Sounds like she had an altercation with him, right here at her front door. We'll check it out as soon as we know a little more."

Charles started to sit down. The commander grabbed his arm and stopped him. "Don't sit. You'll just add to the list of people whose DNA we'll have to process. Let's walk outside."

As they walked through the doorway, Charles said, "I need to get back to work. Keep me updated, Jeff. This makes me sick. She was a good person, a good secretary. Just keep me in the loop."

Once he arrived at this office, he kept the front door locked, altering the sign, indicating they would not reopen until three o'clock. He called his boss to determine if the office could provide him with temporary secretarial help. Once that was done, he dialed Michael's number, praying he answered. His call again went to voice mail. Once it did, he said, "Michael, you need to call me immediately. We have a serious problem we need to discuss, immediately. Don't talk to anyone else before you talk to me."

Ten minutes later, he called back. "Hi, Dad, what's going on?"

"Listen, Layla, my secretary, has been murdered. I'm not even going to ask you if you knew anything about it—I'm going to assume you didn't. I know, however, that you tried to run over her, and that if anyone knows that and hears she's dead, you'll be a prime suspect. Do not talk to anyone about this. If someone asks you about it, you call me immediately. Do you understand?"

"Oh my god. Hell, I didn't do it. When did it happen?"

"Last night."

Michael's tone of conversation changed immediately. "Oh, well, I'm okay then. I was with my girlfriend all night. She's my alibi. She'll be a good one too, Dad."

"You really think a jury will believe a couple of druggies like you two? They find out you tried to run over her, believe me, you'll be prime suspect number one. There isn't a jury in the world that will listen to your drug-addicted girlfriend. You need to come home. You need to go through rehab. That would serve two purposes. It would keep you off the streets and away from the cops, and it would dry you out. You need to come home now, Michael."

He hesitated. "Sure, I'll come home. Thanks for the info. See you soon."

The connection was terminated. He placed his phone on the desk and sat back in his chair. He wasn't coming home. Charles honestly didn't believe Michael had it in him to do something like this, but he would do everything he could to keep his son safe. He would monitor the situation and do all he could to keep his only child out of the way of the ensuing investigation. Charles would now just pray to God they figured out who did this and that, one day soon, Commander Wiley didn't walk in his office and give him the bad news—that it was, in fact Michael that was responsible for one of the most horrific murder scenes he had ever witnessed.

23

I t had only been a few days since he had seen Layla, but every hour seemed like an eternity. He missed her. No matter what he did to fill his hours, she was always on his mind. If there had been a defined identifiable issue, some factor that he could say, without doubt, had ended their involvement, it would have made all this so much easier. If it had been insignificant, he could have apologized, hoping that resolved the problem. If it were a major issue—one that couldn't be resolved—he could have easily walked away. But not to know or understand why they were no longer a couple made it just that much more difficult to forget, to remove her from his memory banks.

Barrett had a difficult day ahead. The weather was not cooperative—it was rainy and chilly. Unfortunately, today he needed to start tailing a client's husband. She had no doubt her husband was having a relationship, and this was the day he told her he would start to make that determination. She had given him her husband's schedule and wanted a full report by nightfall.

As he sat in his office, just prior to the time Joyce would arrive, he clasped his hands behind his head and watched the rain through his only office window. He leaned back and put his feet on the desktop. He needed to move on—forget her, and he would, but this one would be hard. When things were right between them, he was as much at peace as he had ever been in this lifetime. He would remember what that felt like, because it definitely was a feeling he wanted to experience on a permanent basis—obviously, now not with her, but with someone.

He heard his secretary walk through the front door and close her umbrella. He listened as she walked to her desk and turned on her computer. The day had just begun. She would shortly make a new pot of coffee, after he had nearly drained the one he had made at six this morning—all comfortable, familiar sounds, and exactly the way it should be to start a new day.

Joyce walked in his office and took a chair in front of his desk. After a moment of silence, he said, "Well, now, no 'good morning,' 'how are you,' 'how's the day look,' 'what'd ya do last night'? You're looking pretty darn sober this morning, young lady."

"You heard the morning news yet?"

"Ha. You know I never listen to that stuff. I learn about the day's news during the day from you. Why?"

she said, "Better brace yourself. You're not gonna like this."

He turned his chair to face her and unclasped his hands from behind his head. He could tell something substantial had happened. He knew her too well.

"Layla was murdered last night."

He said nothing as he tried to process. "What?"

"She was murdered, Barrett. It was on the news this morning. They gave few details. They only mentioned she was Charles's secretary and that she was found stabbed to death. That's all they said. I didn't figure you knew."

"We're talking about the same Layla, right? I mean, are you sure they—"

"No question, Barrett. It's her."

He hung his head and said softly, "Thanks, Joyce. Thanks for letting me know. Just shut the door as you walk out, will you?"

"Is there anything I can do?"

"No. Just let me have a few minutes."

"Sure." She stood and walked through his office door, closing it softly as she did.

He couldn't think. How is this possible? Who could have done this? He tried to think back through their conversations about anyone she thought might have issues with her. She had never mentioned anyone specifically. Of course, there was that situation the other day when she was almost run over, but after it happened, she figured it actually might not have been an intentional act by the driver. She never mentioned anyone that might have had enough of an issue with her to kill her.

"Barrett, Kris on line 1. You wanna talk to her?"

"No. Tell her I'll call her back."

As he continued to recall conversation after conversation with her, Joyce again interrupted the process.

"What?"

"She said she was coming right over and hung up. She wanted to know if you had heard the news."

"Shit... I don't wanna talk to anyone."

"I'll tell her when she gets here."

Fifteen minutes later, as he continued to think about conversations he had with Layla, and about anything that might have forewarned him she had trouble in her life, the door flew open, and Kris stood there, soaking wet. "We need to talk."

She slammed the door and sat down in front of his desk. He stood. "You know what, this isn't a good time. Now could you please get out? I'll give you a call when I'm ready, and we can discuss this partnership thing then. Now get out."

"Just shut up and sit down. This conversation has nothing to do with a partnership. I'm assuming you already know about Layla. You know they're gonna look pretty closely at you for her murder, don't you? You know that, don't you? Now sit your ass down and let's talk about it."

He stared at her as the words sunk in. Finally, he sat.

"What the hell are you talking about?"

"I got a guy inside the cop department that keeps me up to date. He's a good friend, and he keeps me informed. They know about you and Layla. They know you two were a couple, and that you just broke up. They know that the breakup was very pubic and, apparently, a very emotional event, especially for you."

"Good god, that doesn't mean I killed her. I can't believe this." He stood and walked to the window, then turned toward her as he said, "They honestly believe I might have killed her?"

"That's one of the avenues they're pursuing, yes. And why wouldn't they? You apparently were seen having a fight at Reflect. You apparently were seen coming out of her house while she was screaming at you and you had your hands on her. Not much later, she's dead. Excuse me—not too hard to connect the dots! Now where were you last night? You with anyone?"

He sat down and thought, then turned to her and said, "No. With all this going on with her, I just didn't feel like going anywhere."

"Well, you better get your story straight, bucko, because you're going to be the first one they interrogate. They spent most of late yesterday afternoon and last night in her house, questioning neighbors along with family members and people who worked with her in the district attorney's office. Today they're ready to roll. I wouldn't be surprised they're here before ten o'clock."

"I can't think they'd take me as a serious suspect. I've never ever done anything wrong."

"Every murderer has a first time, you know. You better change your point of view, Barrett. I'm telling you they're coming to get you—or at least question you. Do you and I need to go through anything? Should we rehearse what you're going—"

"Shit no. I'm just gonna tell them the truth. I wonder though if I should call John. I wonder if he should be here."

Barrett called John's cell. The call went to voice mail, and the message indicated he was in court, but would return the call as soon as he was out. He left his name, asking John to call him back as soon as he listened to the message. Kris stood and started pacing the office.

"Okay, now what should we do next? What's your thoughts? What needs to be done to stop this? We need to—"

Barrett stood, leaning over his desk as she paced on the other side. "What the hell are you doing? The problem is never going to go so far as to warrant this kind of planning, of strategizing. I didn't do it, plain and simple."

"You ever been in this kind of situation before?"

"No. I told you that."

She leaned on his desk, her face within a few inches of his. "You have no idea how this works. They'll pressure the shit out of you. If they think you did this, they'll use every trick they have to get you to confess or make statements that incriminate you."

"Oh, bullshit. I can't believe—" Joyce opened the door.

"Barrett, there are a couple of cops here. They need to visit with you."

Kris looked at him and said, "You better not say a fucking word, Barrett, not a fucking word until you have an attorney. Take my word for it. I'm just sayin—"

The door opened wide, and one of the cops said, "You Barrett Armstrong? We need to talk. *Now*. And, ma'am, whoever you are, get out!"

24

This temp they provided him wasn't worth a shit. Charles was stumbling through the day, trying to keep her in line and trying to outline his case against Barrett Armstrong. Who would have ever thought they would be looking at Armstrong? On second thought, with all the issues he noticed Armstrong had when in his office, it wasn't so much of a surprise at all—he appeared to be a smart ass and a know-it-all. It *was* a surprise, however, he was the one Layla was dating—the one she chose over him. How quickly it had all changed. A conviction of Barrett Armstrong would now most likely take his own son off the hook for attempting to run over and murder Layla.

The grand jury would convene in a couple of days. He was in the process of trying to run down witnesses and explain that they were about to be served with a subpoena. While he had them on the phone, he wanted to briefly discuss, in general, their testimony. He would also set up an appointment with them later in the day, to discuss their testimony in detail.

In addition to handling the Armstrong case, which, for obvious reasons, was by far the most important one he was prosecuting, he continued to receive calls and officers stopping by asking about their own cases. But this case, the one involving Lyla's murder, was important on multiple levels, the most important of which was to make sure Armstrong remained the focal point of the investigation. Regardless of how loudly Armstrong screamed about being innocent, which he would—they all did—it was imperative everyone's attention remain focused on Barrett.

"Yes, Clarice, what is it?"

"Well, sir, there's a Mister—"

"Goddammit, speak up, Clarice. I can't hear anything anyway, but if you're gonna continue working here, you better speak louder than a whisper, or your 'first experience in a district attorney's office' will be short-lived."

"Sorry, sorry, Mr. Whitmore. Mr. Winters is on the phone."

He picked up the phone and motioned her out of the office.

"Mr. Winters, this is Charles Whitmore with the district attorney's office. How are you today?"

"Good, good. What's going on?"

"Well, I just wanted to forewarn you, you're about to get a subpoena. I need you to testify concerning an altercation you witnessed a week or so ago at Reflect. You remember that—a couple of people arguing with each other? I don't think you were too far away from their table."

"Yes, yes I remember. What am I being subpoenaed for?"

"We believe that man killed the woman a couple of nights ago. Now, I would really like to talk to you sometime later today before your testimony day after tomorrow. Would there be a time you could come in and visit with me?"

"He *killed* her?"

"That's our belief. She's dead, and we believe he did it."

"Well, sure, I could come in sometime I guess."

"Great. Let me put you in touch with my secretary and have her line up a time for you."

He yelled at Clarice, to pick up line 1 and set the guy up with an appointment later today. He assumed she said "okay" but said it so softly he couldn't hear. The call was terminated shortly thereafter, and Clarice told him the witness would be in his office at three o'clock this afternoon. He then told her to get Mrs. Tipper on the phone. A few minutes later, Clarice whispered she was on line 1, and he picked up.

"Mrs. Tipper?"

"Yes."

"This is Charles Whitmore with the district attorney's office. How are you today?'

She hesitated. "Whatta ya want?"

"Well, ma'am, it's my understanding you were a neighbor to the recently deceased Layla Adams, is that correct?"

"Well, yes, I was. Why you calling *me*? I was gone when it happened. It couldn't been me that done it. I wasn't nowhere near when it happened. I got witnesses that'll—"

"Wait, wait, Mrs. Tipper. We know you had nothing to do with it, but it's my understanding you observed an altercation between her and a young gentleman the night before, is that correct?"

"By alternation, you mean fight? Is that what you're a gitten' at?"

"Altercation, yes an *altercation*—a fight, at the front door. Is that correct?"

"Yes, we did. Me and my husband saw that."

"Okay, great. Now, ma'am, you're about to be served with a subpoena to testify before the grand jury in a couple of days. I would like to visit with you about your testimony later today. Can my secretary set you up with an appointment here in my office?"

"Oh my, I just don't know. I don't got a car. My husband takes it to work."

"That's not a problem. I'll send an officer to pick you up, and he'll also return you home. Let me transfer you to my secretary, and she'll set that all up for you. Just hold on a minute." He put her on hold and yelled at Clarice, who set her up with a ride and an appointment later in the day.

Everything was proceeding nicely. He would contact Commander Wiley and tell him this is a done deal—that Barrett Armstrong was the murderer and to look no further— to concentrate all their efforts on convicting him and only him.

Hopefully, they could fast-track the case, and this would all be nothing but another routine conviction in a matter of a few months. Charles tried Michael's number. He answered on the first ring.

"Michael, you comin' home?"

"Hello to you too, Dad. No, I'm not, so stop askin'. I'm perfectly content right where I am."

"So when will I see you? Are you *ever* coming home?"

He laughed. "I'm not divorcing you, Dad. Sure, I'll be around once in a while. We've found a pretty good source of income now, and I'm working at that, so I don't have much free time. But I'll be home now and then."

"Great. Whatta you doing?"

"Oh, this and that. We would be best off not to discuss it on the phone. I'll tell you later, when we're together."

Charles could only imagine what the two of them were doing. He would withhold judgment until he knew for sure. "Anyone talked to you about Layla?"

"No, no one."

"Well, I think I got it handled. I'm about to indict her boyfriend. So I'm thinking you're out of the woods."

"I was never in 'the woods,' in the first place. I didn't touch her."

"Now, Michael, do you expect me to believe that? You told me you didn't try to run her down either. I know you lied about that."

He hesitated. "I'm telling you I never touched her and I didn't. I may have stretched the truth a little about the car incident, but really, I never touched her."

"Stay out of trouble, son, just stay out of trouble."

"Thanks for the advice. See you soon."

"Michael, I… Michael?"

The call had been terminated. He put the phone down and wondered what his new source of income was. Charles actually was afraid to ask. He had no doubt it was illegal. How could he trust him? Given his history, how could he believe a word Michael said? In addition, he may actually *think* he's telling the truth about Layla, when in fact he killed her while high on something. The way Layla was killed would indicate whoever did it wasn't normal—that their thought process was functioning improperly and illogically. Michael on drugs would fit that description—he had seen him that way. He had seen him out of his mind high on drugs, and part of a description of him when in that condition would include *violent*.

Clarice walked in the door and whispered, "Medical Examiner's office on line 1."

"Thanks."

Whether Michael never came home again, or whether he never saw him again, would have absolutely no effect on trying to save him from a conviction for murder. He would do whatever was necessary to keep him in the shadows and completely out of the spotlight when it came to the untimely death of Layla Adams.

25

C larice walked in his office bringing pleadings for signature. As she set the paperwork on his desk, she said, "John Weatherly just called. He wants to talk to you this morning when you have a second."

As he started to sort through the pile of paperwork she had just brought him, he said, "What time is Jeff Wiley's appointment?"

"Ten."

"Okay, I'll give Weatherly a callback right now. I understand Barrett Armstrong is a good friend of his. I assume he'll be representing him. Maybe we can discuss a few of the issues going forward from here. When you go back to your desk, get him on the phone for me."

As she walked out the door, he couldn't help but consider what a change there had been in the office within just a few days. The efficient Layla was now replaced by the soft-talking, slow, somewhat-mindless Clarice. It had certainly changed the office dynamics. That change had been almost as significant as the change in contact with his son. He had no idea when he would speak with Michael again. If he only knew—if he just had one solid, concrete witness that would place his son out of harm's way the night Layla was murdered, rather than the statements of a bunch of drug-infused souls that most likely couldn't say for certain *where* they were the night she was killed.

"John Weatherly's on line 1, Charles."

"Morning, John. How goes the battle today?"

He laughed. "Not much different than the rest of the week I guess. I thought I'd visit with you concerning the Armstrong matter. Barrett called and said he was afraid he was going to be indicted for the murder of Layla Adams, is that correct?"

"That's correct. He's in jail now. Bond's been set at a million. He told the judge he couldn't make bail, so he sits there until some-one puts it up. The grand jury convenes in the morning. I talked to some of the witnesses yesterday—I have no doubt they'll indict."

"I have no doubt of that either. You know as well as I you don't need much to get that done. Is there any chance of a reduction in bond?"

"Not if I have anything to say about it. You should have seen her, John. It was awful."

"That's what I understand. If they do indict, when do you wanna arraign him?"

"Next week sometime. We'll have it scheduled, and I'll let you know."

"I know this a little premature, but any chance of a bargain?"

Charles hesitated. If he could bargain this out and get a plea on file for her death, then the issue of anyone else committing the crime would be moot. "Sure, we can discuss it if you wish. I'll think about it and let you know. I understand you two been friends a long time."

"Since college. This is completely out of character for him. He would never kill a spider when we were younger. That's why this is all so hard to believe."

Charles said, "The evidence is pretty overwhelming. If you do have something that indicates he wasn't involved, certainly let me know, and I'll take a look at it."

"Okay, I will."

As he terminated the call, if there was evidence indicating he didn't do it, he might consider it, but not for long. This was the man that was going to be convicted of her murder—they weren't going to look any further.

"Charles, Jeff is here."

He stood as the commander walked in his office door and said, "Morning, Jeff. Have a chair."

"Morning, morning. You wanna talk about this Armstrong case? I don't have a lotta time, but I'm ready to go through what we have. Is the grand jury hearing tomorrow morning?"

"Yes. Have your people there to testify by nine thirty, and we'll just take them one at a time until we finish. Tell me what we have at this point."

He opened his file. "Well, we got an established relationship between the two of them. I have a couple of people who will testify they saw them at a couple of different restaurants and they were all over each other."

"Will they be there in the morning?"

"Yes. Then I have that Kris Thompson, who will be a reluctant witness, but I got her to admit to me that he was pretty upset when Armstrong and the victim broke up, and that Layla was the one that called it off."

"She subpoenaed?"

"Yes. Then we have the incident at Reflect. I have a couple of people that witnessed the altercation while Armstrong and Layla were there. They were really specific too, both of them. They should be good witnesses." He continued to review his notes. "Then we have the neighbor that witnessed the altercation at Layla's front door, just before she was murdered. Of course, he grabbed her and was physical with her, which might indicate some type of inherent violent tendencies, even though at that time it was only slight. Layla was also really upset that night, but he was upset enough to grab her and shake her. Now, is all that enough to get an indictment?"

"Yes. I assume you'll have someone testify as to the appearance of the room itself and as to cause of death?"

"Yes."

"In our prior conversations, I understood he has no alibi?"

"None. Of course, his phone shows him at home around the time she was murdered, but he could have left it there when he went to her house. Absolutely no one saw him anywhere else that night. He claims he was home and went nowhere."

"Okay, good. You have an officer to testify to that?"

"Yes, the same one that arrested him."

"You mentioned something about a statement he made. Tell me about that."

"Well, after he was read his rights, and as they were walking out his office door, he said, 'If she treated everyone like she treated me, I can understand why someone might hurt her, but it sure as hell wasn't me.'"

"He actually *said that*?"

"Yes. I assume we can get it in."

"Oh, I'll get it in all right. The guy really cooked his own goose with that one. Are you continuing to investigate?"

"Yes. We will, as we do in every case, investigate right up until the time of trial."

Charles moved forward in his chair. "You're only investigating Armstrong though, correct? You're not still continuing to look for others that might have done this, are you?"

"Oh sure. He denied it. In fact, he vehemently denied it. We'll continue to try to determine if someone else was involved until the case is tried. That's just standard procedure."

"Let me give you a little advice. Tell your people to stop looking for anyone else. We have the man that did this. All he can provide is a general denial. We have enough to convict him. Do *not* waste your time and the time of the men in your department by looking for someone else we're virtually sure doesn't exist. That might be a good idea in other cases, but not this one. I want you to solely concentrate on this man and what he did in this instance, nothing else. Does that make sense to you?"

Commander Wiley cleared his throat. "Well, that's not what we normally do, but if you're absolutely certain we got the right man, then we'll concentrate on getting a conviction and forget about expanding our search to look for any other likely individual."

Charles leaned back in his chair, cupped his hands behind his head, smiled, and said, "Good. That's exactly what I want you to do. Now, let's just plan on meeting tomorrow morning, and we'll start the process. This should be like shootin' ducks in a barrel. We got all we need—he's got nothin'. Don't get any better than that, Jeff. It just don't get any better than that."

26

Kris sat in the back corner of a small coffee shop near the courthouse. Every seat was full, but she had arrived a half hour earlier than necessary, then waited until that one particular table was free before she made her move. The table was farther away from other tables than most, and she wanted at least a small amount of privacy when Art arrived.

She sat with both hands clasped around her cup, starting into space. She thought about her testimony, which had only just ended. The questions were one sided. There was no one there to ask questions from Barrett's point of view. The prosecutor, Charles Whitmore, asked all the questions, and he asked only those questions designed to secure an indictment. He made no effort to point out both sides of each and every issue. She knew what had happened was the appropriate procedure before a grand jury. She just didn't like it. There was no doubt in her mind Barrett had nothing to do with the murder, but at this point, it didn't appear there was much she could do about it. The case was in the hands of Charles Whitmore, and he certainly wasn't going to ask her what she thought about any of it.

As she sat evaluating her testimony, Art approached her table.

"Hi, girlfriend. How are ya?"

She looked up, smiled, but said nothing. He had already picked up his cup of coffee and, after a lack of response, sat down in the chair opposite her, also remaining quiet.

She finally looked up and said, "Oh, hi, how are you? Haven't seen you in a while."

"Hmm, that was indeed a disingenuous greeting. What might be the problem here?"

"Nothing, nothing. What's goin' on in your life?"

"Well, ya know, it's not because I haven't tried to contact you because I have, but you seem to have a problem returning a call, especially lately. Maybe we should start with what's going on in that busy, crazy life of yours, missy."

She never looked up as she said, "Someone I really care for is about to be indicted for murder."

He didn't respond, expecting her to continue. When she said nothing, he said, "You mumble. I've told you that before. Now, again, what's going on in your life, Krissy?"

She finally looked up and said, "I told you. Someone I care for is about to be indicted for murder. *That's* what's going on in my life."

He leaned back in his chair. "You really *know* someone that's in that kind of pickle?"

"Yes, Art, I do. I just got done testifying in front of the grand jury, and I have no doubt before the day's over, he'll be indicted for something he didn't do—an incredible rush to judgment in my opinion. But my opinion doesn't count for much, I'm afraid."

"Okay, girlfriend, let's just rewind. Let's just start this story over from the beginning. Let's go down this path together. You're obviously alone on this little journey, so let Art walk with you. Start at the beginning."

He always made her smile. If there was anything about Art that stood out, it was his ability to make her lighten up—to lighten up when all seemed so dark.

"I have a friend, Barrett Armstrong. He's a private investigator. We've just recently become friends, and in fact, we're talking about combining our businesses together. Our plans were all coming together when he was charged with his former girlfriend's murder. Maybe you heard about it—her name was Layla Adams."

"That the one that was murdered over in Bellevue?"

"Yes."

He sat back, his eyes narrowed, and he pointed his finger at her as he said, "You need to stay away from them murderers, you hear me. I got enough to worry 'bout, without worrying 'bout my friends runnin' with murderers. Holy shit, girl. What you thinkin'?"

"One problem with your warning, Art—he's no more a murderer than I am."

"You don't know that, Kris. How do you know that?"

"*I know. I just know.* What I *don't* know is what I can do to help him. The prosecutor clearly believes he's guilty. I just don't know what to do."

"There's nothing you can do, period. You need to stay out of it. Let the system work without you in the middle of it."

She stood and walked to the counter for a refill. As she walked back, he said, "You're not gonna let it lie, are you?"

"What *should* I do? Think about it, Art—*what should I do?*"

"I'm sorry. Whatta ya mean 'what should you do'? What should *I* do? What does *anyone* do? Hell, I don't know. What's your point here?"

"Come on, Art. Follow me here. What the hell do I *do* for a living? I *investigate.* That's what I do, and I do it pretty damn well, if I do say so myself, although most of the time, it's in *conjunction* with law enforcement and with the legal system, not *contrary* to it."

He took a drink of coffee while he considered her response. "So whatta you gonna do? Where do you go from here?"

"I don't know. I need to think about it. I think first maybe I'll go see his secretary. She's been with him since he started. Maybe I'll quiz her some about him."

"Let me ask you something. How much do you like this guy? You're, I'm sure, doing this without being paid, and for a guy you haven't known that long. What's the deal between the two of you? What am I missing?"

She thought for a moment, then said, "Here's the deal. He's a friend. We were thinking about becoming business partners and, if he gets out of this, probably still will. I know he didn't do this, and I know he has no one helping him figure out who did."

"What about his attorney? What the heck is he doing?"

"I don't know. I'm going to find out though, right after I visit with Barrett's secretary."

136

Art leaned back and said, "You really like this guy, don't you? This is more than just business, isn't it?"

She stood and said, "Gotta go. Got a million things to do. Take care. I'll give you a call."

Joyce was doing what she always did during working hours—answering the phone, taking messages, taking care of walk-ins. Kris sat down in front of her desk, after asking her if she had a few minutes to talk.

"Sorry that took so long. So, Kris, whatta ya need?"

"I need to get Barrett out of this trumped-up charge so we can talk about our partnership. How's it all going here?"

Joyce leaned back and crossed her arms. "I can't believe this is happening. I *know* he did nothing wrong. But my immediate problem is that I've had no contact with him since his arrest. What am I supposed to do with this office? People are dropping in and calling, all asking if this is true—if he's been charged with murder. I don't know what to do. I haven't talked to him since he went to jail."

"I'll talk to him before long. I'm going to see him. I'll ask him about the office and let you know."

"Thank you. I've just been telling new clients maybe they better look elsewhere, and current ones to just hold on until I talk to Barrett."

"Have you talked to John Weatherly? What's he doing?"

"I talked briefly to him, but I think he's probably like all of us—busy with handling this case, but also many others. Outside of just handling the legal issues, I don't think he's doing anything to help Barrett figure this all out."

She thought for a moment, then said, "You know, I think I will."

"Whatta you mean? You 'will' what?"

"Help him. He didn't do this, you know that and so do I. But no one seems to care. They are each doing their own thing, and no one is even considering the possibility he didn't do this. No one is looking for anyone else that might have murdered her. I'm like everyone else—I just don't have the free time to investigate, but I'm going to *find* the time. He's not guilty—we're both certain of that. Can I count on you to help me if I need a little assistance along the way?"

"Sure. Absolutely. Anything to help, Barrett. Where you gonna start?"

"I need to go see him. I haven't had a chance to speak with him since he was arrested. I think I better start with his story and go from there. I've got contacts all over Nashville that owe me a favor." She stood. "But somewhere along the way, I'll most likely need your help. I'll stay in touch."

27

Barrett lie on his back, in his bunk bed, his forearm over his closed eyes, as he processed his dilemma. His current situation was a first on so many levels. First time someone he loved had been murdered. First time behind bars. First time for feeling so frickin' scared and frustrated at the same time. He had no idea what to do or where to turn. John would represent him, which was a plus. But what would *John* do—how far would he really go to actually try to figure out who did this? Barrett knew he didn't have enough money to pay for a full-scale investigation. Most of what he had in savings would need to be used just to pay the basics in attorney fees—he would have little left to investigate.

His family couldn't help. Both his parents were deceased. He had no siblings. It seemed everywhere he turned, he ran into a wall. No one seemed to be interested in who actually killed her. Since he was the one charged, everyone clearly assumed it was him—that seemed to be that—end of story.

"Hey, Armstrong, how ya doin' in there?"

He raised his head. It was the jailer. "Doing fine, Sam, doing fine."

"You want somethin' for lunch? Got some great eats today. Got 'em for ya right here if you want 'em."

"Not hungry, Sam. You go ahead and eat my share. I'll pass."

"You know, you ain't ate much since they put you in there. We need you nice and plump so you'll be all pretty and make some guy a nice sweetheart when you get to the pen. You wanna look your best when you get there, don't you, Armstrong?" He belted out a laugh one could have heard outside the jailhouse.

"Yup, that's what I live for, Sam. But, today, you go ahead and eat my share. Maybe you'll choke on it and die right before my very eyes. Sounds like a great ending to my morning, for sure."

Sam stopped laughing. He turned to walk out the door and said, "That wasn't very nice, Armstrong, not very nice at all."

About an hour later, back came Sam, and this time he said, "You got a visitor. Get up and I'll take you to the meeting room."

"Who is it?"

"Get up, I told you."

"What if I don't wanna see them?"

He unlocked the door and said, "Get your ass up before I beat the livin' hell out of you. You'll learn to follow instructions pretty quick here, Armstrong. You follow them, and you follow them quick or you'll have trouble surviving. Believe me, you won't last long."

Barrett slowly stood, and as he did, the jailer said, "Follow me."

They walked into a room, crowded with small tables and chairs filled with inmates, and those that had come to visit. Obviously, some were attorneys, but there were many who were holding hands with the inmates, obviously in a relationship of some type.

Near the middle of the room sat a table for two, one chair unoccupied, the other occupied by Kris. She continued to wave as he stood looking at all the people in the room. He nodded and walked to her table. As he sat down, he said, "What in the world are you doing here? You surely got better things to do than visit some down-on-his-luck son of a bitch that most likely will never see the light of day, don't you?"

She smiled as she said, "Not really. I'm here 'cause I wanna be, and no other reason. I'm here to help a poor innocent chump charged with something he never did. Hopefully, there's something I can do to get you out of here."

Barrett looked away as he said, "As tight as this case sounds, I'm thinkin' I may never get out. Sounds to me like they got everything pretty well figured out, at least in their minds." He looked up and said, "Did you testify before the grand jury?"

"Yes, yesterday. I had asked John to call me when they came to a conclusion. Have you talked to him yet?"

"No. Have you?"

"Yes."

"I assume they indicted me, or I'd be out by now."

"They did."

"What's the charge?"

She hesitated.

"Come on, I'm gonna hear it from somebody, might as well be you."

"Murder one."

He smiled as he leaned back in his chair. "The big one."

"Yes. I'm assuming John will be here to tell you sometime today."

"Probably."

Neither said anything until she broke the silence when she said, "I'm gonna help you."

"No, you're not. Just leave it to the cops and John. They'll get to the bottom of this."

"They may, you're right. But I'm gonna do my own investigating. I have a little free time, and I wanna help. After all, you were about to be my partner. Besides that, I believe in you. I'm gonna help."

He studied her for a moment and could tell she wasn't going to take no for an answer. "Up to you, I guess. I should tell you though, I don't even know where to begin. I'm still trying to process our breakup and, now on top of that, her murder. And, of course, the frosting on the cake is that I'm now *charged* with her murder. I can tell you one thing I know for certain. For my feeble little mind, that's one hell of a lot to process."

"You need to start figuring this all out. Something smells here. Obviously, you didn't do it, but someone had to have been keeping pretty close watch. It seems to me your argument with her and her death right after that was way too coincidental."

He moved forward in his chair, looked down, clasped his hands together on the table top, and softly said, "I guess so. I just don't know."

She reached out and placed both of her hands over his. "Look at me." He never moved. "Barrett, look at me." He slowly looked up. "I can't do this by myself. I can't figure this out by myself. I need your help. I can only imagine what you've been through. First losing someone you love, and then going through what you're going through now. But I'm here for you. I'll work my ass off for you. I'll investigate until I drop. It's what I do. I investigate and I do it well. But I must have your help. There's no way I can do this alone. You can't give up, not now. This is your life we're talking about here. You need to stay with me. I can do the legwork, but you need to stay with me, help me when I need help, think this all through with me, so I can get your sorry ass out of here."

"But I don't know… I don't know anything… I don't know how—"

"Listen to me, just listen. I can do this. I can do all the legwork and figure this out from outside. Even if you do no more than talk it through, that will be a help. But I can't handle you giving up. I can't handle a quitter. You have to promise you'll stay with me until we get you out, and get you off, or until there's nothing else we can do. Can you do that for me? Can you do that much for me?"

He pulled his hands away. "I can, I guess. It just seems like they have enough to convict me. Maybe I should try to cut a deal or something. Plead to something and get probation. Maybe do what I can to just get out of here. You have no idea what it's like in here."

"Certainly, you can discuss that. But, Barrett, not to burst your bubble, you need to remember you've been charged with murder in the first degree. You really think they're gonna let you plead to something that doesn't require some jail time? Besides that, I can investigate while you're in here, and while you're figuring out that plea issue. We can work simultaneously on both of those aspects."

"You're right. I agree. Whatta you want me to do?"

"You need to think back on all the times you've been together and try to figure out if there was anyone in her past she might have mentioned who might have been a potential problem for her. I'll go ahead and check a few things I already have in mind, but just start there for me, will you?"

Their discussion lasted a few more minutes and until the jailer told them time was up.

As he sat on his bunk, he tried to organize his thoughts. Where would he begin? As he considered his relationship with Layla, there was never a moment he felt she had issues with anyone else, and certainly issues of this magnitude. The only time anything appeared out of place was when she was almost hit by that car, and trying to figure out who did that, when Layla couldn't even figure it out, was most likely impossible.

He couldn't help but smile when he thought about Kris and how determined she was to help him. It was clear she believed in him. At least someone did. And she was right. It wasn't time for him to crawl into a hole and let them do as they wished with him. It was time to fight for what he knew was the truth. If she was committed to helping him, the least he could do was assist her in her efforts.

28

A couple of days after his conversation with Kris, the officers had transported Barrett from his cell to the courthouse, where he sat while defendant after defendant walked up to stand in front of the judge's bench and pled guilty or not guilty as charged. John had met him at the courthouse and waited with him until it was his turn.

Once they called his name, he, along with John, walked forward and waited for the judge to review the file. He had little doubt this judge had plenty of experience. He appeared to be on the far side of ninety years of age. It was clear he was a southern boy through and through. You could cut his southern drawl with a knife, and Barrett had no doubt his early years were spent in southern Alabama or Louisiana. While native Nashvillians had a slight drawl, this guy was over the top.

He wouldn't reduce Barrett's bail. The judge felt the nature of the offense was so heinous the amount was justified. So he would sit in a jail cell until the case was tried or they bargained it out. John wouldn't waive speedy trial, and the trial was set to begin April 18. John was concerned the trial date wasn't far away, but he did feel it was far enough in the future that he had time to adequately prepare. Once the process had been completed, they took Barrett back to his cell. John had indicated he had a few things to handle while at the courthouse, but then would meet Barrett in the conference room at the jailhouse.

A couple of hours later, an officer came for Barrett and took him to the conference room, where John was waiting.

As he approached John's table, he said, "So what's next?"

"Well, the first thing I'm going to do is depose the witnesses that are going to testify against you. I'll take each of their statements under oath and we'll just hope something turns up. After I take their depos, knowing what they are prepared to say will also give me an opportunity to more effectively plan on how I'm going to cross-examine them."

"Are you optimistic? I mean, does that sort of investigating normally yield much for you—has it in other trials?"

John leaned back and said, "It's hard to tell. I'm not expecting a lot, but at this point, it's just hard to tell. I know one thing—I don't want to try the case without knowing what they're gonna say in advance. So we don't really have much choice, whether it ultimately helps or not."

"What about trying to bargain this down to something I can live with and getting me released?"

"I'm gonna talk to Charles about that, but the problem is, I don't have much doubt they won't let you go without pleading to a felony. If you do, you'll lose the right to vote and the right to carry a weapon. Your investigator's license will be revoked, which will affect your ability to make a living, and you'll be a convicted felon, which has all sorts of additional repercussions. I'll talk to him about it, but it just may be better to try the case and let the chips fall."

"Let me know when you've had that discussion."

"I will. Is there anything else you haven't told me? Is there a chance someone may have stopped by your house the night she was murdered—any way in hell you might have some kind of alibi for that night?"

"No. I've thought and thought about that night, but the only thing I wanted to do, while trying to get over Layla, was be alone. I had a drink with Kris earlier in the evening, and that's what I told her then—that I just wanted to be alone. That's what I was doing that night—being alone."

"Okay, I'll see what I can do with Charles. I just wish you had a little more for me."

"I'll be very convincing in front of that jury, I'll tell you that. I'll make damn sure they know I didn't do it, and that I still love her, even today."

John said nothing.

"I *am* going to testify in my own defense, aren't I?"

"We'll see. I don't know at this stage."

Barrett leaned forward. "You *always* have your clients testify. What's so different with my case?"

"I know, I know. But let's just see how the evidence comes in. I don't want you screwin' your own case up. I know how emotional you can be, and I don't want Charles hammering you on cross."

Barrett sat back and folded his arms. "I don't get it. You always have your clients testify. That doesn't make sense to me that you change your position when it comes to my case."

"You know, Barrett, I'm not representing some schmuk off the street I never met before. Nor have I ever represented my best friend... in a murder trial. Just let me think it through first. Let's see what the witnesses have to say."

"Okay. Up to you, but you need to know I have no fear of telling the jury I did nothing wrong. By the way, Kris is doing some investigating on her own."

"Really? What's she doing?"

"Just checking on a few things we discussed—nothing too important. I'm sure she'll review whatever she turns up with you."

"That would be a real good idea, since I'm the one that has to present it at trial if she does find anything. I better go. I'll stay in touch."

He started putting his files in his briefcase as Barrett said, "Hey, you know our conversations have all been one sided. We haven't talked much about you—about your life. Other than the fact you're about to lose your best friend to a jail cell for the rest of his natural life, how's everything going for you?"

"Let me put it this way. You and I are living parallel lives. You've run into a tough time in your life as have I. Maggie kicked me out the other day. She thinks I'm seeing someone else, so she kicked me out of the house."

Barrett said nothing for a moment, obviously collecting his thoughts. "Okay, let me ask you a couple of questions. First, are you seeing someone else? And second, where the hell are you living?"

"No, Barrett, I'm not seeing anyone else. Never have and doubt I ever will. I love her and always have. I moved into one of my attorney friend's basement, until we get things worked out. I have no doubt we'll be just fine, but for now, I'm livin' in a frickin' basement."

"Where the hell did she get the idea you're seeing another woman, if you aren't?"

"She says I'm gone too many nights, and to be honest, I probably am. But every night I'm gone, I'm at that damn office getting ready for something. I make a lot of money, Barrett, and it's only for one reason—I work my ass off. Now, let's move on. I'm getting along fine, and my mess, as well as yours, will all eventually pass. We'll both get everything worked out one way or the other."

John left shortly thereafter, and Barrett was taken back to his cell. John's words, "We'll get it worked out one way or the other," haunted him. He had no doubt John was correct, but he was starting to conclude the method of resolving his own issues, in a manner that would set him free, was slowly turning out to be an improbable solution to an overwhelming problem.

29

It had been a couple of weeks since Barrett's arraignment. Kris had been to see him once, and he mentioned depositions were set to begin in a few weeks. That would still give them enough time before trial to figure out who did this, or at least come up with enough evidence to create reasonable doubt in the minds of the jurors. John had concluded, even if Barrett did testify, it most likely would not create the doubt they needed to get him off—the State just had too much evidence that pointed toward his guilt.

Kris had been crazy busy and had tried to tie down a number of time sensitive issues before starting on Barrett's situation. But now, his case was also quickly becoming time sensitive. The first thing she needed to do was check out the crime scene. Kris knew by now it had been cleared for occupancy by police, and she wondered who might be living there, if anyone. She drove to Bellevue and started looking for Primrose Lane. Her GPS quickly located the street. It was a cul-de-sac off a major four-lane roadway. The street was long and narrow, with no intersecting side roads. If someone turned down Primrose Lane, it was because they wanted to be on that particular street and no other—there was no access to any other street.

As she drove by Layla's house, she noticed a vehicle in the drive-way. She pulled over and parked while watching the residence. A man and woman, appearing to be in their midfifties, were emptying the house of furniture and loading it in a truck. She concluded they were most likely her parents. She stopped in front of the house and parked.

Kris walked to the front door and introduced herself. She soon learned they were indeed Layla's parents. She was invited in, and when they learned she was investigating their daughter's death, they were surprised the investigation hadn't been concluded. They knew about Barrett and had just assumed he had been the correct suspect. Kris told them he might be, but she was investigating it further and wanted to discuss Layla's immediate past with them if they had time.

Over the next hour she learned all about Layla. In fact, she heard way more than she needed to hear. But at the conclusion of the conversation, she knew no more concerning whether anyone may have wanted to harm Layla than she did when she started. One thing was, however, quite clear. As far as law enforcement was concerned, the investigation into Layla's death was over. They hadn't even contacted her parents other than to tell them she was dead and that they had the murderer in custody.

While discussing the facts with Layla's parents, she also determined there would be no estate. Layla had titled everything that had a title in both her name and her father's name. Upon her death, everything passed to him with no further probate necessary. While they visited, she also had Layla's father call the law firm Layla had been associated with prior to her job with the district attorney's office and tell them to provide her with whatever information she might need concerning Layla. Her next stop would be Layla's former employer.

She was fully aware of the location of their offices, having dealt with the firm on many occasions. Kris was on a first-name basis with the office manager, who didn't hesitate to sit with her and discuss Layla and her employment history.

It was clear, especially during her last few months of employment, that Layla was having problems in the office. She complained numerous times about advances made toward her by most every male in the office. But she also complained about her working conditions, about the lack of appropriate pay based upon her experience, and about wanting more time off. It appeared she just wasn't happy with her job. There didn't appear to be anything specific that caused her to quit—it was just everything in general.

Nothing Kris heard at the law office seemed to be significant enough to warrant further investigation. She left with little more information than she came with. As she sat in her car, she felt perhaps one more stop might be in order.

Kris drove to the downtown police precinct and asked for Bob Harvey. They had dated, once or twice, a long time ago. At that time, they quickly determined they would never enjoy a long-term relationship but parted as friends. Since then, they met once or twice a month, just to touch base with each other and enjoy a beer.

"Hi, Bob. You got a few minutes where we could talk in private?"

"Sure. Come with me. I'll get us a cup of coffee. Sugar, no cream, right?"

"Exactly." She followed him to a small conference room and waited until he returned with two cups of coffee.

After catching up on their personal lives and current relationships, Kris said, "I need to talk to you about a case, —one I hope you might have worked on or know something about."

Bob leaned back in his chair as he said, "Which case?"

"The Layla Adams murder."

"I didn't work on it. Sorry, but I really don't know one thing about it. I didn't have anything to do with it."

She looked down—another dead end.

"Why you working on it? It's my understanding they caught the guy and the investigation is over."

"They caught the guy, but I'm not sure they caught the *right* guy. Do you know, was there ever any indication that someone else might have done it?"

"No, at least nothing that I know of."

"Okay, well, if you hear there might have been someone else involved, will you let me know?"

He smiled. "I will. I'll be glad to do that for you."

She stood as he did, but he seemed hesitant.

Bob said, "I will tell you one thing that's a little strange about the case though. I wouldn't tell you this if we were in an interrogation room with the cameras rolling, but in this conference room, we got no cameras, so here you go. The investigating officers were told, not long after the perp was apprehended, not to investigate any aspect of the case any further. They were told they had the right guy and were to leave it alone."

"Is that normal?"

"Not really. Especially when all you have is circumstantial evidence, the charge is murder, and the defendant completely denies it. That was a first for many of us, which is why I heard about it. The case wasn't in my precinct, but I got a buddy who told me he was told to quit investigating. Most of the time the investigation continues, at least on a limited basis, until we reach the point where we are all 100 percent convinced the one we arrested did it. I thought it was the quickest rush to judgment I ever saw. But it wasn't my call, and it wasn't even in my precinct. Besides that, based on what I heard, it really did appear they had the right man. But stopping the investigation so quickly was unorthodox. It caught the attention of quite a few."

"Okay. Thanks, Bob. That's not much to go on. It's a little strange, but I guess nothing anyone could hang their hat on as being *that* unusual."

"It's not normal, that's for sure, at least not for this department. Don't say anything about it. We don't normally share that type of information with anyone."

She left shortly thereafter and drove straight to the jail. She waited in the conference room while they brought Barrett from his cell.

"What'd you find out?"

"Hi. Really not much. I had a chance to talk to Layla's parents at the house, and they didn't give me anything useful at all."

"They live a thousand miles away, and I don't think they were all that close. That's no surprise, I guess."

"I went to her former employer's office and they didn't provide much either. I think Layla was really unhappy there, for many reasons, one of which was she was hit on by most of the attorneys, but I didn't find out anything that might help."

"What about one of those attorneys that hit on her? Maybe they were upset about her not responding."

"You know, I thought about that, but I just don't get that feeling—that there was enough of a problem to create that type of rage. Anyway, I got nothing out of the conference with them, and unless something inadvertently turns up concerning one of the lawyers in the firm, I probably won't pursue it any further."

"So we got nothing."

"Not yet. I've just started though. There was one thing that bothered me a little."

"What's that?"

"I talked to an old flame with the police department, and he told me, in complete confidence, that once you were arrested, the investigating officers were told to stop any further investigation concerning her murder. He told me he was told they had the right guy, and nothing further needed to be done. He also said that was unusual, and that really wasn't normally the way it was done. Especially when the perp swore he didn't do it and all the evidence was circumstantial."

"So what's that mean? Doesn't sound like much to me other than they just really feel I'm the right one."

"The officer I talked to thought it was a little strange, and if he did, then I think we should too."

"Where do we go from here?"

"I don't know. Let me think it through. I do have one really good friend on the force. He was a good friend of my dad's when he was a cop. I've known him forever. He's like a second father. I might go see him and see if he knows anything we should know. He'll tell me if he does, I can guarantee that."

"I didn't even know your dad was a cop. Let me know how that turns out. I did talk to John about a plea. He tells me even if they do agree to a plea, it would probably involve a plea to a felony, and with all the repercussions from that, I might as well just go through the trial."

"So it's really coming down to what I can come up with in my investigation?"

"I'm afraid so, unless John can come up with new evidence, which I don't expect."

She sat back and took a deep breath. All of a sudden, she wasn't doing a "little something" that might help him. All of a sudden, it had turned into an investigation that *had* to turn up something to help him or he would be facing a prison term for the rest of his life. How suddenly everything had changed. Her offer to assist had quickly moved from an offer to simply help a friend to one of *literally trying to save his life.*

30

Charles waited down the street from his home. It was dark enough it would be hard for his son to identify his vehicle. Michael had called and asked if he would be home this evening, to which his father had answered in the affirmative. Charles had been waiting for this opportunity, and thankfully, Michael had given him enough forewarning to make sure everything was ready. He watched while Michael pulled into the driveway in that brown piece of shit he drove, which would soon be nothing more than a pile of metal—nothing even closely resembling the brown vehicle with the broken back window that almost ran over his now-deceased secretary.

He signaled to the officers, who had been told to wait a few minutes after the signal before they made their move. Charles then drove in, behind his son's vehicle, and walked into the kitchen where Michael was just fixing himself supper.

"Michael, how are you?"

Charles walked up behind him and placed his hand on his shoulder. He pulled away, as he continued to fix himself a cold meat sandwich, with accompanying potato chips. "Fine, Dad, just fine. Do you have a minute to talk?"

Charles walked toward the kitchen table and sat down as he said, "Sure, sure, what about? What have you been doing? You said you had a job. Where're you working at?"

Michael walked to the table and sat down. "Well, Dad, I might have gotten myself in a little trouble."

Charles was hesitant to ask, but it was necessary. "What'd you do now? You didn't have anything to do with Layla's murder, did you? Don't tell me you were involved in that, please."

"No, no, I didn't have anything to do with that. I told you I didn't and I didn't."

"So what's the problem?"

As he put his sandwich down and just started to explain that his illegal activities might have caught up with him, two officers walked in the back door. Michael looked at the officers, then at his father. "Dad, what're they doing here?"

"Time for you to dry out, Michael. It's gone on long enough. I filed a petition to have you involuntarily committed, and that's why they're here. Now, I've packed up a few clothes for you and a few necessities I felt you would need. If there are other items you need, let me know, and I'll get them to you."

Michael looked back at the officers, then at Charles. "Why, you old son of a bitch. I should kill you right here. I'm not goin' anywhere with them." He jumped to his feet and started toward the living area, but the officers had already anticipated that move and had him securely in their grip before he reached the doorway. As they walked past Charles on their way to the police cruiser with Michael's suitcase in hand, he quickly looked at his father and said, "You'll pay for this, old man. You'll pay for this."

Charles stood and said, "I'm hoping you'll thank me when it's all over. I hope eventually I get my son back." He watched as they put him in the back seat and drove away. There would be a hearing before long to determine his dependency. They would also then determine whether Michael would remain committed. But Charles and the hearing officer were good friends, and as such, the decision for continued treatment had already been made. With his son safe and secure, Charles knew now he shouldn't have to worry about his involvement with the death of Layla. The vehicle would be destroyed tomorrow. To finish it off, he just needed to convict Armstrong—that would seal the deal completely.

J. B. MILLHOLLIN

The next morning, his first appointment was with John Weatherly. John was precisely on time, and Clarice sent him in Charles's office the moment he arrived. "Morning, John. Haven't seen you since the depos. How'd you think they went? I thought they went quite well."

John took a chair as he said, "I imagine you did, Charles. That doesn't surprise me at all. They concern me, and they're the major reason I'm here."

"I thought the woman that saw the altercation at the front door did a good job. She really laid it all out, at least for us."

"Barrett thought she was way too extreme in testifying to what she observed, but I guess he can testify to that. What about trying to resolve all this? You have any thoughts?"

"Well, you know, we only got about three weeks until trial. The closer it gets, the more prepared I become, and the harder it's going to be for me to agree to anything. We probably should just let the chips fall—just try it and see what happens."

Charles really wanted to resolve the matter right here and now, but he didn't want to appear too receptive. He needed a plea. A plea would close the case and let his son off the hook once and for all.

John said, "Are you gonna offer anything?"

"What about murder two. I'll ask the court for leniency, indicating this guy has never been in trouble before, and let the judge rule as he wishes."

"Hell, that would most likely end up with him dying in prison. He isn't gonna buy that. You gotta come up with something better than that."

Charles thought for a moment and finally said, "I might be able to go with voluntary manslaughter, but I'd have to get approval from my boss and check on the police department's feeling about it too. He'd do time, but at least he'd get out while he still had a little of his life left. I might be able to go there, but I would need approval first."

He held his breath while John thought it over, just hoping he'd bite, and this case would end. "Let me talk to Barrett and see what he says. He still swears he didn't do it, but I'll visit with him. Could we get around admitting he did it?"

"No. That's got to be in the record. We aren't going to use an Alford plea and indicate he's pleading guilty not because he necessarily did it, but because the evidence establishing that he committed the crime is overwhelming. I want him to admit he killed her."

John left shortly thereafter, and Charles was left wondering what Armstrong would do. As he sat considering what turn this case would take next, his phone rang.

"Dad, I get one call. Get me out of here. I mean out. You put me here. Now get me out. I can't stay here." Charles tried to calm him down. He stayed on the line until their time was up, and the call was terminated on Michael's end. He felt sorry for him, but he also hoped they would be able to pull him out of the downward spiral he was in. If Armstrong would just plead guilty, and Michael would just dry out, this whole situation, which all started with the mistake he made when he hired Layla, would, thankfully, finally come to an end.

31

L ater that same afternoon, as Kris was meeting with Barrett, John also joined the two of them. She had been with Barrett for almost an hour, talking mostly about the case, but also other miscellaneous items. Through it all, Barrett's depressed state of mind was obvious. She wasn't sure if she could keep him focused on what they needed to do to favorably resolve all these issues. It was apparent he was having some serious mental issues concerning his current situation.

"Hi, John. You have a chance to meet with Charles?"

John took a seat. "I did, and what he said isn't what you're gonna wanna hear. He wants you to plead guilty to voluntary manslaughter and also admit you killed her."

Kris spoke before Barrett even had a chance. "Are you shitting me? He's not pleading to manslaughter, and he sure as hell isn't going to admit to something he didn't do."

Barrett looked down, remaining silent.

Noticing his hesitation, she looked at him and said, "Right?"

Again, Barrett failed to respond. Kris said, "Barrett, Goddammit, am I right? You're not going to admit to something you didn't do and spend literally years in prison, are you?"

"Whatta you think, John?"

"You know the options as well as I do. But I don't think Charles is gonna drop the charges any further. It's up to you. You tell me what direction you want me to take, and that's what I'll do."

Barrett thought for a moment then said, "It looks to me like there's no way out other than just trying the case and explaining I didn't do it. I'm not going to plead to murder, and I'm not going to plead to anything if I have to admit I killed her because I didn't. If I could plead to something, just to get out and not admit I killed her, I would, but I'm not admitting to something I didn't do, especially if I have to go to prison anyway."

Kris smiled and softly said, "Yes!"

John looked at her briefly, then at Barrett, as he said, "I understand. I'll tell him we just aren't going to plead, and that will take care of that. Any thoughts about the depos? I haven't had a chance to visit with you to any extent since they were taken."

"Not really. That woman that saw us arguing at her house was really embellishing the actual incident, but I guess you'll have a chance to point that out at the time of trial, right?"

"Yes. That was not the time to argue with her. That's what depos are for—to find out what the witnesses are going to say and prepare accordingly. I can handle her at the time of trial."

"So have we exhausted all the possibilities of a plea then?"

"I think so, Barrett. I'm afraid we'll just have to take our chances with a jury."

"Have you got everyone subpoenaed we're calling to testify?"

"Yes. As you know, most of them will testify as to the type of relationship you had with Layla and as to your character. We really have no one to testify as to the actual events of that night."

Kris spoke up. "Either do they. Everything they have is circumstantial."

John smiled as he said, "That's true, Kris, that's very true. That's also all they need to convict, but it's definitely a circumstantial case through and through. The next time I come, I'll bring you a jury list so you can go through the potential jurors. I'm going to need to know if you know any of them or if you've had a problem with any of them. I'll go through the jury selection process with you then too."

"Are you doing anything to uncover who might have done this?"

"Barrett, it's all I can do to have time to prepare your case in court. No, I don't have the manpower in the office to investigate, and you don't have the money to hire outside help. Besides that, I thought Kris was helping in that area."

Kris said, "I am, but it wouldn't hurt to have help. I can only do so much."

"I'm doing all I can on the legal end of this for you. I can't do much more. I'll go through the proposed jury instructions with you when I come to see you next time. I've been working on those this week, and they're almost ready."

"I don't even know what those are. I have no doubt you're doing all you can for me. Thanks."

John left, leaving only Kris and Barrett to continue the discussion. "I'm meeting with my cop buddy this afternoon. Hopefully, he'll have something for me. I'm running out of ideas, so I'm just hoping somewhere along the way, I'll run into something that can jump start my investigation. I'll visit with him and then stop back later today."

Thomas Williams had been a family friend for as long as Kris could remember. He was a cop and had been for over twenty-five years. He had been best of friends with her father prior to her father's death in the line of duty, and since his death, he had made it his responsibility to check up on Kris from time to time.

She had called and agreed to meet him at two thirty in his precinct office. Upon arrival, he escorted her to one of the conference rooms.

"Kris, how are things? How's the detective business going for you?"

Thomas had been wounded five years ago. The resulting leg injury left him available only to perform office work. He had made it clear he didn't like remaining within the walls of the precinct building, but he needed to remain active and wanted to remain in the law enforcement business, regardless of the type of job he was given.

"Good, Tom, good. How's everything around here?"

"Oh, fine. I get a little bored now and again, but I'm just glad they keep me around. Without a family, sitting at home day after day would be hard for me to handle. What brings you here today? You don't normally come to see me here."

"Need to ask you about a case. You heard, I assume, about the Layla Adams murder, haven't you?"

"Oh, yeah. Most all of us have heard about that one, whether we were involved or not."

"Okay, well my good friend has been charged with her murder. The case is completely circumstantial. I know the guy well. He didn't do it. I have a feeling we're missing something, but I can't put my finger on it. You know anything about it, the facts, the investigation—anything at all?"

Thomas looked at her for a moment, then stood, and walked over to close the door. Upon sitting back down, he said, "This can't come from me, Kris. I have no doubt it won't, or I wouldn't tell you in the first place. I'm sure if I give you this information, what I'm about to tell you will come out at some point in time, but I *cannot* be the one it came from, okay?"

Kris moved forward in her chair. "Absolutely."

"This has happened before."

She hesitated. "What?"

"This same crime happened before. About ten years ago. Same factual situation. It happened here, in Nashville, and not in Bellevue, but the factual situation was almost identical."

Kris tried to comprehend. "Where did it happen?"

"Right off West End Avenue."

"They catch the guy?"

"No."

Kris sat back as she considered what he had just told her. "Why hasn't this come out? Why hasn't anyone brought this up?"

"Well, first of all, the specifics of the crime have never been released to the press. I don't know if they would have been smart enough to put two and two together anyway. Second, everyone was told right after your friend was apprehended not to investigate any further—that we had the right guy, end of story. Of course, Commander Wiley is in charge of the Bellevue precinct, so he isn't part of our precinct, and besides that, he wasn't even here when the first one happened. But I know for a fact he told his officers to forget investigating the case, and when they did, we did. They had been told to just go with the evidence they had and forget about anything else, so that's what we all did."

"But, Tom, it obviously isn't Barrett that did this. Whoever did the first one did this one."

"Maybe, maybe not. They have all the evidence they need to convict him on this charge, so I'm thinking they don't care what happened ten years ago. It least that's what I'm *thinking* they are thinking. Doesn't matter anyway. They have what they need to convict, and that's what they're going with. Didn't this guy live here ten years ago?"

"Yes, I think so."

"So there's no reason he couldn't have done that one too. Sometimes you wanna just let sleeping dogs lay, Kris. He could still be charged with the first one since there's no statute of limitations on murder."

"I understand that. But this is too important to let lie. I'll need to discuss it with Barrett and see what he wants to do. I wonder why this person would have waited so long to do this again?"

"Oh hell, Kris, it's hard to tell. Maybe he left the area for a while. Maybe there was a significant change in his life—who knows."

"Is there a folder on this?"

"I imagine there are a number of folders and files. It was a big case at the time. It's been looked at a couple of times since then, as a cold case, but no one has ever been able to come up with anything."

Kris thought for a second. "Tom, I need that information. Is it just statements and pictures of the scene? Does the file or folders actually contain evidence?"

"No, it's just the officer's reports, pictures, and things of that nature. The actual evidentiary items are kept locked up."

"So if you loaned me the files so I could go them item by item and, it wouldn't affect the chain of custody concerning evidentiary items?"

"No. But, Kris, I can't give you that stuff. Good god, I get caught I'm done here."

"You won't. I'll make copies of everything and get it all back to you within a day." She moved forward and said, "I really need this,

Tom. I need to do all I can to help this guy. I know he's been wrongfully charged, and he needs all the help he can get."

Tom sat back, smiled, and said, "Drive 'round to the back door about six o'clock. I'll box everything up. Probably take a couple of boxes—there's a lot of information. It's pretty slow 'bout that time, and I'll slip it into the back seat of your car. If they see it on the video covering the alley, I'll just tell them it was some of your dad's stuff that was still here at the station. They'll never take the time to follow up. Make copies of what you need. I need it all back the next day. You know my car. It's always in the lot. Just stick the boxes in the back seat. I'll leave it unlocked and then just bring the boxes through the front door later in the day. I don't think they'll question me. Been here too long."

"Thank you, Tom. Thank you so much."

They both stood. She put her arms around him. "You've always been there for me. Believe me, no one's going to know a thing about this—ever."

Late that afternoon, she drove down the alley, the door opened, and Tom slid two large boxes into the back seat. Tonight, she would copy it and return all originals the next evening. She would need time to look through the specifics, but the only issue right now is that it happened once before. Surely, that factor coming into play, in and of itself, would be enough for the State to reconsider its position, at least to the point of dropping the charge down to one Barrett could plead to and get out of jail. Hopefully, this would be all they needed to turn this disaster in a new direction and end this nightmare.

32

Kris had contacted Barrett and indicated she needed to see him. They set up a time to meet in the conference room at the jail. When she arrived, the jailer brought him to her. As he reached the table, she stood and hugged him.

"How ya doin', Barrett? You look like you've lost ten pounds since they locked you up. You feelin' okay?"

"Never been better. The food is better than my own cookin', and the company I keep is second to none. Never been happier. And you?" he asked sarcastically.

They both smiled as Kris said softly, "I do have some good news. I went to the station and talked to my friend. He gave me some interesting information. This same crime happened here in Nashville ten years ago, and it was never solved."

He moved forward in his chair as he said, "Whatta you mean this same crime? You mean exactly the same thing as happened with Layla?"

"Exactly. I looked at the crime scene pics last night, and they're duplicates of what you described to me the scene looked like at Layla's house."

"So this has happened at least once before? They apparently never caught whoever was involved in that one."

"No. And the strange thing is they have stopped the investigation into your situation. I've been told that's not normal. Normally, when the defendant denies his guilt in a case like this they continue to investigate right up until the time of trial. This just doesn't make sense. You did live here ten years ago, right?"

"Yes. I was going to Belmont at the time. I don't remember anything about that murder though. I'm sure I didn't know the victim or I would have heard something about it."

"I have two huge boxes full of material concerning the investigation. I had a chance to look at the pics and make copies of everything last night, but that was about it. I just really wanted to make sure the circumstances were exactly like you described them as concerned your situation, and they were. I'll dig back into the rest of the materials later, but once I found out everything was the same, I wanted to see if that might make a difference in how they approached your case. I called John's office earlier this morning. He's to meet us here and discuss this shortly."

John arrived about fifteen minutes later, and as he sat down, he said, "Good morning, you two. Now what's so important it was necessary I run over here this early in the morning?"

Kris said, "John, did you know this same crime occurred about ten years ago?"

"What same crime?"

"The same crime that they are investing Barrett for—just a different woman."

"Hell no, I didn't know. How'd you find that out? Where'd you get that kind of information?"

"Doesn't matter. I got crime scene photos, the whole works. The crime scene is exactly the way Barrett described the one with Layla. Kind of funny no one's ever mentioned that. Now they've shut down investigating Layla's murder any further, and no one seems to want to talk about the fact this has occurred before."

"Barrett, do you remember when this happened?"

"No. I don't remember a damn thing about it."

"Okay, now let's see. That would have been between our junior and senior years in college. I was here, and I remember maybe a murder, but I don't remember much about the details." He sat back as he considered these new facts. He started to smile. "Wait a minute. What year did you go to Australia with your parents? They were both still alive then. Wasn't it that summer? Wasn't it between your junior and senior years?"

Barrett leaned forward in his chair. "By god, it was. It was that summer, and I was gone almost a whole month—I was gone from near the end of June to near the end of July. When did you say this happened?"

Kris said, "July 14, 2006."

"Hell, I wasn't even in the fucking country! I couldn't have done it. Do you know if the specific details were released to the general public?"

Kris said, "My contact said they weren't. That was one of the things he told me not to do, was to release any information concerning the first offense. I've probably already gone too far there, but I'm prepared to do *anything* to help here, Barrett."

"If the details weren't released and I wasn't around when the first one occurred, how could I have gotten this crime scene to turn out like the first one?"

"You couldn't have, plain and simple." John stood. "I need to go see Charles right now. I'll demand he make time to see me later this morning. I'll be back after I've talked to him. Keep your fingers crossed."

About 2:00 p.m., John contacted Kris and told her to meet him at the conference room in the jail at three o'clock. She was waiting with Barrett when he arrived.

As he sat, Kris said, "So what happened? We've both been on pins and needles since we split up this morning. What'd he say?"

John leaned back, folded his arms, scowled, and said, "Nothing good I'm afraid. I told him about it happening once before ten years ago. He wasn't familiar with the situation. He wasn't here then, and of course, when they stopped this investigation, nobody brought up the one ten years ago."

Barrett was sitting on the edge of his chair, as he said, "Go on. What did he say about it when you told him?"

"Really nothing. He just waited for me to finish. I told him about it, and it was if he was waiting for the punch line. He looked at me quizzically and said, 'Go on.'"

"I said, 'That's what I came to tell you—that this crime has happened before in exactly the same manner. Barrett wasn't even in the country. The details weren't released to the public. He couldn't have known about the specifics. Therefore, there was an excellent chance he didn't do this. The investigation needs to be reopened.'"

"What did he say?"

"He said, 'In my opinion, we have the right guy. I don't know anything about the first one, and don't care.' He said, 'Somehow, you got the information concerning the first crime scene, and if you did, Barrett could have gotten it too.' He absolutely turned a deaf ear. He thinks you're the one that did it, and that's the end of that."

Barrett sat back and took a deep breath. Kris looked at him, then at John, as she said, "Can you go over his head? Can you talk to the district attorney and tell him what's going on? Would he listen? Do you know him?"

"I know him, but I know he's going to defer to Charles. Charles has been around a long time, and he's highly respected. I know, without a doubt, the district attorney is going to let his most successful assistant make the decision, and Charles has made it. He nearly threw me out of his office. As I continued to argue with him, he finally stood and said, 'I'll see you in court.' I walked out of the room and called you, Kris. No, he's come to the conclusion you're the one, Barrett, and he doesn't give a shit about what happened ten years ago. He made it clear he wasn't going to waste the officer's time continuing to investigate a case that, in his opinion, had already been solved. So we're still on for the eighteenth. Sorry. I really thought that might change the whole scenario."

Barrett looked away. Kris grabbed his hand. "Don't give up yet. This isn't over. This isn't over by a long shot. Someone else did that first one. We can bring that up at the time of trial right, John?"

John hesitated. "We'll see. It's really irrelevant in court. The issue is whether *he* did what he's been charged with, and a case that occurred ten years ago doesn't have much to do with this one, so we'll just have to see whether the judge allows evidence concerning the first one. It's going to be entirely up to the judge." All three sat in silence until John said, "I need to go. Barrett, if I don't see you by the end of the week, I'll be back the first of next to go through the jury list with you and explain the jury instructions. Hang in."

John walked away, leaving the two of them alone. Once he left, they talked about other ongoing investigations in their own line of work and about their clients, but it was all small talk and paled in comparison to the major issue.

Kris left thirty minutes later, but as she left, she turned and watched a defeated man being led back to his cell. Unfortunately, after today, it was hard for her to lift him up. She did the best she could, but after the conference with John, she too found it hard to feel upbeat about Barrett's case. She only hoped something came up soon, because time was growing short, and to be honest, at this point in time, Barrett's situation looked just short of disastrous, even to her.

33

He just didn't care how he looked. What difference did it make? Barrett Armstrong waited to meet with Kris, the only friend he apparently had left in the world, and then he would meet with his attorney. He was dressed in clothing the jailer had provided when he was incarcerated, which were five sizes too big. They would have fallen off if it weren't for some god-awful belt Kris had purchased for him at a nearby K-Mart. He hadn't shaved in a month, and his hair hadn't been cut since he had been arrested. Barrett knew quite well what the whole picture looked like. He just didn't care.

Trial was scheduled to begin in a few days. Today he would visit one last time with his attorney, review whatever he had to review with him, and talk to Kris about the results of her investigation. He had seen neither of them for a week. Kris had called and wanted to stop by a couple of times, but he told her he had more pressing things to do. His attorney had also called, and he had put him off until today. Barrett had denied and denied, but he knew he needed to meet with him one last time, and today was as good as any.

He had lost whatever drive in life he was incarcerated with. It had slowly dwindled to the point it no longer existed. Nothing mattered—absolutely nothing. And to be honest, he had found his new approach to life much easier to deal with. No expectations, no foreseeable future, no drive to succeed—just a "whatever happens, happens" type of attitude, which was just fine with him. He didn't give a damn anymore.

Barrett watched as John waved to him while he sauntered across the conference room floor, slowly making his way to the table.

"Good morning. You ready for your final primer?"

"I guess. Let's make it short and sweet. I got a lot going on today."

John smiled. "Now, come on, let's keep up the spirits. Who knows how this might all turn out." He looked Barrett over from top to bottom. "You know this new early-American look isn't going to work for the trial—you know that, don't you?"

"Whatta ya want me to do? How do you want me to look?"

"You need to get your hair cut, shave, and put on some decent clothes. You stink—anyone told you that—you stink. You need to shower. You need to look human again. You've lost contact with the rest of us."

Barrett leaned back in his chair, crossed his arms, and said, "I'll do what I can. Can't promise anything 'cause I just got a lot to do between now and then, but if I get some time I'll clean up for ya."

"I'm sure you'll be just fine. Now do you understand what's going to happen when this all starts?"

"Go through it again—briefly."

"We'll start picking a jury on the first day. That's really important. They'll be the ones that decide whether you spend the rest of your life in prison or not, so we need to get it right. It may take a week to make sure we have the right people. Don't hurry me. I'll just need to take the time I need to get the job done right. I have your list of people that you've marked and don't want on the panel, so I'll be careful to try and have them removed if any of their names are called."

"During the trial, can I stop you and ask you questions when I need to?"

"Yes, and I would encourage that. I want you to know what's going on."

"What happens after jury selection?"

"The attorneys will give their opening comments, and the State will start to call their witnesses. The main witnesses will be the neighbor and the man at Reflect. They'll establish motive and your physical contact with her when you were upset. Once the State has finished, we'll get a chance to call our witnesses, of which we don't have many, but then we'll need to decide whether you should testify. If the evidence appears inadequate, I'll not call you, and if it looks overwhelming, then you'll need to testify. We'll decide that at the time."

"I thought you *always* had the defendant testify. I thought that's what you told me."

"I always want the defendant to be *willing* to testify. The situation is always case by case. We just need to see where we're at when we get there. I'm anticipating at this point, you will testify, and when you do, I'll have you bring up that murder ten years ago. We can develop it from there, if the judge allows the testimony into evidence. Now, let's go through the jury instructions and make sure you understand each one of them. The judge is going to read these to the jury right before closing arguments. They'll tell the jury what the law is and what they're responsibilities as jurors are." John pulled the instructions from his briefcase, and for the next hour, they laboriously plodded through each and every instruction. Just as they finished the last one, Barrett saw Kris walking across the conference room floor.

As she approached, she said, "Morning, boys, how goes the war today?"

John looked up, smiled, and said, "Nice to see you, Kris. I was just finishing up with him. Your turn."

Kris sat down and said, "How's it all looking, John?"

"We don't have much to work with. I'm just hoping for the best. We'll present what we have and go from there. I need to get back to the office. Barrett, if anything comes up before the trial, call me. Otherwise, I'll see you at the courthouse."

In silence, they both watched John walk until he disappeared through the doorway and out of sight. Kris turned to Barrett and reached out, taking his hand.

"You look awful." When he failed to respond, again she said, "Barrett, do you know that—you look horrible."

"C'mon, Kris, tell me something I don't already know." He pulled his hand away.

Kris looked down ever so briefly and said nothing. After a moment, she looked him in the eyes and quietly said, "You need to remember one thing, Barrett. I've been here with you from day one. When no one else cared about what was happening to you, other than the attorney you are *paying* to be with you, I've been here through it all. Just keep that in mind." As she finished her statement, she started to cry and stood to leave.

He reached up and grabbed her hand as he said, "You're right. I'm sorry." He stood and embraced her. "I'm sorry, you're right. You've stayed with me and hung in there with me from the very beginning. Don't leave. Stay awhile."

She sat back down, wiped away a tear, smiled, and said, "You stink. You need a shower. Now sit down, and let's go through what's going to happen in the next week or so." Together, they went through the process that would take place during the trial.

As they finished discussing the legal issues, Barrett said, "How're you coming with the information you got from the police department?"

"There's so much there. I'm trying to look through it, but it's difficult because I'm not sure what I'm even looking for. I'm half through. I'll get it reviewed and finished up by the time the trial starts. It's a chore, and I don't wanna bring any of it here for you to look over, because I can't take the chance one of the officers will take it from you, look at it, and wonder where the information came from. I have to do it and do it myself. I'll review it all before the trial starts. I promise."

"I'm not expecting much, just so you know."

She looked him over. "What's this new Daniel Boone persona? You gonna clean up and put on some clean clothes. Maybe shave? You know— all those things so many people your age do now?"

He looked down, and when he looked at her, with tears in his eyes, he quickly turned away. She grabbed his hand and whispered, "Barrett, it's gonna be all right. It's gonna be all right. Just hang in there. Keep fighting until you're free. We'll get there."

She stayed but a few more minutes and then told him she might see him here before the trial started, but most of her time away from work would be spent on that box of materials she got from the department.

He told her that was fine, and he would see her when everything started, if not sooner. He watched her walk away. She had turned into a good friend—no, maybe more than a friend. He trusted her, he cared for her, he was close to her. But as the officer took him by the arm and escorted him back to his cell, he just figured it didn't much matter. After she had visited with him once a month in prison for a few months, the visits would stop, she would find someone new, and his contact with the rest of world would end. How different this all might have been if he had just become involved with *her* before he met Layla. The end of his relationship with Layla was not the first time he had suffered as a result of ending a relationship with a woman, but it was sure as hell the most dramatic.

34

Kris Thompson had gone to bed at ten thirty, which was the precise moment her eyes had reached the point they were so tired from reviewing paperwork associated with the first murder, she couldn't keep them open. She was halfway through copies she had made from the second box and had yet to find anything that would help Barrett's case. Of course, it was difficult looking for something when you really had no idea what you were looking for. She was, however, determined to carry on, having nowhere else to look for information that might help him.

Once she did go to bed, she tried to fall asleep for over an hour with no success. Kris finally made a phone call to her friend Art, who, as she knew would be the case, was still awake and watching reruns of the *Johnny Carson Show*. He agreed to meet her for a late-night cup of coffee at a small diner near downtown Nashville that remained open all night.

He walked in as she waited and, while still walking to the table, said, "What the hell's wrong with you? You're normally in bed by ten o'clock or ten thirty and sleeping five minutes later."

As he sat down, she said, "I tried to sleep, but couldn't. I'm still going through material which I'm hoping will somehow help Barrett's case." She wasn't about to tell him what materials she was reviewing or where they came from, since she had promised her friend Tom Williams that's exactly what she would do. "I'm through about half of what I need to review, but I just couldn't get to sleep. I sat through two full days of that bullshit trial already, and I'm bracing for another day of it today."

"How far along are they?"

"They just finished picking a jury. They're just ready to do opening statements, but it's to be a short day. The judge and the attorneys are working on something called instructions to the jury, which they think will take most of the afternoon. After that, they'll start taking testimony."

"How do things look?"

"Not much has changed. I'm really concerned. Not only am I concerned about him, but I'm concerned about the lack of attention I'm giving my own business. Being gone is definitely affecting it. So not only am I losing business, I'm losing..." She started to tear up as she pulled a tissue from her pocket.

"Losing him? Is that what you were about to say? You in love with him?"

"No, no, he's just... a..."

Art leaned back in his chair. "Don't give me that bullshit. Just say it—you're in love with a guy who's about to be convicted of murder and sent up the river for the rest of his natural life."

She wiped away the last of the tears, glared at him and said, "Okay, okay I do care for him. More than I wish to admit. But there's more to it than that. This guy is guilty of nothing, but no one will listen. I'm not sure, but I believe his own attorney thinks he's guilty."

"So what're you gonna do in the morning?"

"I'll go back to the courthouse for opening statements and then to work for what's left of the day. I'll try to put out all the fires I can, and then go back home to review more information concerning his case. Until it's over, one way or the other, my priority will be Barrett and only Barrett."

"How's this guy feel 'bout you? Any indication?"

"No, and to be honest, it doesn't matter. If he gets off, we'll just figure this all out, but it's the injustice that concerns me... with a little bit of love mixed in. It's complicated. I can't even figure out my own feelings, but I know one thing. I'm going to spend whatever time is necessary to help get him off until there are no other available options."

"Why the hell don't you just admit you're completely in love with him and make that part of it just that much easier instead of continuing to fight it? Just accept what's damn obvious to me."

She turned away and whispered, "You're probably right. Leave it up to me to fall for a guy whose only lover for the next sixty years will probably be some 240-pound bruiser named Bubba."

Kris sat through opening statements the next morning. Charles took two hours outlining his case witness by witness. John took twenty minutes. At the conclusion of the statements, once everyone had left, except Barrett, John, and the officer getting ready to take him back to his cell, Kris walked up behind Barrett and said, "I gotta go. I'll be back later this afternoon. I'll just see you at the jail."

Barrett stood, walked back to the railing separating the visitors from the participants, and said, "Do you have to go now? Can you meet me at the jail in a few minutes? I won't be here much longer."

As she continued to lean against the railing, he placed one of his hands over hers. She looked down as she realized what he had done. As Kris looked up, she started to smile and said, "Don't you worry. I won't be gone long. I need to check in at the office and then keep reviewing the files I got from the sheriff's office. I'll see you soon. Rest assured, Barrett, I'll be right here with you, until we sort this mess all out—right here with you."

He looked away and said, softly, "Thank you."

Kris spent a couple of hours at her office and then drove home to sort out the remaining paperwork in the boxes, hopefully finding something, anything, to shed some light on who might have been involved in the first killing.

She had piles scattered all over her living room—statements in one pile, pictures in another, officers' notes in yet a third pile. They had used all the resources available while trying to determine who had killed her, but in the end, all they had were two big boxes of paper, and no perpetrator. She was just ready to finish for the afternoon. She wanted to read a couple of more statements, then run over and see Barrett before she grabbed a bite to eat for supper and drove back to the office where she would spend her evening sorting through messages.

She picked up one last statement and read it. Nothing remarkable was noted, until she looked at the very top, at the area indicating whose statement had been taken. Her eyes widened as she did. She read it again. She stood and walked over to her copier, made a copy, then returned to the box. She sorted through the remaining paperwork until she found the second doc she needed and quickly made a copy of it.

Thirty minutes later, she was sitting at a small table in the conference room, and they were just bringing Barrett across the room to join her. As he sat, he said, "Well, what'd you think of John's opening? Pretty short, wasn't it? I didn't think there was much to it, but he told me they don't amount to anything anyway. Hell, I don't know much about it, but—"

"Stop. I got something I need to show you. This is probably no big deal, but I thought you should be aware. I have a couple of statements I need to have you read."

"Statements from what—from whom?"

She sat forward in her chair and said, "Statements from the first murder. I found them this afternoon."

"Okay. Are they relevant? I mean, do they impact what I've been charged with?"

"Not yet, but I guess I just find them interesting. Here's the first one. It's the one I'm concerned about. We'll talk about the second one later."

She pushed the statement across the table. Barrett picked it up and started reading. The further he read, the more he concentrated. As he reached the end of the statement, he leaned forward in his chair and said, "What the fuck does this mean? I don't understand this? *He was dating her?*"

He read on, then said, "Because he was dating her at the time, I can understand they may have needed to take his statement. But that's all negated because he says he had someone for an alibi. That should have ended his involvement as a suspect."

"Here's the second statement from Oren Lee, the guy that was his alibi." She shoved it across the table. Barrett hurriedly picked it up and read it. He sat back and said, "Well, that should have ended any question about his involvement."

"You're probably right, but as I continued to search through the file, I noticed the cops decided to reinterview this Lee. However when they went to talk to him, some thirty days later, he had disappeared. There's another note in the file indicating they continued to try to contact this Lee to reconfirm his statement, but he was never located. The cops just let it drop, figuring they had his statement and it was enough of an alibi to put an end to that issue."

"Both statements say he had been dating the victim."

"Correct. I don't have any doubt he wasn't involved in the murder, but why didn't he tell us about this?"

"I don't know."

"Should we confront him about it?"

"No. I don't want this to even be *mentioned* at this point, at least not yet. Can you follow up on this? I mean, the fact he never mentioned it to us is a little strange, to say the least."

"Absolutely. I'll keep looking."

"Keep me informed."

Barrett again looked down at the statement dated over ten years ago. The name at the top continued to hold his attention. The individual interviewed, the individual dating the victim at that time was none other than John Weatherly, his attorney.

35

Kris sat quietly while the prosecutor began to question Don Winters. He was one of many that had witnessed the argument at Reflect. Yesterday, the State had called the medical examiner who testified as to cause of death. One of the interesting, but sickening elements of his testimony was that he had been able to determine Layla had been sexually assaulted post-mortem. She turned to look at jurors after that unsavory element of testimony. Many of them looked away, and it was obvious that fact affected a number of them.

Charles then called a string of law enforcement officers who testified as to what they observed at the murder scene and placed into evidence pictures of the victim, which were disturbing to say the least. He then called a couple of Barrett's former clients who testified how quickly Barrett could lose his temper. They reiterated situations that they personally observed, or which directly involved them. John had objected to their testimony, but Judge Hanson, who seemed inclined to allow most everything into evidence, overruled the objection and allowed it all. The State also called witnesses that had been at Reflect that night and who had observed what happened from across the room, but who weren't able to hear what was being said. They testified they could tell Layla and Barrett were involved in a very public dispute but couldn't hear exactly what they were saying. Mr. Winters and his wife happened to be only a table away and heard it all.

After the witness had been sworn, and the basics as to his qualifications had been entered into the record, Charles said, "Now,

Mr. Winters, where were you situated the night you observed the argument?"

Don Winters had testified he was employed with a major Nashville corporation and crunched numbers for them day and night. Kris could tell by the way he testified he was clearly detail oriented, and she expected his testimony to confirm that his attention to detail at work most likely carried over into his personal life as well.

"I would say we were approximately six or six and one half feet from both of them. There were no tables between us. I was facing them and was able to hear most everything they said because they were speaking loudly."

"Can you tell us what you heard them say?"

"Sure. She said they were through. She said that more than once. From his body language, he seemed to be upset with what she was saying. She just finally stood and again said, 'We are through' and walked off."

"What did you observe about his demeanor?"

"He appeared to me to be upset, not angry, just upset. It was obvious what she was saying was upsetting to him."

"Nothing further."

"Do you wish to cross, Mr. Weatherly?"

"I do, Your Honor." John stood as he continued. "Did you ever observe any form of violence—any actions by him that were physical and were directed toward her?"

"No."

"Did he ever raise his voice to her?"

"No. Now *she* did raise her voice as the conversation continued. It was as if he just wasn't getting it—like she was having to tell him time after time that their relationship was over."

"But even after the last time she said 'We are through,' did he try to touch her or make any kind of aggressive physical movement in her direction?"

"No."

"I have nothing further, Your Honor."

Kris watched as he left the witness stand, concluding that both attorneys had made their point, but knowing that this witness was only the start of the State's case—Mr. Winter's statement was just a short introduction to the testimony that was to follow.

"The State calls John Tipper to the stand to be sworn and testify." John Tipper and his wife were the neighbors that had observed the altercation on Layla's front steps. If all their testimony were allowed into the record, he would be an important witness for the State and one that could extensively damage Barrett's position.

After his personal information had been introduced into the record, Charles started his examination concerning the facts with, "Where do you live as concerns the house belonging to Layla Adams?"

"Next door."

"Do you recall the day she was murdered?"

"Very well."

"What occurred that day that caught your attention and which involved the defendant?"

"Well, we had just arrived home, the little woman and I, and I seen him and her on the front porch of her house."

"And by him, I assume you're talking about the defendant in this case, Barrett Armstrong?"

"Yes."

"Tell us what you saw."

"Well, I was getting out of my car, and they were discussing their relationship. She was ending it. He obviously didn't want to end it, but she was a makin' it clear it was over."

"Was there any physical contact?"

"Yes."

"Tell us what happened."

"Well, as the voices got louder, he just finally reached over and shook the hell out of her."

Barrett leaned over to John and whispered, "That's not true. That's not what happened. I grabbed her shoulder, but I never shook her."

"Did he use both hands?"

"He sure did. Just shook the hell out of her, with both hands, real mean like."

"Did it appear to you he was mad, upset?"

"Oh, there was no doubt in my mind he was mad as hell."

"Objection."

"Overruled. The witness has a right to his opinion and to testify as to what he saw. Proceed."

"Were you surprised when she ended up dead?"

"Objection."

"Overruled."

"But, Your Honor, what difference does it make if he was surprised. It's irrelevant."

"You'll get your chance, Mr. Weatherly. Overruled. Proceed."

The judge continually made it clear he was going to remain very liberal with what the State introduced into evidence. Kris only hoped he would be as liberal with Barrett and the case he presented.

"No, I wasn't surprised. I think if he would have had a chance, and could have done it without anyone around, he would have killed her right then. He was plume mad."

"Nothing further, Your Honor."

"Cross?"

"Not at this time. I do reserve the right to call him later, and I want him available then." Charles agreed to make him available and the witness was excused.

As the witness left the room, Barrett whispered, "Why didn't you cross-examine him? His testimony wasn't accurate. He lied. I don't understand."

John turned and said, "Do you really think I was going to be able to get him to change his story? Besides that, I don't want that testimony emphasized. I have the right to call him back if we wish. Now let me try the case, Barrett. We'll talk about it later."

The last witness for the day was Officer Ted Zorley. Again, once all foundational evidence had been entered into the record, Charles asked, "Were you the officer that arrested Mr. Armstrong?"

"Yes."

"Where was he arrested?"

"At his office here in Nashville."

"Did you read him his rights as you were arresting him?"

"Yes."

"And after you read him his rights, did he say anything to you?"

"Yes."

"And was this in response to a question or anything you might have said to him?"

"No."

"Can you tell us what he said?"

"He said, 'If she treated me like she treated others, I can understand why someone might hurt her.' Those were his exact words."

"Did he say anything else?"

"No."

"Nothing further, Your Honor."

"Cross?"

John stood. "Now, Officer, he didn't say he hurt her, did he?"

"No, but the—"

"Just stop right there. He didn't say he hurt her, did he?"

"No, he didn't."

John sat, looked at his notes, and said, "Nothing further, Your Honor."

"Redirect, Mr. Whitmore?"

"No, Your Honor, the State has but a couple of additional witnesses, but because of a scheduling issue, they won't be able to testify until tomorrow morning. We felt what we have presented today might have taken longer than it did. If it's acceptable to the court and council, we would like to recess until tomorrow morning."

"Any objection, Mr. Weatherly?"

"None."

"We will be adjourned until tomorrow morning."

Kris softy said to Barrett as the jurors filed out, "I'll see you at the jailhouse," to which Barrett nodded affirmatively.

As Kris walked toward the door, she noticed Chad McNamara just standing, preparing to leave the courtroom. She stopped, walked toward him, and said, "Mr. McNamara, what are you doing here? Do you have an interest in this case?"

He smiled and said, "No, not really. Just curious, that's all. Just curious."

"What are you curious about—the facts, the people, the judge?"

"No, no none of that. I can't discuss my interest really, but it was good to see you."

As they walked through the courtroom door, she said, "Good seeing you." He walked away quickly, in the opposite direction she did. She wondered why he was taking time out of his busy schedule to attend the trial of a man he knew virtually nothing about. But she didn't have time to dwell on it—too much to do.

After she had run a couple of errands, she drove to the jail. Barrett and John were still talking when she arrived, although John was standing to leave. Once he was out the door, Kris said, "How'd you think everything went today?"

"About as expected I guess. I knew what most of them were going to say before they testified. There weren't any surprises, although that one neighbor did lie about what happened."

"I noticed John never even cross-examined him. Wonder why?"

"I don't know. I asked him that same question twice. Both times he said he could recall him as a witness, but he just didn't want to place undue emphasis on that part of the evidence. I thought it was strange, but he seems to know what he's doing."

"I sure as hell hope so. I'm going to take a little trip tomorrow and visit with the parents of Oren Lee. I called them and told them I was coming. They said they would both be there when I arrived."

"Why you going to see them?"

"I just wanna know what they have to say about their son's position concerning that first murder, and what happened when Oren disappeared. Nothing earth-shattering, but I do wanna visit with them. I'll stop back here when I get done. It doesn't sound as though I'm going to miss much tomorrow in court."

"Just more of the same—just another day of everyone looking at me and saying I murdered the woman I loved. Nope, you aren't going to miss much, that's for sure."

36

The drive to Goodlettsville, just north of Nashville, took little time, and as a result, Kris didn't have much of an opportunity to process all that had happened in court. Many times, she would use her drive time to assess, evaluate, and review work or personal issues, but today, the trip was just too short for that to happen.

The Lees lived well—their home was upper-middle class, and the yard and surrounding grounds were extensive. There were a couple of BMWs sitting in the drive. Money was clearly not an issue for this family.

Mrs. Lee met her at the door, and Mr. Lee was waiting in the dining room as she escorted Kris into the home. After they handed her a cup of coffee, Mrs. Lee said, "You didn't provide much information on the phone, Kris. You mentioned something about our son Oren, but little else. What's the purpose of your visit?"

Kris was having trouble functioning beyond just taking in the beauty of the home. These people didn't just have money—they were *rich*. As she reengaged in conversation, she said, "I'm looking into the murder of Cassie Wilson, which occurred about ten years ago. Do you remember that happening?"

Mr. Lee quickly said, "Yes, very well. Our son spoke of it. He disappeared not long after that. Yes, we remember when it happened. Why are you looking into it?"

"Because the circumstances of that murder were very similar to another murder that took place a few months ago here in Nashville. You probably didn't recognize the similarities because the facts weren't set forth in the newspaper. You say your son discussed the Wilson murder with you?"

"He didn't discuss it, but he did mention it. Unfortunately, we weren't on the best of terms with him at the time. In fact, other than paying his bills at Vanderbilt, we had shut him off. He was living here, but we didn't like the friends he carried on with, and there were a number of problems we had with him, some of which centered around just having too much money. So we told him to get a job, which he did. Didn't pay much, but it at least structured him a little, which was what we wanted."

"What did he say about the crime?"

Mrs. Lee spoke up and said, "Well, actually, one of his friends, John Weatherly, was dating the woman. So we learned what was going on from Oren who got his information from John. He didn't say much to us, but what we did know, we learned from Oren through John."

"What was his relationship with John like?"

They looked at each other.

Mr. Lee said, "John was a strange kid. He and Oren were good friends right up until Oren disappeared. John was in our house many times, but he was just different. I know now he's a lawyer and doing well, but back then, there was a time or two we asked Oren if he would quit running with him. He never did, but if he hadn't disappeared, we were going to prohibit him from being with John."

"When you say he was strange, whatta you mean?"

"He just seemed sneaky. He was quiet when around us. Of course, he always had plenty of money. I never turned my back on him. I just didn't trust him as far as I could throw him."

"If it's not too difficult to discuss, what happened to your son?"

He said, "We don't know. One day he was here, the next he was gone. He never contacted us again. They never found a body. He just disappeared. We still hope he will return or contact us some day. We weren't on the best of terms." He wiped away a tear as it made its way down his cheek. "That was really the sad part of it—we weren't on the best of terms when he disappeared. I have wished so

many times... so many times... that we had been on better terms...
that..."

"I understand. I'm so sorry. Have you talked with John about
his disappearance? Did he know anything?"

"The police talked to him, but they said he had no idea either.
He said Oren was there, and then he just disappeared. Of course,
he blamed us. We found out he blamed us for running him off. We
never personally spoke to John after Oren disappeared."

The discussion lasted only a few more minutes. She thanked
them for their time and then left for a short meeting with Barrett
before heading back to her office.

As they sat together, Kris said, "I had a nice visit with Mr. and
Mrs. Lee earlier today. They're the parents of Oren Lee, the witness
that provided an alibi for John when that girl was murdered ten years
ago. Nice people."

Barrett, clearly not fully engaged in the content of the conversation, said, "Oh. What'd they have to say?"

"They just said Oren and John were good friends when John's
girlfriend was murdered. Oren provided an alibi and then just disappeared. Don't you think that's a little strange?"

"What part? What part of that is strange? Sure, it's too bad the
murder happened. It's too bad John was dating her. It's too bad this
Oren guy disappeared, but what part's strange?"

"Well, first of all, it's strange John never told us any of this, don't
you think?"

"Not really. Why would he? It doesn't involve the facts of my
case. It's irrelevant."

"Yeah, but then his eyewitness disappears—you don't think
that's a little strange?"

"Hell, I don't know. No, I don't think it's strange—sad, but not
strange, I guess."

"They told me they had cut Oren off—that they weren't giving
him money. If the kid was broke, and John said he would pay him to
be his alibi, and then John got rid of him... does that make sense to
you? Is it logical?"

Barrett thought for a minute, finally turning to Kris and say-ing, "Look. John is the best friend I ever had. I don't remember him talking about this Oren guy, ever. He's my attorney, and one of the best in Nashville. If you really think he was somehow involved in that first murder, you're going to have to come up with one hell of a lot more than what you already have to convince me. Now, you going to be in court with me tomorrow, or do you have other more important things to do?"

"I'll be there, like I have every day—I'll be there."

As Kris left the jail later that afternoon, she continued to review her conversation with the Lees. Barrett might not think there's much to all this, but she did. And she wasn't about to let it lie without doing at least a small amount of additional investigating. It was all they had to work with, and the fact that Barrett didn't think it amounted to anything wasn't nearly enough for her to stop digging.

37

The State, after presenting testimony from Mr. Winters, along with a few other witnesses from the restaurant, rested. John then presented his obligatory motion for acquittal, based primarily on the lack of any eyewitness testimony, and what he felt was an overabundance of irrelevant, circumstantial evidence. The judge promptly overruled the motion and then informed the attorneys he was unavailable Monday, so they would resume testimony on Tuesday. That left Monday for Barrett, Kris, and John to prepare one last day and to contact witnesses that had already been subpoenaed, with specific information concerning when they would need to appear and testify.

John arrived around ten o'clock, and the discussion concerning the next court day's activities began in earnest once he took a chair. "You know it's just too bad the security system in your town house building wasn't up and running that night. That could have confirmed you stayed home. That might have been all we needed."

"I know, John, you're not telling me anything new. Of course, we discussed that issue a month ago. Nothing we can do about it now."

"You know, it's really too bad you weren't on your computer at some point during the evening. That might have helped too. We might have been able to establish you were home on it rather than out killing your girlfriend."

"Again, John, we've been down this road before. I wasn't on it. You know that because you've asked me that ten times, and every time, I tell you I wasn't on it. I went home and did absolutely nothing, but mope over the end of our relationship. You know, you *knew* all that when you took the case. You *knew* it would be tough, but here we are going over the same things time after time. Let's figure out what the hell we *are* going to do, as opposed to what we *aren't* going to do. Now who's testifying tomorrow? Let's get them called and figure this out."

"You're right, Barrett. Okay, I'll contact those three women you dated. Let's put them on first. I talked to all three of them, and they all told me you were nothing but a gentleman while you were dating. Even when your relationship ended with them, they said you handled it well, whether they ended it or you did. I think we should start out with something positive."

"That's a good idea."

"I'll contact all three and tell them when to be here. Then I think we should call those three former clients that are subpoenaed. I also talked to them and they're willing to testify you never ever lost your temper or got upset while they employed you. They all said you were very even-tempered. I'm not sure how far Judge Hanson will go in allowing all that into evidence, but the State opened up the issue of character, and I'm thinking the judge will be consistent and very liberal all the way through the trial."

"What then?"

"I think we should put Kris on the stand and have her testify concerning her business involvement with you."

He turned and looked at Kris. "That's your only interaction with Barrett, isn't it, Kris, because that's why I'm calling you—for business purposes."

"Yes."

"You two aren't involved romantically, are you?"

She hesitated as she turned a slight shade of red before she finally said, "No, of course not."

"That's correct, isn't it, Barrett? You two aren't involved, are you? I want the jury to hear from her as a professional, not as your lover."

Barrett looked at Kris then faced John and said, "We aren't involved."

Barrett wasn't entirely sure—until now. Kris had made it clear through her glances, through her overall demeanor, that there was more to her persistence, her assistance in the case, than just business. He felt their relationship had been changing for quite some time, but until now, he just wasn't sure. Now he knew. It was obvious their relationship had changed. He definitely had feelings for her—feelings that went beyond a simple business relationship. But he knew this wasn't the time nor the place to become involved in light of the fact he may very well be going to prison for a long, long time.

Kris and Barrett continued to look at each other, without saying a word, as John said, "Okay, then, I think we're set, at least for the next couple of days. Once they're done testifying, I may call you, Barrett. We'll just see how everything goes."

Barrett quickly turned his full attention to John. "I wanna testify. If I'm going down, I'm going down swinging. I don't want there to be any question about whether I do or don't testify. I'm *going* to testify. That's not even subject to discussion."

"Okay, okay, I understand. I'll put you on last. We'll go through your testimony right before I put you on."

With the planning at an end, the three generally discussed what was going on outside prison, giving Barrett an idea of what he was and wasn't missing. As the conversation wound down, John stood to leave.

"By the way, John, how are you and Maggie getting along?"

"Not well. I think the marriage is over. She won't even talk to me anymore. I hate it, but I can't do it all myself. I better go. I'll see you tomorrow morning in court."

As he picked up his briefcase, Kris said, "John, do you remember that murder ten years ago—the one involving Cassie Wilson?"

Without hesitation, he said, "No, not really."

"Did you know her? That would have been about the time you were going to Vanderbilt. Had you happened to run across her?"

"Yes, I knew her. Been a long time ago. I went out with her once or twice. She was a nice girl. It was awful what happened to her. I need to get back to the office. I'll see you tomorrow."

Once he walked out the door, Kris leaned forward in her chair and said, "I'm telling you he knows something. No doubt in my mind."

Barrett smiled. "Really? Based on that conversation, you've determined he knows something?"

"Why didn't he say that he had given a statement? He had the opportunity. He could have mentioned that. Why didn't he?"

"Why didn't you ask him? You could have asked him about his friend Owen too, but you didn't."

"I just expected him to tell us… to tell us what his involvement was and explain why he hasn't mentioned it before. He knows more than he's letting on, Barrett."

"Well, he might, but it looks like you're going to have to pull it out of him."

"You're really not on board here, are you?"

"No, I'm sorry, but I'm not. It's just too hard for me to imagine my best friend, as well as I know him, being a sadistic murderer. I'm not going to suggest it to him *in any manner.* You come up with something else and we can discuss it then."

Kris stood and, with hands on hips, said, "Well, I'm telling you one more thing I *am* going to do. I'm going to see his estranged wife—what's her name, Mary, Martha?"

Barrett smiled. "Maggie. Her name is Maggie."

"She'll tell me about him you can bank on that. I'll let you know what she says."

Barrett, continuing to smile, stood, and put his arms around her. "You do that, Kris. You just do that."

He could feel the tension leave her body, as her arms first dropped to her side and slowly found their way around him. Simultaneously, she moved closer against his body—as close as she could move.

He leaned back, looked down at her, and said, "I really don't know what I would have done without you, Kris."

She let go of him and moved back, as she said defiantly, "This isn't over, Barrett. I know what I'm doing. I know he knows something. I'll be back after I talk to Maggie."

She turned and walked away as Barrett yelled, "I'll be here!" He watched her walk out the door as he whispered, "I'll be here."

38

U pon arriving at her office, Kris was greeted with a mountain of messages from clients that had walked in or called in to determine the status of their investigation. There were many of those individuals that had time-sensitive issues, and she knew she needed to pay attention, but their issues didn't involve a life-and-death situation as Barrett's did. At least that was how she was justifying placing a higher priority on Barrett's case.

She returned a number of calls and set up appointments for those who had personally walked in the office. She just hoped, because of circumstances involving Barrett's case, she wouldn't need to change any of those new appointments after she was the one that set it up. But his case had and would continue to have priority until it was finished, one way or the other.

Once she had completed her calls and discussed a number of office issues with her secretary, she looked online for a phone number for Maggie Weatherly. She had access to a number of sites that provided, for a fee, the numbers she needed in her business activities, and her cell number was not difficult to locate. The call went to voice mail, so she left a detailed message, indicating she needed to visit with her—that it concerned Barrett's pending case and her estranged husband. Within a few minutes, she received a callback.

"Hi, Maggie. You obviously got my message."

"Yes, I did. What is it you're trying to determine—who are you?"

"I'm a private investigator, and I'm looking into Barrett's case. I'm sure you've heard about it—Layla Adams was murdered and—"

"Yes, I know all about it, but how does it involve John? I don't understand."

"Do you have some time tomorrow morning? I'm going to have a problem getting out of the office today, but could I visit with you tomorrow morning, as early as possible?"

"Well, I guess. What about nine o'clock?"

"Give me your new address."

Maggie provided her address, which was on Douglas Avenue in East Nashville, and Kris told her she would see her tomorrow morning. She remained in her office until seven o'clock. Once she locked the door, she drove to Final Stop, a small bar located in Nashville, where Art was waiting for her. He had her drink already on the table when she arrived.

"You look beat. Long day?"

Kris slowly slid into the booth Art had been able to secure when he arrived and let out a sigh, as she grabbed the glass. "Yes, today was a long day. One I'd just as soon forget. The defense starts presenting testimony before long, and at some point, I'm going to have to testify. The case has developed a life of its own—it just seems to go on and on."

"What are your thoughts—winning, losing?"

"Losing. I think we're on the wrong side of this one. I'm doing all I can to help, but I feel like I'm just spinning my wheels."

"What have you determined concerning the first murder—anything at all?"

"I honestly believe his attorney knows something about it. I have this feeling that the guy was somehow involved, but *feeling* it and *proving* it are two different things. Of course, Barrett thinks I'm nuts, which doesn't help."

"So what do you know about his attorney and this woman ten years ago?"

"I know he knew her. I know he was questioned about her disappearance. I know he apparently was a strange child and young adult. I know the kid providing his alibi for the night in question disappeared soon after giving a statement to law enforcement and has never been heard from again. Those are the things I *know*. Obviously, there are many blanks to fill in, and of course, I have no idea about any facts of any nature that tie John into Layla. I just got a theory and a few facts to back me up—it's far short of what I need to actually prove anything, but I honestly believe the guy's involved."

"You have any time at all for a life of your own? You look beat." He smiled. "Is the case consuming you, or is that just your new, permanent look?"

"Funny. Yes, it's consuming me, but there's no doubt in my mind something's really off here. I'm going to continue to remain *consumed* until I figure it out or until there's nowhere else to turn."

"Can you somehow draw a connection between John and this Layla? You would need to do that, you know. Do you know, if this John had been with Layla prior to her death? I mean, was he seen with her, ever?"

Kris thought for a moment. "Hmm. I hadn't even thought of that. I wonder if he *has* been with her. If he was, I wonder if he screwed up and was with her in public prior to her murder."

Their conversation lasted only a few more minutes, until Kris informed him she needed to go home and get some sleep. She did go home, but sleep was almost impossible. Art's comment about John having been seen with Layla just kept the wheels turning all night.

The next morning, after checking in at the office, she drove to the address Maggie had provided her and knocked on the door of her home at precisely 9:00 a.m. Maggie Weatherly immediately answered and, after introductions, lead her to a small, but well-furnished living room.

Once they were seated, Kris said, "I'm really sorry to bother you, but I have a few questions for you concerning John. I would appreciate this conversation not leave this room."

"Not a problem with that. What do you wanna know?"

"Can you tell me what the issues were, involving you and John? Why the breakup?"

"Why do you wanna know? What's going on?"

"Are you familiar with Barrett's case"

"Not really. I haven't followed it at all. I just know he's been charged with something. To be honest, lately, I've lost track of most everything in life except my own issues."

"I can understand that. Let me bring you up to date. He's been charged with the murder of Layla Adams. I now find out that ten years ago, there was a murder in which the factual situation was identical to the one involving Layla. While reviewing statements, I did notice during that same time period, John was dating the woman at the time of her murder. He, of course, was never charged, but I'm just looking into that murder a little further."

Maggie sat forward in her chair. "Do you think he was involved? You don't honestly believe he was involved in either murder, do you?"

"I don't know. I don't have enough facts yet to conclude anything. Now, can you tell me about your breakup?"

She hesitated, processing what she had just been told. After an uncomfortable silence, she said softly, "It was all those nights away from home—and the other women. Many of them. I knew about them, but I just denied, denied, and denied, until I couldn't deny anymore."

"How did you find out?"

"The longer we were married, the more nights he would be gone. Sometimes he would get home at ten o'clock, sometimes midnight, and sometimes not at all. He always told me he was working. He told me not to call the office phone, to call him on his cell, but I got tired of him never answering so I just quit trying to run him down. I finally started keeping a calendar so if he asked for custody, I would have something concrete to show the court concerning the number of nights he wasn't home."

Her heart skipped a beat. "Really? So do you have that calendar handy?"

"Sure."

"Would you check a date for me? Would you check the night of February 19?"

Maggie stood and left the room. When she returned, she had the calendar in hand and said, "He was gone all night that night. I show I tried to reach him twice and he never answered either time."

Kris took a deep breath. "Let me ask you another question. Was there any place in particular he took his 'women' for a drink—a bar or restaurant he normally went to or do you know?"

"I know he's taken them to a little bar, I think it's called Andy's in a hotel in west Nashville just off Main Street, but that's the only one I know of. He tried to get away from the area where his office was located. I know that's where he went because I followed him—more than once. I never confronted him there, but I know that's where he took his 'women' friends."

"I know which bar you mean. Okay, just one more thing. Do you have a picture of him I could borrow?"

"Sure, let me get one."

When she returned, she had a small picture she handed to Kris as she said, "You don't really think he was involved with this Layla, do you? I mean you honestly don't believe he murdered her, do you?"

"I don't know. I do know that Barrett didn't do it. I know him well enough by now to know he couldn't have harmed her, which means someone else did." She stood and held out her hand. "Thank you so much for your time. By the way, hang on to that calendar."

Maggie smiled as she shook her hand and said, "Don't worry about that. It's here in safekeeping, and that's where it'll stay."

As Kris left her house, she called and was allowed to speak to Barrett. She asked him if he had any pictures of Layla and himself. After he quizzed her about what she was doing, he finally gave her the entry code to his garage and the location of some small pictures they had taken while in a photo booth at the Wilson County fair, which he had retained.

Once she arrived at his home, she punched in the access code. As she walked into his house, she couldn't help but notice it was a complete mess, as she had expected. She walked straight to his bedroom, and there, as he had told her, were the pictures of the two of them.

She stood looking at the picture. She couldn't help but notice how happy they both were—how involved they both were with each other. Now, just a few short months later, she was dead, and he was involved in a fight for his very survival.

39

ourt had recessed for their noon break. Charles Whitmore
had taken advantage of the break to walk back to his office
rather than spending his time preparing for the defense witnesses, which were scheduled to testify during the afternoon session.
He started to review messages but had only read through half of them
before he read the one that caused him to stop and lean back in his
chair.

Michael had left the halfway house where he had been living,
and no one had heard from him for days. No one from the facility
had called to tell him until today. His instincts were to call them to
determine exactly why he hadn't been contacted immediately. But
as he thought it through, he concluded for him to call them now to
ascertain who had failed to do their job would benefit no one—he
was gone, and they had no idea where he was.

As far as Michael was concerned, Charles had gone as far as he
was going to go. He only hoped his son was safe and would contact
him in the near future. He would help no more unless his son asked
for it. He knew he had gone beyond the line by suppressing information in Layla's case, but that too was water under the bridge. He
would continue to push for a conviction concerning Armstrong until
it was finished, but would do nothing more.

Charles had Clarice work through the noon hour to help him
with messages he didn't understand and update him concerning
other matters that were pending and needed at least a small degree
of attention.

"Jeff is here. Do you want him to come on in or wait a few moments?"

"No, send him in. I don't have much time left."

Clarice opened the door, and Jeff walked in as he said, "Afternoon, Charles. How goes the battle?"

"Good, good, Jeff, have a chair."

Once he was seated, he said, "How's the trial coming? Any surprises?"

"Really, it's going well. The State has rested. All the witnesses we called presented themselves well, and Weatherly had no luck during cross-examination at all. To be honest, he used little effort on any of them. I was surprised. He's known for his aggressive cross, but that hasn't shown up at all, at least for now. They started putting their witnesses on this morning, but they've presented little that concerns me. All in all, everything is going well. You uncovered anything that might help us concerning the trial?"

"No, nothing else has turned up. Of course, we've quit investigating, pursuant to your request, and as a result, we have nothing more than what I've already given you. I do, however, wanna discuss that prior incident that happened ten years ago. I wasn't here then, but I had a couple of guys in the department tell me about it. You know, it does sound remarkably similar to the Adams case. Does the defense know about the murder that so closely resembles this one? Did you disclose it?"

"No, and we aren't going to disclose it now. I learned of it after we provided all the information they asked for during discovery, and while I'm bound to disclose any new evidence I learn about after I provide all our information, I'm not going to say a word about it. If someone brings it up, I'll just tell them I didn't think it was relevant and didn't learn about it until after the verdict. I don't want anyone from your department mentioning it either."

"But aren't we bound to provide that type of information? Aren't they entitled to know about it?"

"Let me ask you a question. Do you think Barrett Armstrong killed Layla? Do you think he's guilty?"

He hesitated for a moment considering his response, then finally said, "Let me just say all the evidence points to him, yes."

Charles smiled and said, "Then why fuck up a good conviction with irrelevant bullshit that happened ten years ago, and which we both know has nothing to do with the facts of *this* case. Not disclosing that to them doesn't bother me in the least. By the way, you heard anything about Michael? I guess he took off and no one's seen him since."

"Okay, first things first. I won't say anything about the prior incident as you have requested, but this is on you, Charles. Any repercussions that come about by not disclosing the prior incident is all on you. In response to your question, no, I haven't heard a word about him. I just hope he's okay, and that the treatment he went through was beneficial. He needed it, and if it wasn't effective, I'm afraid you'll have your hands full this time."

"I'm done. I've done all I can for him. The rest is up to him. As concerns the case, that's fine. If there are any repercussions, I'll be glad to tell them it's my problem, not yours."

The conversation lasted only a few minutes longer, and Charles noticed it was almost time for court to reconvene. Clarice brought some files in for him to review later in the afternoon, once court had recessed for the day. As she left his office, he watched her walk through the door. For the first time since he hired her, he considered how much more effective she had become as a secretary. They were starting to work together, as a team, rather than remaining continually at odds with each other. She walked back in with additional files, and as she started to walk away, he said, "Clarice, I guess we've never talked much about our personal lives. I know you're not married, but are you involved with anyone?"

She stopped, turned around, and smiled as she said, "No, Mr. Whitmore, I'm not. Almost got there a few times, but just never worked out."

"First of all, call me Charles. You've been here long enough, there's no reason to be on a last-name basis. Now... Clarice, what are you doing after work? You have time to catch a little supper with me tonight? Maybe we can discuss a few matters involving the office and just get to know each other a little better. Whatta ya think?"

"Well, I guess I could do that. You want me to meet you somewhere after I close up the office?"

"Tell you what. I should get out of court around four thirty. Why don't I just walk back here? We can close up the office together, and I'll take you to a little restaurant that's quiet, where we can discuss business, or whatever might come up."

"I'll be ready."

As he stood, he thought about the trial and all that was going on around him. He was about to secure a conviction, one that would certainly catch the eye of the public and his boss. He had dismissed any further thoughts of helping his son—he had done all he could do to help him. In addition to both those positive issues, he was about to start a relationship with a young, good-looking woman. All in all, just a pretty darn good day—just a pretty good day, indeed.

40

Kris sat through the afternoon session, listening as Barrett's old girlfriends testify as to his character, followed by former clients who testified as to his trustworthiness and temperament. The witnesses did well, and Charles Whitmore did little to cross-examine any of them. The only point he continued to bring home was that they knew nothing about the facts of this case, which they didn't.

She spoke briefly to Barrett as she left the courtroom, then hurried back to the office to determine what had happened in her absence. After reviewing her messages, none of which were earth-shattering, she grabbed a Big Mac on the way home. Kris had intended on traveling back to the jail to visit with Barrett and review what she had found out from Maggie. Although not enough to be significant, the fact John was gone all night the night Layla was murdered just added one more log to her fire.

While she consumed her sandwich, she sat down on her couch with the second box of data from the Cassie Wilson murder in front of her and started going through what was left to review. After she had looked through a portion of what remained, she thought maybe she would just rest her eyes a moment.

If the morning sun hadn't awakened her, she would have slept until noon. She sat up and quickly looked at the time. She had forty-five minutes to shower, dress, and drive to the courthouse. John told her to be there an hour before everything started so they might once again review her testimony. She literally ran to the shower, throwing yesterday's clothes off as she did. Once dried off, she threw on a change of clothing, rushed her makeup, and ran to her car.

She arrived only ten minutes after they had planned, and John went through her testimony, hurriedly, one last time.

A half hour later, she walked confidently to the witness chair and took her seat waiting for Barrett's attorney to begin.

"Please state your name for the record."

"Kris Thompson."

John stood and smiled at her, as he made sure he entered into the record all the foundational issues necessary for her testimony to continue. Once completed, he said, "I would like to discuss your relationship with Barrett Armstrong, the defendant in this case. How do you know him?"

"Business associate."

"Are you related? Are you involved in any other manner other than through business?"

"No."

"How are you involved with him in the business world?"

"I've had contact with him concerning cases we have both worked."

"How long have you known him?"

"I'd say 'bout six months."

"Have you formed an opinion concerning his truthfulness?"

"Never ever heard him not tell the truth."

"What about his tendency to lose his temper or be violent?"

"He's never lost his temper around me. He's extremely even-tempered. And as concerns violence, that's a joke. There's not a violent bone in his body."

"Have you discussed your businesses with each other?"

"Yes. In fact, we were considering a partnership. Barrett's business, like mine, has grown significantly in the past few months, and I approached him concerning the formation of a partnership. We were in the middle of that discussion when Layla was murdered."

"Did you know the victim?"

"No."

"Did you know Barrett was involved with her?"

"Oh, yes, he had made that clear."

"How?"

"He was really in love with her, and it was obvious."

"Did he discuss her desire to end the relationship?"

"Yes. He discussed it and showed frustration with her failing to express a reason for ending it. He just couldn't understand what had happened. He wanted her to tell him what the problem was, but she wouldn't discuss it."

"What'd you notice concerning his attitude about the breakup?"

"He seemed fine about it, but he just wanted a reason. He was upset, but when he's upset, it involves him moping around and whining rather than losing his temper or discussing doing harm to someone. He would have never ever done what he is accused of in this case—that's just not the way he resolves his problems."

"Thank you, Ms. Thompson. Nothing further."

"Cross, Mr. Whitmore?"

"Yes, just a few questions. Now, ma'am, you weren't with him when Layla Adams was murdered, were you?"

"No."

"So, you, in fact, have no idea, other than what he tells you, where he was that night, do you?"

"No, but—"

"Your 'no' is enough. Please just answer the question asked. Were you here when the neighbor testified that Barrett grabbed the victim and shook her? Did you hear that testimony?"

"I did, but—"

"Your 'I did' will suffice. Was that an action that is contrary to what you would have expected from Mr. Armstrong?"

"Yes. I have never seen him react like that—to anything."

He smiled and said, "Well, then, maybe you just don't know him as well as you thought you did, Ms. Thompson. Nothing further."

John had no redirect, and Kris left the stand feeling she had done little to help the cause but knowing she had done all she could.

Court was in recess until Monday when Barrett would be first to testify and would also be the last of the defense witnesses. Once John had reviewed what the procedure would be after the defense rested, he left, leaving only the two of them.

"I've got something I've been dying to tell you. You know, I told you I was going to visit with Maggie?"

"Yes. Did you go? How is she? How are the kids?" He looked away. "You know, I really miss them. They've been an important part of my life, up until now anyway. I wish—"

"Hold it! Do you mind if I jump in here—I mean there's something that came out of our meeting we need to discuss."

He turned to look at her, smiled, and said, "Okay, okay, go on. What'd she have to say?"

"She told me he was gone all night the night Layla was murdered."

"All night?"

"Yup. She tried to reach him a couple of times, but finally just quit trying."

"Well, is that out of the ordinary for him? Is he gone all night on a regular basis?"

"She keeps a calendar. That's how she knew he was gone."

"Why'd she need the calendar?"

"Because she felt this divorce was inevitable, and that he might ask for custody. She wanted to keep track of the times he was gone part of or all of the night."

"Was he gone that much?"

"She said right before they separated, it was most every night. She knew there were other women involved, many other women, and she just couldn't take it anymore."

"So the fact he happened to be gone that night wasn't unusual. It just happened to be the night she was murdered—a coincidence. Is that what you're telling me?"

She sat back in her chair and considered his remark. "Do you want me to continue looking into this for you? I've about had enough."

"Well... yes... but..."

Her voice became elevated as she said, "It's part of the overall picture, Barrett. He was involved with the woman that was murdered ten years ago in an incident that mirrors this murder. He doesn't tell us about it. He's gone the night Layla's murdered—it's all fitting together. Can't you see it? Can't you put this all together like I can? He knows something, Barrett, or he was involved. You know, I think you're too much a part of the problem to look at it objectively. I'm not. I'm removed from it, and I'm telling you there's a significant issue here."

He smiled. "You know you're pretty damn cute when you get angry. Not that I'm trying to make you angry just to see how cute you can really be. But you really are kind of appealing when you're mad."

She leaned forward and said softly, "You know, sometimes you just really piss me off—you know that? Sometimes, you really get to me. I'm out of here."

She stood to leave. He grabbed her hand. "Wait a minute. Don't go. Stay a little longer."

She pulled free. "I'll see you Monday. I've got things to do, places to go, *intelligent, smart, reasonable* people to see. Don't call me. I'll call you."

As she walked away, he yelled, "Wait a minute! Don't leave upset. Wait, Kris."

Kris just kept walking. She didn't have time for his attitude. She needed to figure out a time she could meet with the manager of Andy's. Perhaps he could shed some light on John, how often he was in the bar, the women he brought in. Her time was growing short. They were ready for Barrett's testimony, and if she didn't come up with something significant quickly, she was afraid her time with him, with the man she was in love with, would be spent looking at each other through the bars of a prison and not across the sheets of their bed, as she had hoped.

41

Kris waited until eleven o'clock before she called Andy's. The phone rang a number of times, but once someone answered, she asked for the manager or the employee in charge of the bar on weekdays between the hours of 5:00 and 8:00 p.m. She was told that particular individual varied somewhat on a weekly basis, but Jack Beard was the one in charge most weeks. If he needed to be away, or was on vacation, someone else took over, but by and large, it was Jack in charge. Kris asked if he might be available later in the day and was told, if she came in around three o'clock, he would most likely be there. She could visit with him then if she wished. Kris indicated she would call around then and make sure he was there before she drove to the bar. She needed to finish reviewing the contents of the box of information concerning the first murder and started doing that as soon as she hung up. She finished at two thirty, finding nothing of significance, and waited another thirty minutes before she called back. Jack was there and was available if she could come now.

Twenty minutes later, she was seated at a small table waiting for him to join her. The bar was well lit, very comfortable, but small. It would hold no more than fifty to sixty people at any one time.

"You must be Kris."

She stood as he approached and said, "You must be Jack."

He smiled and extended his hand. Once they shook hands, they sat down opposite each other and he said, "You were a little vague concerning what type of information you were wanting from me. You aren't with a law enforcement agency?"

She continued to stare. He was more than handsome. He was beautiful. Tall, dark hair, blue eyes, good physique—at least physically he was as good as it gets.

"Kris. You okay?" He brought her back to reality in a hurry.

"Yes, yes, I'm fine. No, I'm a private investigator. Let me ask you, do you remember hearing about the murder of someone by the name of Layla Adams a few months ago?"

"Not really. I don't read the paper or listen to the news much. My hours are mostly spent here. This place takes all my time, either getting ready for tomorrow or taking care of today. Fill me in."

"Hey, Jack, I'm taking off," one of the employees yelled at him as he walked through the back-room door and headed toward their table.

"No problem, John. I'll see you later today."

As he reached the table, the new participant in the conversation leaned down and kissed him. Kris quickly concluded Jack was still damn good-looking, but clearly unavailable.

"Sorry about that. Lot's going on this time of day. We open at four o'clock."

"I understand. A woman by the name of Layla Adams was murdered a few months ago. I'm a good friend of the man that was charged with her murder. His trial is going on right now. I'm trying to come up with additional facts that might help exonerate him."

Jack smiled and said, "Waited a little too long, didn't you?"

"Just let it suffice to say, hopefully, it's not too late. Let me ask you..." She reached in her blouse pocket, pulled out a picture of John Weatherly and handed it to him.

"You know this guy?"

He took the picture and said, "John Weatherly? Sure. Everyone around here knows him. Regular customer. In here about two or three times a week."

"He normally come in alone?"

He placed the picture on the table and said, "Why?"

"Because I've been told, by his wife incidentally, that he frequently comes in here with a woman, not his wife. She also told me he brings in a new face about every week."

"She told you that?"

"Yes."

"Is this all confidential?"

"It is unless it's determined he did something wrong—like broke the law in some manner. Otherwise, I could care less who he runs with. Besides that, this place is a public place. *He* apparently didn't elect to keep anything a secret. Why should *you*?"

"Good point. Yes, he's brought women in here with him many times. I would say, on average, it's a different one about every other month. We don't ask. He doesn't explain. He's a good customer, and we keep it at that."

"Here. Take a look at the woman in this picture. Does she look familiar at all?"

He took the picture and reviewed it for five long seconds before he said, "She kind of looks familiar, but I'm just not sure. She might have been in here. Why?"

"That's Layla Adams. She's the woman that was murdered. Look carefully and think! Do you remember seeing her, and if you do, can you remember who she might have been with?"

He continued to stare at the picture before he finally said, "I don't know… I'm just not sure, but I do believe I've seen her. I'm just not that sure."

"Let me ask you… do you have a security system in house?"

He laid the picture down and said, "Sure."

"I realize this may be a lot to ask, but it's a matter of life and death and—"

"You want me to check and see if she shows up? Nope. Can't be done. Too many hours. It'll take too long. I can't commit anyone to that much time watching video."

"It wouldn't be watching all the footage you have. It would only be for a period of about three weeks and only Monday through Friday. It would be only those days prior to February 19 and only between the hours of, say, five o'clock to eight o'clock. If she doesn't appear during that timeframe, I would have no idea where to look."

He hesitated. Finally, he said, "No, I just can't do—"

"Look. We're desperate here. This is literally a matter of life and death. It's only about three hours a day, for fifteen days. Please, Jack, I'm begging you…"

He turned away deep in thought. After what seemed to Kris an eternity, he turned to look at her and said, "Okay, I'll call in someone to look over the video but only during those hours and only for those days. I'll get him in here tomorrow morning and give you a call one way or the other, hopefully sometime tomorrow afternoon. But if nothing shows up, I'm done. I'm not going to go any further."

She grabbed his hand, smiled, and said, "I'd give you a kiss if I thought it was a positive for you, but I'm not real sure that would be appreciated."

He laughed and said, "Thanks, but I'm good without it. Let's see what turns up. I'll give you a call tomorrow."

She waited all day but heard nothing. Kris knew it would take time looking over even that small amount of video, and she had wanted to see Barrett before the day was over. It was now too late to see him, but hopefully, the day wasn't a total loss—hopefully, the call from Jack might still come and, more importantly, would be productive.

Finally, as she ate an abbreviated supper and watched the evening news, her cell rang.

"Yes, hello, Jack?"

"Hi, Kris. You got some time to run down here? I think there's something you should see."

"Be right down."

She jumped up, couldn't find the remote, and decided not to take the time to look—she just left the TV on. She got in her vehicle and exceeded the speed limit all the way, reaching Andy's about twenty minutes later. The bar was closed, so she knocked on the door until he appeared.

"Come with me."

She followed him through the bar into the back room.

"Have a seat."

As both sat down in front of a monitor, he said, "This is footage of exactly two weeks prior to the nineteenth of February. Watch this."

Kris watched spellbound, as the front door of Andy's opened and Layla, followed by John, walked through the door, finding a small booth in the corner of the room.

"Oh, my, god."

Jack said, "Let me fast-forward. Now this is about thirty minutes later."

Clearly, the conversation was intensifying. Neither appeared happy. Finally, she started to move away from him. He tried to reach for her, but she got up and walked toward the door. John stood and walked after her, but after apparently rethinking his situation, just returned to the table.

Jack said, "We reviewed footage after that day, but they were never in here again after that."

"It appears to me they got into an argument of some kind. No wonder she never married. She apparently fought with every man she had any contact with. That's exactly what I was looking for." She turned toward Jack. "Thank you so much. Now, can you make me a copy of only that portion of the footage?"

"Here you go. Already did. I transferred it to this flash drive."

She stood. "Stand up."

He stood. "You ready to leave?"

She hugged him. "I don't care what sex you're interested in, you deserve that, and you're just gonna have to suck it up and take it."

He hugged her back as he laughed and said, "How 'bout a drink? You got a few minutes. I'm not quite ready to head home." One drink turned into a couple, and Kris finally arrived home around ten o'clock. She needed to be at the courthouse early tomorrow morning and discuss her discovery with Barrett.

As she lie in bed, thinking of the video, she could almost hear Barrett now. "It's not enough. It doesn't prove he killed her." He would, again, be correct. If she could just put Layla and John together that night. As she started to drift off, she, again, wondered if she there was a way she could prove they were together that night... that night... that...

42

Barrett walked slowly to the witness chair. He appeared guilty. He appeared defeated. He certainly didn't appear to be an innocent man that was anxious to tell his side of the tale.

Kris was sitting directly behind John, watching both men as John started with his direct examination of Barrett, an endeavor that would most likely either send Barrett to jail for the rest of his life… or save him.

Once the foundational requirements were completely satisfied and the basics of Barrett's background had been entered into the record, John said, "Tell us about your relationships with women, Mr. Armstrong. You had many serious relationships in your life?"

"No, not really." He was clearly a beaten man. His voice was so soft you could barely hear him speak, and his eyes, which many times told someone all they needed to know about him, appeared glazed, lifeless.

"Never been married?"

"No."

"Engaged, or ever consider getting engaged to someone you were dating?"

"Nope. Never gave it a thought, until Layla."

Kris had hoped to arrive early enough to have Barrett to herself before John arrived, but no such luck. He was there when she got there, and she certainly wasn't going to tell Barrett what she had found out with him there or even in the same building. She would get the opportunity; she just needed to be patient.

"Tell me about Layla. How did you meet?"

How could she determine whether John was with her that night? Her mind wandered to Layla's home, the street, the cul-de-sac where she lived. There was only one way in, and that was off Jackson Boulevard. There were no other streets that accessed her location. The area surrounding Layla's neighborhood was heavily wooded and contained a number of small streams. It would be nearly impossible for someone to traverse that area in the dark and even more difficult for someone like John, who was overweight and whose idea of "working out" was most likely getting out of bed in the morning.

"Did you go out with anyone other than her from the time you two started dating until she died?"

Jackson Boulevard was heavily traveled. There were no parking spaces on that street. John would have needed to drive to an area nearby, then walk in if he didn't want his car to be seen in front of her house.

"Tell us what happened at Reflect the last time the two of you were together."

"Well, it started out innocently enough. She was to meet me there and we were to have supper. She had never previously given me any indication there was a problem. In fact, I was going to ask her about the possibility of marriage—that's how much I cared for her. Not once in my life had I even considered the thought of marriage until I met her."

If John couldn't walk to her house using the overland route, he would have had no choice but to drive as close as he could get and then walk the rest of the way. He didn't dare park on Jackson—there were no parking spaces along the side of the roadway, and he couldn't have left his vehicle parked on the shoulder.

"Okay, I understand. Now, tell us about the incident at her home the day she was murdered."

As she continued to consider the layout of the area, she concluded he would have had no choice but to have parked on her street. He would have needed to make sure no one was watching—the late hour would most likely guarantee that—and then park his car on her street, walking the rest of the way to her home.

"I didn't shake her. I just *told* you that. I can say it again if you wish, but that witness wasn't telling the truth. I only put my hand on her shoulder, hoping it would calm her down."

Suddenly, as she continued to mull over her conclusion, she wondered if anyone on the street had a security system in their home. If they did, it most likely would have covered their front yard and driveway. John would have parked as far away from her home as he could have, and if someone on the street had a home security system, which had a view of their driveway and front yard, it just might have caught him parking, then walking toward Layla's home.

It was near the noon break. She didn't want to explain to both John and Barrett where she was going and lie about it, so she quietly stood, then walked out the courtroom door, without ever making eye contact with Barrett.

Most of the time, Kris left the courthouse about the same time John left. She was familiar with his car, at least with the color. It was late model, but with only the aid of an occasional streetlight along the street, she figured all that they might see is a car and, hopefully, John leaving it—particulars would not be visible.

She drove to Jackson Boulevard, then turned off Jackson onto Layla's street. She proceeded to the conclusion of the cul-de-sac and counted fifteen homes situated along her street. There was no way John was stupid enough to have parked in front of the house next door or even two away, so she discounted the two homes on either side of Layla's home.

Kris then drove back down to the commencement of the street off Jackson Boulevard, left her car, and walked to the first home. She knocked on the door.

It opened only a crack, with the brass door chain still visible, when an old but firm voice said, "Can I help you?"

"Hi, ma'am, my name is Kris Thompson. I'm a private investigator looking into the death of your neighbor down the street, Layla Adams. Do you have just a moment to visit?"

"They caught that guy. Now, move on. Good seeing you."

She started to close the door as Kris said, "No, no, please wait. They caught *a* guy. They didn't catch *the* guy. Please give me just a moment and I'll leave you be. Just hear me out. I'll stay right here. I don't need to come in."

The door stopped moving. Again, she peeked through the small opening and said, "Go on."

"Ma'am, they have the wrong man. I've been investigating this matter since she was murdered. All I'm trying to do is make sure the actual killer that did this is apprehended. You can help. You can help make sure that happens."

"I'm a little too old, honey, to be fucking around playing detective. I'm eighty-five years old. I wish I could help, but I just don't think I can. Now, move on. Good seeing you."

"Wait, wait, do you have a home security system in your home?"

Again, the door stopped moving, and again, she peaked around the edge. "I do. And it's catching every move you make."

"Okay, okay, what's your name?"

"Bertha Phillips. And I want you to know I have a dog that's real mean if you try to get in here."

"I don't wanna come in." She reached in her jacket pocket and pulled out a card. "First of all, here's my card explaining who I am. I need you to do me a favor. Do you know how to work the security system?"

She took the card. "Why, hell, yes. What the fuck you think I am, some dummy? Yes, I know how to work it."

Kris smiled. "Okay, here's what I'd like you to do. We feel the man that did this might have parked on this street the night of the murder and walked to her home. If one of the cameras in your system is aimed at your driveway, or front yard, it might have picked up his car, maybe even him, the night she was murdered. I would just ask you to look at your footage for that night and tell me if you see anything unusual. Can you do that for me?"

"What night was it?"

"The night of February 19. It would most likely been between the hours of 10:00 p.m. and 4:00 a.m. If you find something, just call the number. Now, ma'am, this is important... really important, and I need to know what you find as soon as possible."

"Okay, I understand. Now move on. Nice seeing you." She shut the door, and Kris heard her bolt it—double lock it—as she started to walk away.

For the next three hours, she knocked on every door on the street, other than those near Layla's house. There was no one available in six of the homes. She left a card in the door and asked them to call as soon as they could. Someone answered the door at two of the homes, but wouldn't speak to her, quickly slamming the door in her face, when she told them what she wanted. The remaining homes had someone present, but only three had security systems. She said the same thing to those people she said to Bertha Phillips. The occupants of those homes indicated they would review the footage and try to respond to her yet today if they found anything.

As she drove back to the courthouse, she was tired and discouraged. She heard not one word of encouragement from any of those homes where she stopped. She had probably spent the last three hours in vain, but it was the last straw. She had no idea how else she might establish John was near the house the night Layla was murdered.

Upon returning to the courthouse and taking her seat in the courtroom, she noticed Whitmore was in the middle of cross-examination. It was near 4:00 p.m., and the judge adjourned for the day. John told Barrett that he had matters that needed taken care of at the office and he would see him here, in the morning, when he figured Charles would end his cross. John indicated then he would get a chance on redirect, to clean up any loose ends that still might exist.

Kris told Barrett she would meet him in the conference room, and fifteen minutes later, they were sitting across the table from each other.

"I need to tell you something—something I uncovered about John."

"What's that?"

"John was seeing Layla."

"Oh, bullshit. You can't prove that."

"The hell I can't. I have a video that shows them together about two weeks before she was murdered."

216

Barrett sat back in his chair, trying to sort it all out, and finally said, "Well, that's a shock to me. I guess it don't mean he killed her, but I can't believe he was seeing her."

"Figured you'd say that."

"I wish we had something that ties him to the scene or in some way ties him into the murder."

"I'm working on that. But don't you think we have enough to at least get another attorney—to fire him and hire someone else?"

"Not going down that road. It's too late and we don't have enough to *prove* he did anything. Besides, I think he's doing a good job. Let me think on it tonight. You be here tomorrow?"

"Certainly."

He stood as did she. He put his arms around her, and said, "Jesus, Kris, I don't know what to do. I trusted him. What should I do?"

"I got something else going on right now, Barrett. Hopefully, I should hear something tonight. I'll let you know. But if this doesn't pan out, I just hope to hell you're right. I hope he's creating reasonable doubt."

Barrett leaned back, looked at her, then kissed her. "Don't know what I'd do without you. I really don't."

She smiled. "I finally fall in love, and not just a little, but head over heels, and it had to be with you."

He smiled, kissed her again, and she pulled away. Kris never turned around. He didn't need to see the tears streaming down her cheeks. He already had enough on his mind, and all of it, way more important than some stupid, emotional woman.

43

Kris Thompson sat in the front row of seats in the courtroom, trying to stay awake. It wasn't that the cross by Whitmore or the answers by Barrett weren't interesting, it was that she had been awake most of the night waiting for her cell to ring. She figured, because of the advanced age of many of the people on the block where Layla lived, they most likely all went to bed early. But she still couldn't sleep, hoping she was wrong— hoping that instead of sleeping, they had all labored over hour after hour of video, looking for that unknown man, driving his nondescript vehicle, and stopping on the street near Layla's home, on his mission to kill their neighbor. When she thought about it that way, she realized what a long shot her theory really was, but having come to that conclusion still didn't help her sleep.

"Mr. Armstrong, I'm confused. Why did you make that statement to law enforcement about someone hurting her 'if Layla treated them as she did you'? Obviously, you were hurt by the termination of your relationship. That statement makes it clear you were. Why are we to assume you didn't do something you figured someone else would have, if they were in your shoes?"

"It was a stupid statement. I don't know why I made it because I would never hurt anyone, ever—under those circumstances."

"So you might *hurt* someone, just not under *those* circumstances? Is that what you're saying? What type of circumstances *would* it take, Mr. Armstrong?"

"That's not what I meant."

218

John had told both of them before the start of the proceedings this morning that once Whitmore finished with his cross, he would be able to question Barrett one more time—redirect, he called it. But then the evidentiery portion of the trial was most likely over. From there on, it would simply be a matter of closing statements and instructions to the jury. Time was almost up. Her cell buzzed quietly in her slack's pocket. She pulled it out and took a quick glance. Immediately after, she slowly stood and walked out of the courtroom through the back door. The caller was Mrs. Phillips. She had terminated the call and left no message. Kris immediately returned the call.

"Mrs. Phillips, Kris Thompson. I see you called."

"Yes, I did. I wasn't gonna talk to that goddamn machine and leave a message. I figured you'd call back. I found something you need to look at. I have no idea if it's what you want, but you need to see it."

"I'll be right there. I'm at the courthouse now, but I'll be right there."

Mrs. Phillips terminated the call. Kris literally ran to her vehicle.

The trip to Bertha's house took forever. She often cursed at the increase in traffic throughout the city of Nashville, but today, she minced no words in describing to her vehicle how she felt about the difficult task of getting from point A to point B in the city.

Once she arrived, Mrs. Phillips greeted her, but only after a fourth prolonged knock. As she opened the door, she said, "You need to know, Kris, I'm not as quick as I used to be. Just hold on to your panties, if women your age still wear them. Sooner or later, I'll be along."

"Sorry, Mrs. Phillips. I'm just a little anxious I guess. Can you show me what you have?"

"Call me Bertha—everyone else does."

She turned and walked toward a computer screen sitting on a table along the far wall of her living room. The house appeared well kept. The walls were filled with pictures of people from another time, another era.

"Come with me. I've pulled a chair up for you to sit by me while I show you what I've found."

They walked, slowly, toward the two chairs in front of the darkened monitor. Once they arrived, she sat down and jiggled the mouse, activating the monitor.

"This is video of the night Layla was murdered. Now watch."

The time on the screen was 1:32 a.m. As the video started to play, a vehicle drove in front of Bertha's house, passed her driveway a few feet, and parked. The video was in black and white. Only the headlights of the vehicle, one street light, and a permanent low-voltage light over Bertha's garage provided any light in the area. The driver turned the engine off, shut off the lights, then exited the vehicle. As the individual walked up the street, there was no way anyone could identify who it was. It was simply too dark. Bertha stopped the video.

Kris said, "Well, that's interesting, but I'm not sure it's much help. Can't tell who it is. It could be anyone, including the man that's charged."

"Just hold on there, missy."

She hit the Fast-Forward button and the video leaped ahead. She finally stopped it at 3:05 a.m. Less than thirty seconds after she restarted the video, a figure walked back into the picture and walked straight to the vehicle. The individual started the engine and turned on the lights. As of yet, there was certainly nothing that would help identify the driver. The individual then backed up and turned into Bertha's driveway to turn around. When the individual backed up, in her driveway, in front of the garage, the light above Bertha's garage door shown directly upon the back of the vehicle. Kris took a deep breath. While you couldn't make out the driver, you could clearly make out the license plate and the number contained thereon. Bertha stopped the video.

"I might not have been able to get a face, but I got you a license plate number."

"Oh my god, you did, you did." She grabbed Bertha and hugged her. "Can you make a copy of that video?"

She reached over, grabbed a flash drive, and handed it to her. "Way, way ahead of you, Kris. By now, I figured you'd determined I ain't no goddamn dummy. Had it ready this morning about two thirty, but knowing people your age as I do, I didn't want to awaken you from your beauty sleep."

Kris hurriedly said her goodbyes to Bertha, explaining if the video was needed she would be in touch. She drove back to the court-house as quickly as traffic would allow. Upon finding a place to park, she walked to the area where John parked his vehicle. Officers of the court had their own parking lot, and John's car, a red Mercedes, would not be hard to locate. She had memorized the plate num-ber from the video, and as she approached John's vehicle, her heart skipped a beat. What if it wasn't his? What then? She prayed it would be the same.

She walked toward his vehicle and smiled. The numbers and letters were identical! It was John's car! He was there the night she was murdered! As she walked in the courtroom, she figured they would need to tie down the fact that he was in possession of the car that night. She didn't want him explaining that he had loaned it to someone else and didn't have it at the time Layla was murdered. That would need to be established before the video came into play.

She walked into a courtroom, which contained only a few spec-tators and a panel of jurors talking among themselves. She asked if they were in recess. The court attendant indicated the district attor-ney had just finished cross, so they took a short break before redirect.

Kris walked to the conference room she knew they were using and knocked. John opened it and she walked in.

"Morning, Kris. Barrett and I were just going through the last few questions I'm going to ask him before we rest. Have a seat."

As Kris sat down, she looked at Barrett, then turned toward John. "Could Barrett and I have just a few moments alone? Would that be okay, John?"

"Why?"

Kris looked at Barrett, smiled, then again turned toward John, and said, "Please. Just give us a few moments."

John looked at both of them, then he too started to smile. "Okay, I get it. Sure. I'll give you two a little time alone. We don't have long. I'll knock when the court's ready to reconvene."

Kris watched as John walked out, shutting the door behind him. "Kris what's going on?"

She took his hand and whispered, "Barrett, we got him."

"We got who, where?"

"Barrett, I have a video in my pocket that shows John's car parked on the street where Layla lived from about 1:00 a.m. until after 3:00 a.m. the night she was murdered."

He pulled his hand away and looked at her in disbelief. "You actually saw him... you saw him on her street that night?"

"No, I couldn't see his face. But I was able to see the plate on the car, and I just checked it against his plate. It's his car. There's no question about it. We'll have to tie down the fact that he had possession of it that night, but it's definitely his car. *We got him, Barrett, we got him.* We just have to figure out how the hell to finish this off."

They talked for as long as John gave them, trying to figure out their next step. He knocked on the door, and together they walked into the courtroom. Once Barrett was seated in the witness chair, the judge said, "Anything additional, Mr. Weatherly? Do you have any redirect?"

John stood. "Yes, Your Honor, just one more question. Mr. Armstrong, do you again confirm you were not involved in any way with Layla Adam's murder?"

"Yes."

"And more specifically, I would ask you one last time—*did you murder Layla Adams.*"

Barrett looked down and hesitated.

"*Did you murder Layla Armstrong, Barrett?* Please answer the question."

Barrett leaned forward in his chair, looked directly at him, and said, "No, John, I didn't. *But you did.*"

44

No one said a word, as everyone continued to stare at the witness. After a few uncomfortable seconds of silence, John smiled and said, "You must have misunderstood the question. Again, you had nothing to do with the murder of Layla Adams, correct?"

"Yes, that's correct. I couldn't have murdered her because you did."

This time the courtroom erupted in conversation. Every juror was talking to the one next to them, trying to make sure they heard and understood exactly what the witness just said. Charles, along with the judge, looked at John who just shrugged his shoulders in disbelief.

After a few seconds of total chaos, the judge rapped his gavel on the sounding block and said, "Quiet. I want it quiet in here right now." No one even looked at him, as they continued their conversation in the jury box. Again, he slammed down the gavel. "I said I want it quiet in here, *now*."

Slowly the room's level of volume decreased, and once it had reached the judge's satisfaction, he looked at Barrett and said, "Just answer the question asked, young man, no more, no less."

Barrett turned, looked at the judge, and said, "I already have. I couldn't have killed her because John did. Now, I want a continuance and I want a new attorney."

The judge looked at both attorneys who offered nothing whatsoever. He then turned to the witness and said, "Are you serious? Are you just trying to delay the trial, because if you are—?"

"Nope. I'm dead serious. I want a new attorney, and I want some additional time."

The judge just hung his head while everyone waited for some direction from him as to further proceedings. When he looked up, he turned to the jurors, and said, "Folks, we're at recess for a few minutes until we get this all sorted out. Don't leave the courtroom. We'll reconvene in a few minutes. I wanna see the attorneys, the court reporter, and the defendant in chambers, *now*."

The judge walked down from the bench and through the courtroom door. Each juror continued their unfinished conversation with the juror next to them, and the attorneys rose to walk back to chambers. Barrett left the stand and walked to where Kris was now standing, just beyond the short barrier separating the participants from the spectators.

"Whatta you want me to do, Barrett?"

He smiled and said, "I think we caused a little uproar, didn't we? Why don't you meet me in the conference room? I'll figure out what's going to happen from here on and meet you there."

"Okay."

She reached out and grabbed his hand. "Good luck."

Barrett smiled and said, "At least we got their attention. I'm not real sure where we go from here, but we at least raised a little hell."

"That we did."

The officer approached Barrett and said, "We better go on in. Everyone else is in there."

Barrett released her hand, and both he and the officer walked through the back door of the courtroom, into the judge's chambers.

The judge and both attorneys were huddled over the judge's desk, clearly discussing the inconvenient problem Barrett had just created. When he entered the room, the deputy nodded toward an empty chair, and Barrett took a seat. The whispers stopped, and all three involved in the conversation found their seats.

The judge looked at the court reporter and said, "I want you to take all of this down."

He turned to look at the defendant and said, "Now, Mr. Armstrong, what the hell are you doing here? What's this nonsense all about concerning John? You know, your performance in there a few minutes ago isn't going to stop these proceedings. We're almost finished, and you're not going to put off your conviction by using these kinds of tactics, do you understand me?"

"Yes, sir, I do. But I didn't commit this crime."

"Oh, I understand, Mr. Armstrong. *I get it*, and so does everyone else in the courtroom. We all understand you didn't do it. But blaming your attorney isn't going to get you anywhere. You think we're all a bunch of idiots? Now, we're going back in there and finish this up, do you understand?"

"Not really. I want this case continued until I have a chance to proceed with my defense. I haven't rested right? I mean, as I understand it, as long as I haven't rested, I can still present witnesses on my behalf. Am I correct or not?"

"Yes, Mr. Armstrong, you're correct. The defense hasn't rested, so your attorney may call witnesses on your behalf. Is that what you want John to do?"

"No. I told you he's the one that killed her. I do *not* want him as my attorney. I want someone else. I need to find a different attorney to help me."

The judge sat back in his chair, hesitated as he chose his words carefully, then said, "Look, Mr. Armstrong. This case is literally at an end. I'm not going to continue it. I'll allow you to terminate your attorney if you wish. That's your choice. But I'm not continuing this case while you find an attorney. I find your claim about John committing this crime absolutely ludicrous—simply a method for you to avoid the inevitable. If you have someone in mind that will step in and represent you, go call him. There are literally no witnesses left of which I am aware. This case is over, and I'm not going to start all over again a week, two weeks down the road because of your obvious attempt to delay the verdict. Do you understand?"

Barrett thought for a moment, considering his options, which appeared to be extremely limited, before he said, "Fine. I'll represent myself. I can do that, can't I? Can I represent myself? I know of no attorney that's going to step into this situation with no time to prepare. They would be a fool if they did."

"Sure. You can represent yourself if you wish. Lessor fools than you have represented themselves. Is that what you wish to do?"

"Yes. Doesn't sound to me like I have any other options. Do I have the right to serve subpoenas on people?"

"Yes."

"Would you mind if I had the rest of the day to prepare, at least to some extent, and to get my subpoenas issued?"

The judge considered his request and finally said, "I'll give you until tomorrow morning, and not a second longer. I'll call the public defender's office and have them send someone over to help you if you need help, but all he's going to do is sit there, unless there's an obvious issue you need to discuss with him. I'm not releasing you from jail to do this. You'll need to figure out how to get your witnesses subpoenaed while you're in jail."

"I understand. I have someone that can help me."

"Now, just to make sure I understand. You're going to not only establish reasonable doubt concerning your involvement in this murder, but you're also going to establish John did this. Is that the gist of it?"

"That's correct, Your Honor."

John said, "Barrett, what're you doing? How in God's name did you ever come to the conclusion I did this? I don't understand."

"You will. Believe me, you will."

"John, in light of this allegation, even though it's, in my opinion, completely without merit, I *do* want you in the courtroom while the trial is going on. The fact that I'm releasing you from any further responsibility concerning your representation of the defendant doesn't mean you can be somewhere else while this is going on. I want you here."

"Wouldn't miss this for the world, Judge. I'll be here."

"I'm going to go in and release the jurors for today. I'll tell them to be here at nine o'clock tomorrow morning. Mr. Armstrong, you better be ready to go, because you aren't getting another minute to prepare. Do you understand me?"

"Yes, Your Honor. I'll be as ready as I can be, even in light of the fact you are only giving me basically this afternoon to prepare. I'll be ready."

"If your assertions in court this morning, and in here, weren't so absolutely ridiculous, I would have given you more time. But you'll waste no more than half a day of this court's time to prepare. Now, Officer, take him to the courtroom or conference room wherever he wants to go for now. Then take him to jail and have him back here, seated and ready to proceed at nine o'clock tomorrow morning. We're done here."

Barrett had the officer take him to the conference room where Kris was waiting. As he sat down, Kris said, "Well, where are we?"

He smiled and said, "You got about twenty-four hours to save my life."

45

"I can do that. Not a problem. Don't worry one second. I'll come through." She put her arms around him, and whispered, "Who am I kidding? I have no fucking idea what I'm doing."

He leaned back as he continued to embrace her, smiled, and said, "Either do I. Not a clue. We're going to have to figure this out as we go along."

She pulled free from his embrace and said, as she walked out the door, "I'll be right back."

"Wait a minute. We need to get to work. We don't have any time to mess around."

She heard him, but didn't feel she had time to discuss where she was going or what she was doing. He would just have to wait.

She hurried down the steps and out the door, heading to the parking lot. She wanted to make sure she got there before John did. Once she arrived, she pulled out her cell, made sure she was close enough to read every letter, every number, then snapped a picture of his vehicle's license plate. She figured, before it was over, the plate would be a necessary element of the evidence. She wanted it available when it was needed rather than trying to locate the vehicle if John decided it was time to ditch it, one way or the other.

Kris opened the door to the conference room and found that the population contained within the room had doubled. John was now sitting, talking to his former client.

"What's going on?"

"Really, nothing. John wanted to talk about what the hell I was doing, and I just told him we weren't talking about anything. I suggested that the days of talking between us were over. He was still trying to convince me we should talk this through."

"Here, let me help. Get your ass out of here, and I mean right now."

Kris walked to the door and opened it, showing him the way out.

"As you wish." John smiled at her as he walked by, and Kris slammed the door after he walked through.

"Where'd you go?"

"I went down and took a picture of his license plate. I didn't wanna have to chase that car all over hell when we needed evidence concerning the number. Now, what's the deal? What's going on?"

"We're on our own. The judge gave us until tomorrow morning and that's it. He thinks this is all a joke and wouldn't continue it any further. He's also not appointing an attorney or giving me time to find one. He clearly thinks I'm guilty. It's all up to us, Kris. I have no idea what I'm doing, but we have no choice."

Kris said, "Okay, if that's the hand we've been dealt, so be it. The first thing I think we need to do is get out some subpoenas. Since we have no attorney, and you are acting as your own, I'm thinking you should walk down to the clerk's office and get the subpoenas we need. Why don't you go get about six and bring them back here? We can fill them out. I know how that works. The officer will probably go with you, but that's fine. I'll wait here until you return. By the way, have the officer check with the judge to make sure we can continue to work here the rest of the afternoon."

Barrett left, and as he did, Kris started making notes on a legal pad someone occupying the room before them had left behind. Barrett was gone about twenty minutes and returned with a handful of papers.

"The judge said we could stay here until four thirty, and then I was to be escorted back to the jail. I had the clerk issue six subpoenas. What now?"

"Let's get them made out for everyone to appear at either nine o'clock or one o'clock. I can watch out for them as they come in and direct them to a conference room until it's time for them to testify."

"Okay. Who should we start with?"

"You know, let's put my friend Tom Williams on first. You can ask him all about that prior murder ten years ago. Then maybe I can testify John never said a word about the prior incident, and even when confronted, he didn't think it was relevant. Then you could get on the stand and testify you couldn't have committed the first murder because you were out of the county and then introduce your passport into evidence."

"Okay. So, Tom, you, and me for tomorrow morning. What about John? The judge told him to be here anyway, but the subpoena will ensure he'll be here. Should he be next?"

"Yes, then John. Let's have him testify about his car and whether it's always in his possession, before we put Bertha on the stand to testify it was his car in her driveway. While he's on there, you can ask him about the prior incident and anything else you want about both crimes."

"That should fill up the morning. What about the afternoon?"

"Then let's call Maggie. She can testify he was gone that whole night. Right after her, let's call Jack Beard. He can testify they were seen in his bar together only shortly before her murder. Then after him, let's put Bertha on the stand. I don't know how she'll react to having to testify, but if she carries the persona I know, to the witness stand, she'll have no problem whatsoever."

"Sounds good. I've about got these filled out. What are you going to do with them?"

"I've got a good friend that I've dealt with many times who serves papers. I'll take them to him and tell him he has no choice, but to serve them all this afternoon."

She kissed him, and he said, "Good luck. I'll just wait here until I hear back from you."

She walked out the door, and as she did, she saw Chad McNamara walking toward her. "Kris, what's going on? I wanted to sit in on the morning's activities, but no one's in the courtroom."

"I don't have time to explain. We'll be in session again tomorrow morning. By the way, sometime you need to tell me why you're interested in this case."

He smiled. "Oh, I will, I will. I'll be back in the morning."

Kris waved goodbye as she walked away. She immediately drove to her friend's place of business. He was available, and once she told him what she needed, he walked out the front door with her, on his way to serve everyone as quickly as he could. She told him to contact her as soon as everyone was served.

Kris found a place to park and walked to the conference room with phone in hand.

"Is everyone served?"

Kris said, "Just got the subpoenas delivered to the process server. I'm going to call everyone and alert them as to what's going on. I have no doubt they will not resist testifying, but I just want to forewarn everyone what it's all about, especially Bertha—I don't want her shooting the server through the door, and if she thinks he might harm her, I'm afraid that's what she'll do."

Everyone had been contacted by Kris and been served by late afternoon. They all indicated they would be there and on time. The stage was set.

Kris told Barrett she was going home and wouldn't see him later that evening. She wanted to write down all the important points she felt he needed to cover with each witness and suggested he do the same. They agreed to meet at 8:00 a.m. in the conference room to compare notes and make final preparations.

As Kris drove home, she felt somewhat confident. For the first time since this all started, she felt they were finally headed in the right direction. Whether this direction would be the direction to Barrett's freedom was another story, but at least, for the first time since it all started, they appeared to be headed down the correct path.

46

Everyone was seated and ready to proceed. The judge had appointed Gary Comstock, from the public defender's office, to assist Barrett on a question-by-question basis, but nothing more. He had made it clear that Barrett wanted to represent himself, and that was exactly what was going to happen. Gary would be there to answer an occasional question, most likely concerning procedure, and nothing else.

Barrett had an opportunity to visit with the public defender in the conference room prior to the commencement of proceedings. But Barrett felt the visit, which lasted all of fifteen minutes, amounted to nothing more than a simple primer concerning the basics of courtroom 101. His advice would most likely amount to virtually no assistance at all once the battle in the courtroom began today.

The judge rapped his gavel, and everyone started to quiet down. Once the noise had reached an acceptable level, the judge said, "Ladies and gentlemen, we've had a change in circumstances that I need to explain.

"First of all, you see Mr. Weatherly sitting in the front row of the observer's seats rather than up here with Mr. Armstrong. The defendant has decided to represent himself during the remaining portion of this trial. I have asked Mr. Gary Comstock, attorney with the public defender's office, to sit near him and assist him if he needs help as the trial continues. Do not conclude anything from this. The defendant wants to represent himself, and he has the right to do so. The trial may not proceed quite as smoothly as it has, but we'll get through it. Now, the defendant hasn't finished presenting witnesses—he hasn't rested yet—so, Mr. Armstrong, if you're ready to call your first witness, please do so."

Barrett stood, turned to the rear of the courtroom, and in a voice anyone could have heard in Dallas, yelled, "The defense calls Tom Williams to the stand."

Tom stood and, with an obvious limp, walked slowly toward the front of the courtroom, where he was sworn in and seated. As he waited for the first question, the judge looked at Barrett and said, "You don't have to yell out for your witnesses, Mr. Armstrong. Just say their name and they can come forward. You're not calling up the cows. The courtroom is small, and we can all hear you if you use your quiet voice."

"Sure, I understand, Judge. Now can I just go ahead and ask him a question?"

"Yes, please proceed."

"Your name's Tom Williams, right?"

"Now just wait another minute, Mr. Armstrong. Ask him what his name is. Don't tell him and proceed in a like manner the rest of the trial. Don't tell the witness the answer when you ask him a question, do you understand?"

"I think so, Your Honor. Sorry."

He again addressed the witness. "Can you tell us your name?"

"There you go, Mr. Armstrong, that's the way to do it."

"Yes, I can. My name is Thomas Williams."

"And you're a cop, right?"

The judge looked down at Barrett and said, "Mr. Armstrong, what did you just learn not two minutes ago?"

"Darn it, Judge, darn it. Mr. Williams, what's your occupation?"

The judge nodded his approval and turned to the witness for his response.

"Well, for twenty years, I worked for the Nashville Police Department. As of last week, they felt they didn't need me any longer, and I was terminated. About five years ago, I was injured in the line of duty and had been relegated to office work only—mainly in records. They did me a favor letting me work there for that long, in light of my disability, so I couldn't hardly be upset when they finally terminated me."

"Why are you here today, Mr. Williams?"

"Because your friend, Kris Thompson, subpoenaed me."

"And why was that?"

"Because I worked in records and have information she wants made a part of the record in this case."

"What kind of information?"

"Information concerning a murder that was committed over ten years ago."

At that point, Charles stood and said, "Objection, Your Honor. This line of questioning is immaterial. What do we need to know about a murder that's over ten years old? Obviously, it has nothing to do what the facts of this case."

The judge looked at Charles and said, "How do we know? He hasn't even been allowed to tell us what facts he has or might have. Besides that, Mr. Whitmore, I allowed quite a bit of leeway when your witnesses testified, and I intend on doing the same with the defense. Now, keep still and let's find out what he knows. Proceed, Mr. Armstrong."

"Whose murder was it, Mr. Williams?"

"A young lady by the name of Cassie Wilson."

"What happened to her?"

"She was murdered in exactly the same manner Lyla Adams was."

"How do you know that?"

"I've seen the pictures entered into evidence in this case, and I've compared them to pictures that were taken in the *Wilson* case."

Barrett stood and picked up some papers sitting on the table in front of him. "Here, look at these, Mr. Williams, and tell me what you see."

"Wait a minute, Mr. Armstrong. Let's do it the right way. Hand them to the court reporter and ask her to mark them. Then let the witness identify the pictures by the numbers when they testify. Do you understand?"

"I do, Your Honor."

Barrett handed the pictures to the court reporter, who then marked each one as an exhibit. He handed them back to Barrett, who handed them to Tom as he said, "Now, Tom, can you tell us what these depict?"

"Sure. They're pictures of a murder scene concerning a murder that happened about ten years ago."

"Where did they come from?"

"From a file we have at the station, which involved that murder."

"Was the murder ever solved?"

"No."

"Was information concerning the crime scene ever released to the public?"

"No. That's not unusual in a crime of this nature. It was extremely graphic, and the department wanted to keep the details under wraps for investigative purposes."

"Have you had a chance to review the pictures of the crime scene involving Layla Adams?"

"Yes."

"What did you observe?"

"The scenes were identical. Everything was positioned in an identical manner."

"Your Honor, can I show these to the jury?"

"No. You can introduce them into the record now, but we'll wait and show them to the jury at the conclusion of the trial."

"I would move to introduce these pictures into the record then."

"Any objection, Mr. Whitmore?"

"May I see them?"

"Certainly."

Charles came forward and looked at each picture carefully, before looking up at the judge and saying, "Your Honor, I still don't see the relevancy, and would object on that basis."

"Well, I'm just starting to see the relevancy, Mr. Whitmore. Overruled. Proceed, Mr. Armstrong."

"During the course of that same investigation, did the department have a chance to interview people—people that might know something about the crime?"

"Sure. There were hundreds eventually interviewed, and all their statements were in our files."

"Was one of those people interviewed in this courtroom now?"

"Yes."

"Can you point him out?"

"Yes." He pointed toward the first row of observer's seats, as he said, "John Weatherly."

Barrett handed a paper to the court reporter and asked him to mark it. He then handed it to Tom and said, "Is this the... I mean, what is this?"

Tom looked at the exhibit and said, "That's the statement John gave at the time."

"Why was he asked to give a statement?"

"Because he was dating the girl that was murdered."

"And did John have an alibi?"

"Yes, he did. His alibi was provided by one Owen Lee, who said John was with him most of that night. As the investigation proceeded, the department decided they needed to further tie down John's alibi. But when they went to look for Mr. Lee, he had disappeared. To the best of my knowledge, he was never found."

"Was John what you might call a 'person of interest'?"

"Absolutely. At the time, the department felt he knew way more than he was telling us, but he had that friend, that Oren Lee, who told us he was with him all night. That's the one area they were pursuing when the witness disappeared."

"That's all I have, Your Honor." As he started to sit down, he said, "Wait. Just one more question. Did the medical examiner notice any sign of post-mortem sexual activity?"

"Matter of fact, he did. In fact, there was some talk at the time about that perhaps being the reason for the murder. A few of the officers thought that was actually what the murderer might have been after in the first place. But of course, nothing was ever proven along those lines. Sometimes that's how some of these guys get their kicks, you know. Pretty sad, but a fact."

"Each to their own I guess. Thank you, nothing further."

"Mr. Whitmore, cross?"

"Just a few questions, Judge." He stood as he said, "Now, Mr. Williams, do you have any information concerning *this* case—concerning the charges filed against Mr. Armstrong?"

"Well, no, but—"

"Stop. Thank you. The fact is, Mr. Armstrong could have committed that murder too, couldn't he—the one ten years ago?"

"Hell, I don't know."

"Answer the question. As far as you know, Barrett Armstrong *could* have killed this Cassie Wilson too, correct?"

"Well, I guess."

"Even if he hadn't, he might have found out, on his own, enough about the first killing, to have duplicated it the second time, correct?"

"That would have been nearly impossible. This file has been sealed for ten years and no one outside law enforcement has been allowed to review the contents."

"You allowed Ms. Thompson to review the contents, didn't you? Someone else might have allowed another individual to review the file too, as far as you know. Isn't that correct?"

"Highly unlikely."

"Maybe so, but the truth is, you know absolutely nothing about this case, do you?"

Tom sat forward in his chair, obviously considering his words carefully, and finally said, "I'll tell you one thing, Mr. Prosecutor— one thing I know for certain. I'm willing to stake my professional reputation on the fact that whoever killed Cassie Wilson also killed Layla Adams. I don't know nothin' 'bout this case, but I do know that—*of that much I am absolutely certain.*"

47

Tom stepped down. Barrett indicated there were a couple of issues he needed to discuss with both the judge and the prosecutor. The judge decided to take a break and answer those questions in chambers. The questions he had, involved taking the stand and making a statement concerning his location during the time period surrounding the murder of Cassie Wilson. He wasn't certain whether he should just make a statement or whether it should be handled in question-and-answer form.

The judge told Gary to ask him questions rather than Barrett making a statement. The judge felt Comstock could do that and still not be considered Barrett's attorney, a procedure to which Charles agreed. Once that had been resolved, the judge told them he needed to return a few telephone calls and would be along shortly. Barrett walked back in the courtroom and noticed Tom and Kris conversing near the back of the room.

"Thanks, Tom. You did a good job," Barrett whispered.

Kris smiled and said, "Of course, I didn't get to hear his testimony since I'm going to testify, but it sounds as if you handled yourself pretty well for being all washed up."

Tom said, "I meant what I testified to. Whoever committed that first crime committed the second one... no doubt in my mind."

"I didn't know you'd been terminated. Whatta you doing now?"

"Kris, I may have a bum leg, but I'm not dead. I'm looking for something to do. I'm not gonna sit on my ass all day at home watching reruns of *Little House on the Prairie*, I can tell you that. The only thing this leg stops me from doing is running."

"If I ever get out of jail, I'll keep you in mind. Never know when I may need extra help. Now, Kris, you ready to go. You're next."

As they discussed her testimony, the judge walked back through the courtroom door. Barrett walked forward to take his position at the defendant's table.

"Everyone ready to proceed? Mr. Armstrong, call your next witness."

"I would call Kris Thompson to the stand."

Kris walked forward, and as she did, the judge said, "Ms. Thompson, you're still under oath."

As she sat, Barrett said, "Now, ma'am, have you been in the conference rooms with me every time I've met with my attorney, John Weatherly?"

"There might have been a time or two I missed, but by and large, I've been there every time, yes."

"Were you the one that first brought up the issue of a prior identical murder ten years ago—the Cassie Wilson murder?"

"Yes. Until I brought it up, it hadn't been mentioned."

"Did you find that strange?"

"Yes, I did. It was identical to the Adams murder, and John was a party of interest, yet he never ever brought it up. Even when I asked him about it, he just brushed it off as being insignificant."

"Did you bring it up on a number of occasions?"

"Yes."

"Why?"

"Because, obviously, both murders could have been somehow connected, and the connection could be the murderer. But John just never showed any interest. He never even checked into it, or asked *me* to, which I would have, if asked."

"Did he ever mention he had made a statement or been involved with Cassie Wilson in any respect, even during small talk?"

"No. And believe me, that seemed really strange."

"Nothing else, Judge."

"Cross, Mr. Whitmore?"

"No."

"Next witness?"

"Me."

The judge said, "Come on up here. Remember, you're still under oath."

Once he was seated, Gary said, "Let's talk about your involvement in the *Cassie Wilson* case. Did you know her?"

"No. I remember now that John was dating her back then, but I hadn't had a chance to meet her before she was murdered."

"Did you learn about the specifics of the crime, the details, at any point in time from anyone?"

"No. The details weren't ever in the paper, and John never discussed it."

"There were statements made by Tom Williams concerning the specifics of the crime, and specifically concerning the fact that details were not released. Of course, he also testified, in his opinion, the same person committed both crimes. You heard him say that, correct?"

"I did, yes."

"Do you remember that time period?"

"Very well."

"Why?"

"Because I was enjoying one of the few trips I took with my parents before they were both killed in a car accident."

"Where were you when the Wilson murder occurred?"

"In Australia."

Barrett could hear the jurors whispering after his response, as Charles stood and said, "Objection. What proof do you have of that? That statement is self-serving and—"

"Sit down, Mr. Whitmore, you'll have your turn. The objection you made and the objections you were going to make concerning this issue are overruled. Now proceed, Mr. Comstock."

Gary smiled and said, "Thank you, Your Honor. Mr. Armstrong, what proof do you have you weren't in the country?"

"My passport." He pulled his passport from his shirt pocket and handed it to the court reporter.

Gary said, "Could you please mark that for us?"

Once it was marked and returned to the witness, he said, "What does that passport show, Mr. Armstrong?"

Barrett turned a few pages and said, "Right here. Right here." He pointed toward one of the pages, looked at the jury, and said, "It says right here I was gone for six weeks. The murder took place right smack dab in the middle of that time period."

"Judge, we would ask that the passport be introduced into the record."

Charles stood and said, "Can I see it?"

"Certainly," Judge Hanson responded.

Charles walked to the witness stand, took the passport, and reviewed it.

"No objection, Your Honor." Charles returned to his chair while the judge reviewed the passport. The judge laid the exhibit down and said nothing. Finally, Gary said, "Judge, might I continue?"

The judge looked down at Charles and said, "Mr. Whitmore, did you know about the Wilson murder?"

Charles stood and said, "No, not until now."

"No one told you about it? No one from the police department said anything to you about it?"

Charles looked down and, when he looked up at the judge, said, "This is really the first I've heard of any of this."

"You know, Mr. Whitmore, it seems strange to me no one has brought this up. The former cop, Tom Williams, testified he knew all about it, but you didn't? I'll discuss this issue with you later. Please continue, Mr. Comstock."

Gary continued to examine Barrett concerning other lesser issues involving his relationship with John and his knowledge of the prior murder for the next half hour, at which time the judge took a noon break.

Kris, Barrett, and Gary all walked across the hall to the conference room. Kris said she would run to get them some sandwiches for lunch and had no more than left the room, when someone knocked on the door. Barrett opened it and said, "Whatta ya want, John?"

"Can we talk for a moment?"

"No, now go."

"Just for the sake of our friendship over the years if nothing else—just give me a couple of minutes."

Barrett looked at him for a few seconds and then said, "Come on in. You got *two minutes*. Whatta ya want?"

John walked in clearly as confident, as self-assured as he was the day the trial started. He sat down and said, "Barrett, I have no idea what you're doing. I didn't kill Layla, and I sure as hell didn't kill Cassie. You've proven nothing so far, and I have no doubt you'll prove nothing the rest of the way. If I can get you some kind of plea, would you consider it?"

Barrett sat down and said, "A plea? To what?"

"Maybe manslaughter or something like that? I still might be able to help you here, but if you go much farther, I'm done. You're not going to ruin my reputation in that courtroom over this bullshit without me putting up a fight, and believe me, you don't want to be on the other side when I get pissed off."

"I'm not pleading to anything. Your time's up. Go get pissed off outside. I got some planning to do with an attorney that knows his ass from a hole in the ground." He stood and pointed toward the door. "Now, git."

John smiled that self-assured, cocky smile Barrett had seen so many times before, stood, and walked toward the door. "Don't make me take matters into my own hands over this stupid case, Barrett. Just don't go there."

Barrett walked to the door, opened up, and shoved John out with a push on his back. "Don't come back. We're done here!" He walked back to take his chair, when again there was a knock on the door. Barrett wheeled around and threw open the door as he said, "You rotten son of a bitch, what did I... Oh, hi, Charles. I thought you were John. Whatta ya need?"

"Can we talk?"

"Hell, I guess so. Come on in. Have a seat."

Charles walked in the room and took the chair John had just vacated.

"Barrett, I wonder if we should put a lid on this trial. Maybe I could offer you something that would end it all."

Barrett wondered if John and Charles had discussed the possibility of a plea before John ever walked in. This all seemed way to coincidental.

"Whatta ya wanna do, Charles?"

"How 'bout a plea to manslaughter or felony assault? We could clear this all up quickly, and you wouldn't need to do much time."

Again, Barrett stood and said, "Get out."

"You don't even wanna discuss it?"

Barrett walked to the door, opened it, and said, "Get out."

Charles stood, and as he walked through the door, he said, "Okay. Your funeral, not mine."

Barrett slammed the door behind him.

Gary said, "You're mighty popular all of a sudden."

A few minutes later, the door opened and Kris walked in with lunch. "Anything going on in here?"

Barrett said, "Absolutely nothing of any importance. Now, who testifies first this afternoon?"

48

Maggie Weatherly sat quietly, obviously nervous, but stoic and well under control. Once the noon break had ended, Barrett called her as the first witness of the afternoon session. As of yet, she hadn't said a word, but her appearance, her demeanor, already added a touch of class, of credibility, to the defendant's case.

Barrett started with the obvious. "Your name, please?"

"Maggie Weatherly."

"Your relationship to John Weatherly?"

"I'm his wife. Not for long, but for now, I'm his wife."

"How long have you and John been married?"

"A little over nine years."

"Apparently, things aren't going well?"

"No, we're separated, and the hearing terminating our marriage is in about a week."

"Children?"

"Yes. Two."

"Is custody an issue with the two of you?"

"No. I had anticipated it would be, but eventually, he didn't resist giving me full custody. He'll have the right of visitation, but that's it, and that's all he really wanted anyway."

"At one time, did you believe custody was going to be an issue?"

Charles stood. "Your Honor, what in the world does this woman's divorce and custody of her children have to do with this case. This is preposterous."

Barrett jumped up and said, "You know, if you'd let me do this, instead of jumping in all the time, it would be a hell of a lot—"

"Stop. Just stop, Mr. Armstrong. You keep still. I handle matters like this, not you. Mr. Whitmore, be seated. I'm sure we'll soon learn what he's trying to establish, and if it's all irrelevant, I'll have it stricken. Now sit down and listen like the rest of us. Mr. Armstrong, please continue."

"So believing custody might be a problem, what steps did you take to help avoid that issue?"

"John was gone many, many nights. Sometimes he was gone just during the evenings and sometimes all night. He always told me he was working, and I believed him, but after six or seven years of that, I became suspicious. I started having him followed and, subsequently, determined there were other women involved. Those nights weren't spent working. They were spent with other women."

"How often would that happen?"

"Often enough that I knew it would be impossible for me to just remember what nights he was gone without a record. So I started using a calendar to keep track of the nights he was gone, whether it was just until late in the evening or all night. I figured if I could show the court how much he was gone, his request for custody would go right out the window. That's exactly what happened. He was going to ask for full custody until he saw the calendar."

"Do you have that calendar with you?"

"Yes."

"Could you check it for the night of February 19, the night of the Layla Adams murder, and let me know what it reflects?"

Maggie flipped through the pages, until she came to the appropriate month, looked down the page, and finally said, "He was gone all night that night. I tried to call him a couple of times with no response. He didn't come home until morning."

"Did you ever try to track his phone and determine where he had been during any of those nights?"

"Yes, but his phone was always at the office. He never took it with him when he left the office at night."

"Nothing further."

"Cross, Mr. Whitmore?"

Charles thought for only a moment before he said, "Nothing, Your Honor."

Maggie walked down from the witness stand, and as she walked by Barrett, he looked up at her and said, "Thank you."

She smiled and walked on by, as the judge said, "Next witness, Mr. Armstrong."

"John Weatherly."

Every juror's head turned, in unison, toward the next witness. John stood and walked forward to be sworn. Once completed, he walked to the witness stand and sat down, appearing as calm and collected as an innocent man should appear.

"Could you state your name, please?"

"John Weatherly."

Barrett, with paper in hand, walked to the court reporter and said, "Could you mark this, please? That's the right way, correct, Judge?"

"I'll let you know if you do something the wrong way. You just keep moving forward unless I stop you."

"Yes, sir. Now, Mr. Weatherly, I'm handing you a piece of paper containing letters and numbers. Can you tell us what those are?"

He looked at the paper, then back at Barrett. "No. I have no idea."

"Could they be the letters and numbers on your vehicle license plate?"

He looked again. "Oh, I guess they are. I didn't think of that. Yes, that's my license plate number on my own car. Why?"

"Now, Mr. Weatherly, let Mr. Armstrong ask the questions here. You know the rules."

"I would like this to be admitted as an exhibit. Mr. Weatherly, what vehicle does that go with—I mean which vehicle is that on?"

"My Mercedes."

"Who drives that, only you or do you let others drive it when they need it for a special event?"

"No, not that one. I'm the only one that ever drives it. I didn't even let my wife drive it—never have."

Barrett sat down. He knew that would, most likely, be the only issue John admitted that would help the cause. Then again, that's all he called him for—to identify the number and that the vehicle was in his possession at all times. But he figured he would test the waters anyway—since he had the time. He wasn't going anywhere, but back to jail anyway.

"Did you know Cassie Wilson?"

"Yes."

"Did you kill her?"

John smiled and said, "No, Barrett, I didn't."

"You know Layla Adams?"

"Just through you—while you were dating her."

"You ever take her out—I mean like on a date?"

John looked away and said, "No, Barrett, I never dated her."

"Never took her out for say a drink or something like that?"

The witness looked at Barrett, no longer smiling, and said, "Absolutely not."

"You at her house the night she died?"

"Of course not."

"Where were you? Obviously, you weren't home that night."

"I have no idea. I didn't keep a calendar like Maggie did. But I assume I was at the office and just stayed there all night, like I have many times."

"Nothing further."

"Any questions, Mr. Whitmore?"

"Nothing, Your Honor."

The court had to discuss a few issues with the clerk of court concerning submission of the case to the jury and took an early noon break. Once Barrett and Kris were behind a closed conference room door, he took her in his arms and kissed her.

"Well, are we making any progress?" he asked her.

"I want another one of those."

"Which those?"

"Those what you just did."

He smiled and kissed her again. They both sat down. Kris said, "You did really good, Barrett. John didn't appear worried while he testified, but he will tomorrow morning, especially when Bertha testifies."

"When is she to be here?"

"Since the judge told us he had other business to attend to this afternoon, I told both Jack and her to be here by nine o'clock. She had someone that would drive her, or I would have gone and got her."

"I just hope everything comes into evidence the way it's supposed to. If it does, we can rest and let the jury decide." She took his hand. "You're doing great. I'm proud of you."

"Couldn't have done any of this without you. I told you that two months ago, and I'm still telling you that today."

She smiled. "I just hope it works… I just hope it all works."

49

Barrett had unfortunately endured a sleepless night. Not that commotion within the jail during the evenings was unusual but adding the noise to the mental anxiety he had concerning the following day, did not create an environment conducive to sleep.

Today, they would present testimony from both Jack and Bertha. Hopefully, it would be as dramatic as Kris predicted. Once both witnesses had concluded their testimony, the court would read what the judge termed "instructions" to the jury, there would be closing statements by both parties, and the jury would decide his fate.

The court had given him a copy of the instructions, and he had reviewed them with Gary, but even after the review, he didn't know much more than he did when he was initially handed the paperwork. They apparently were just written instructions the judge would hand to the jury, giving them some idea what they could and couldn't do in this particular case. The instruction that caught his eye was the one that said they *could* find him guilty of murder—that was the one he remembered as he tried to sleep. The others were all a blur.

Jack was just now sauntering to the witness stand. Good-looking, great physique, but Kris had lamented he was unavailable. She hoped her comments about Jack's physical appearance would elicit a reaction from Barrett, which it did. He smiled, as he remembered how he grabbed her, kissed her, and told her to remember she was involved… with him… for at least one more day.

Once he was sworn in and general information concerning the witness had been entered into the record, Barrett said, "So how long have you been the manager at Andy's?"

"Going on two years now."

"Whatta ya do?"

"I generally supervise—mostly the shift from around 4:00 p.m. until we close, which is in the neighborhood of midnight, give or take."

"Do you actually deal with the public or just remain in the background?"

Jack smiled and said, "I do whatever needs to be done, from waiting on tables to throwing out the trash. It's up to me to see that everything runs smoothly, and I do whatever needs to be done to accomplish that goal, each and every night."

Barrett stood, pointed toward John, and said, "I would ask you if you know the man seated in the front row of the observer's seats."

Jack looked toward John and said, "Absolutely. I know him well. It's John Weatherly. He's a great customer. Comes in frequently after work."

Judge Hanson said, "Let the record reflect the witness is identifying Attorney John Weatherly, now seated directly behind the council tables."

"How long has he been a good customer?"

"As long as I've been a manager. Well over two years."

"You say he's a good customer—when he comes in, does he normally come alone?"

"Very seldom."

"Who's normally with him?"

"Varies from day to day, month to month. It's always a woman, but the one he's with varies. Normally, he'll bring in the same one for a month or so, then it changes."

"Your Honor, I would like to show the video we now have from one of those nights. It's been marked as an exhibit and has already been viewed by you and by Mr. Whitmore. I would ask the court attendant to bring in the big-screen computer to show that video and ask the witness questions concerning same."

"Mr. Whitmore, you've had an opportunity to view the video. Do you have an objection? Since it's already been marked, please refer to the number of the exhibit if you do wish to object."

Charles, slowly turned and looked at John, who shrugged his shoulders, clearly uncertain as to what was to follow. He then turned, faced the court, and said, "No, Your Honor, I have no objection."

"Bring in the computer."

The court attendant disappeared for a few moments, and when he returned, he wheeled the cart with the computer to an area where all the major participants could see the screen, including the jury. John couldn't view the screen, so he stood and walked toward the defendant's council table to get a better view of what was about to be played.

The judge said, "Please turn it on. The witness may guide us through the video as it plays."

As the video began, Jack said, "This is about two weeks before the night of Layla Adams's death. As you can see, there's not a lot of activity that night. There, walking through the door is John, along with Layla Adams."

At that point, John walked behind the council table and back to his seat.

"They both walk to the table guided by one of the waiters, and both take a seat as you can see. Judge, if it's acceptable to you, if the court attendant could fast-forward the video a few minutes, it might speed this all up. Not much happens while they are sitting there."

"Go ahead."

The court attendant moved the video forward, until Layla started to stand. At that point, Jack said, "Slow it down to normal speed now. As you can see she walks away from the table by herself. He follows for a moment, then stops, turns, and walks back to his table. You can shut it off now. Nothing else happens that involves Layla."

Barrett said, "So John Weatherly and Layla Adams were together shortly before she was murdered, is that correct?"

"Yes, and that wasn't the only time they were there together either. There were other times before that when they were noticed by the help as being in the bar."

"So, if Mr. Weatherly said he never spent time with Layla Adams prior to her death, he would most likely, based on the video, not be telling the truth, correct?"

"That would be correct."

All eyes turned toward John, who sat, with his arms crossed, still staring at the witness, emotionless.

"Nothing further, Judge."

"Mr. Whitmore, any cross?"

"No, Your Honor, I guess not."

"Any objection to introducing the video into the record?"

Charles looked down for only a moment, before he slowly looked at the judge and said, "No, Your Honor."

The judge turned to the witness and said, "You're excused. Next witness."

"Your Honor, we would call Bertha Phillips."

Barrett nodded to Kris, who walked out the back door of the courtroom. When she returned, she had Bertha hanging on her arm, walking slowly, carefully, to the front of the courtroom. Once she arrived, she was directed to the witness chair, and everyone waited while she settled in. Barrett had the opportunity to visit with her before the day's proceedings commenced—to explain the procedure so nothing would take her by surprise when she took the stand.

Once seated, she took her time as she smoothed out her dress and settled in. Barrett then led her through all the basic information, which was necessary before she could continue to testify as concerned the specifics of her testimony.

Once that was completed, he said, "Now, Ms. Phillips, did you know Layla Adams?"

"Well, I knew who she was, but I didn't really know her."

"Where is your home in proximity to the Adams house?"

"I am the very first one on the block. She lived on down the street."

"And do you live alone?"

"I do. My husband died about ten years ago. I've had plenty of opportunities since then to have a man move in with me, but I always found most of them to be trite, blood-sucking bastards, so I never let any one of them move in." She turned to the judge, smiled, and said, "If you get my drift."

The jury broke out in laughter, continuing to laugh, until the judge slammed down his gavel.

"Moving on, Bertha, do you have a security system in your home?"

"Yes. Had it professionally installed. I tried to climb a ladder a few years ago, and it scared the living bejesus out of me. So I just had them do it."

"Does one of the cameras you had installed point toward the street and your driveway?"

"Yes, it does."

Barrett stood. "Judge, again, as was the situation with the prior witness, the court and Mr. Whitmore have had a chance to view the video from her security camera. It's been marked, and I would ask that the court attendant plug in the flash drive and play the video."

"Any objection, Mr. Whitmore?"

"No, Your Honor."

The court attendant started playing the video, and Mrs. Phillips said, "As you can see, it's dated the night of the murder of Layla Adams."

It all unfolded slowly—first, the car, then the figure in the night, and later, the vehicle backing into her driveway. As the car, while in the driveway, stopped for just a moment before it started moving forward to proceed back the way it initially came from, Barrett said, "Stop the video."

The court attendant did as he was told. Squarely in the middle of the screen was the vehicle and its license plate, easily readable to any one viewing it. Barrett stood, walked to the table containing exhibits, and picked up the paper containing John's license plate number. He handed it to Mrs. Phillips and said, "Now, Mrs. Phillips, could you read those series of numbers and letters, which are on the license plate for the vehicle of John Weatherly?"

Barrett watched the jury as she read the license plate number. The further she went, the nosier the jury became as each one discussed the connection involving the plate and the video.

Finally, the judge rapped his gavel and everyone stopped talking.

"Do you have anything more for Mrs. Phillips?"

"No, Your Honor."

"Mr. Whitmore?"

"Nothing."

"Mr. Whitmore, do you have an objection or can the video be introduced into the record?"

"No objection, Your Honor."

"So be it. You are excused, Mrs. Phillips. Thank you for your time."

She turned and looked at the judge and said, "Are you married?"

He smiled and said, "Actually, I'm not, Mrs. Phillips. Thank you for your time today."

"Maybe you and I could get together one of these days. Have a drink and just see where that takes us. Whatta ya think?"

Every member of the jury laughed, as did the judge, who then said, "Maybe so, Mrs. Phillips, but for right now, I'm just a little busy. Why don't you step down, and we can discuss that later?"

Barrett knew that could not have gone any better. Everything he needed to get into the record had been admitted. He wondered what was going through John's mind. The record had established time after time he had lied to the court and jury throughout most all of his testimony.

Barrett turned to see what his reaction to all of the testimony was, and when he did, he smiled. The fact that John Weatherly had left the courtroom would only further confirm his guilt. Barrett had no idea when he left. He didn't remember seeing him when Mrs. Phillips was testifying, but at the time, John was far from the subject of his attention. He was gone now, and that would certainly be a point he would discuss during his closing statement.

50

He sat with Kris, holding her hand, until the last possible minute. He didn't want to let her go, but when visiting hours were over, they were over. There was no appeal, no "do-over."

Later that night, as he lie in his bunk, he thought about the journey. What a horrific set of events. But the trip would all most likely come to a crashing halt tomorrow, one way or the other.

The judge had explained those remaining matters that yet needed to be completed. Once finished, the case would be submitted to the jury. He told them they would have all the time they needed to come to a verdict. Barrett just hoped their decision would come sooner rather than later. He had had about all the drama he could handle for one lifetime.

The next morning, Kris was already waiting for him in the conference room when he arrived. The deputy was late in transporting him today, and he knew it would only be a short time before they told him court was ready to convene.

He kissed Kris and held on, not wanting to let go of the security she offered. For the last few months, he had been living in a world of uncertainty. She offered the only security he could find.

"Well, this is it. I guess they first do this instruction thing with the jury, Whitmore and I sum everything up for them, and the jury does their thing." He turned to look out a window. "I hope when this is all over, looking out a window isn't the only way I have of looking at the rest of the world."

"Hey, come back here. Look at me." As he turned to look at her, she said, "Let's look at this in a positive manner. We submitted all the evidence we could find, which is now in the hands of that jury. They'll do what's right. Just be strong in your closing statement. Point out the issues we proved, which involve John, and we'll just let the chips fall."

There was a knock on the door. Both knew what that meant—it was time.

They were escorted across the hall to the courtroom, where the jury and judge were already waiting. As Barrett looked around the courtroom, he noticed John was still missing. Barrett figured he had most likely made it all the way to the Mexican border by now.

Once seated, the judge read the instructions to the jury. With the copy he had been given the day before, both Kris and he followed along as the judge read each instruction, line by line. They were mostly a never-ending guide of legal jargon setting forth those conclusions of law, which the jury could and couldn't reach during their deliberations. He had found one particular instruction that he wanted to use in his closing, hoping the jury would follow it closely.

Once the instructions had been read, the judge indicated to the jury that each party was ready to provide a closing statement summarizing their case and suggesting a conclusion.

The closing statement from Charles took over an hour. In it, he continued to insist Barrett was guilty. Barrett noticed many of the jurors wouldn't maintain eye contact with Charles, which he hoped was a factor in his favor.

Once his closing was completed, the judge looked at Barrett and said, "Your turn, son."

Barrett stood and took with him the one sheet of paper containing the instruction he wanted to emphasize. His hands shook. His voice quivered as he said, "Ladies and gentlemen of the jury. As you have observed in the last few days, I have tried to do the best I can to explain to you my position—my point of view concerning Layla's death. I obviously had no idea what I was doing. I'm not an attorney. I had to figure this all out as I went along.

"But I do know two things. First, I know I didn't do this—I didn't kill Layla. Now, in that respect, I know I didn't have an alibi for that night. But, on the other hand, is that really unusual—for someone to not always have an alibi for where they were at any particular time? I was home—alone. I didn't talk to anyone, which was understandable because of my circumstances at the time. I was upset over the breakup, but to kill someone just because they terminated a relationship with me, whether it was personal or business, would mean I would have potentially already killed, maybe, a thousand people."

He noticed a couple of the jurors smile.

"Hell, I haven't *ever* had a successful relationship with a woman. And the number of times I've had a client terminate my services and go somewhere else, I couldn't even begin to count. But I never killed anyone over it. To move from relationship to relationship, whether it's business or personal—well, that's just life, and to say I killed someone that terminated a relationship with me is ridiculous.

"Second, there's more to this trial than whether *I* did it. Witness after witness, from Jack Williams, through Bertha Phillips, told you who *did* kill Layla Adams. They told you how John had been with her when he had testified, under oath, he hadn't. They told you how he had dated her, which John said he hadn't. They testified as to how he had been a person of interest in an almost-identical murder ten years ago, which John never disclosed to anyone involved in these proceedings.

"I also need to point out he's gone from the courtroom. I realize the fact that he left the courtroom doesn't prove anything, but when you add it all up, I would ask you, what *does* that say about his guilt or innocence. You tell me—why didn't he stick around? The issues going on in this courtroom directly affected his credibility, his position as a lawyer. The testimony that was offered in this courtroom wasn't *important enough* for him to continue to remain and hear what was being said about him concerning his commission of two murders? If he wasn't involved, as serious as all this was, wouldn't you have thought he would have stuck around to defend himself? Where is he? Where'd he go? Why didn't he at least offer a response?"

Barrett stood quietly, hands on the banister separating him from the jury, head down, as he said, "And he was the best friend I ever had... for years... I would have, and did, trust him with my life."

He looked at the jury and held up that single piece of paper he had in his hands. "Folks, this is instruction number 21. You need to read it very carefully. You need to study it very closely. What it says is that if you have a reasonable doubt in your minds about my guilt, you must find me not guilty. It's pretty simple—*if you have doubt, you must find me not guilty.*

"I would suggest to you the evidence established reasonable doubt concerning my involvement, and not only that, it also established beyond a reasonable doubt who *did* commit the crime. I would ask you to find me not guilty and let the law go after the man that committed this crime. Thank you."

Barrett turned and walked back to his chair. The courtroom was filled with silence until the judge told the jury to take their set of instructions and follow the court attendant. The deputy took Barrett to the conference room, where Kris joined him.

She walked in, hugged him, and said, "You did great. You said all you needed to say, Barrett. There's nothing else we can do."

"At least we have a chance. Without you, I would be nowhere. You are an incredible person... and an incredible investigator. Thank you. Thank you for all you've done for me, and for all you've meant to me."

They had expected to wait, perhaps into next week. They had no idea a knock on the door would come an hour after the case had been submitted. The deputy took them back to the courtroom, where the judge and jury were already seated.

Once Barrett sat down, the judge said, "Mr. Foreman, it's my understanding you've reached a verdict."

One of the male members of the jury panel stood and said, "We have, Your Honor."

The judge said, "Give your verdict to the court attendant."

Barrett thought he was going to be sick. He looked for a waste basket in which he could throw up. He didn't think he could make it to the bathroom. His hands, his whole body was sweating.

The judge, once he had received the verdict from the court attendant, opened it, and read it first to himself, before he read it aloud.

"We the jury, in the entitled matter, find the defendant *not guilty.*"

Kris jumped up and yelled, "*Yes, yes, yes!*"

The judge looked at her and said, "Sit down before I throw you out of here."

Kris took her seat, as the judge looked at the jury and asked, "Is this the verdict of each and every member of the jury?"

"It is, Your Honor. But we also have a special request. We would ask the court to order law enforcement to start an investigation concerning John Weatherly and his involvement in this case. We would have convicted *him* if we could have."

"I understand. I wanna thank the members of the jury. You are now free to go."

As soon as the jury left the courtroom, the judge looked at Barrett and said, "Mr. Armstrong, you're a free man. You need to go back to the jail where you can pick up your personal items and you're done. By the way, you did a fine job representing yourself. And that lady friend of yours—I have a feeling she's the one you can thank."

"Thank you, Your Honor."

"By the way, Charles, I need to see you in chambers. I had a talk with Commander Wiley last night. He enlightened me concerning some of the issues in this case, and before I report your conduct to the bar association, I wanna hear your side, do you understand?"

Charles whispered, "I do, Judge."

Barrett walked toward Kris, and as he did, he noticed some movement in the back of the courtroom. It was Chad McNamara. Kris noticed him at the same time and said, "Hey, I wanna talk to you."

Chad smiled and said, "I'll meet you two outside the courthouse."

Kris turned her attention to Barrett, throwing her arms around his neck and kissing him. "Well, that's that, Mr. Armstrong. What now?"

"Let's get out of here, go have a beer, and discuss the rest of our lives."

"Show me the way!"

51

Hand in hand they walked out into the sunlight of a beautiful spring day— Not a cloud in the sky, not a breath of wind. Barrett stopped. Kris was ready to step off the top step of the steps leading downward from the courthouse to the street below, but his hesitation stopped her in her tracks.

She turned and said, "What're you doing? Why'd you stop?"

He said nothing.

She said, "Hey, wake up. What's going on? What're you doing?"

He let loose of her hand and sat down on the step, continuing to look at the city, at the sky, the trees, anything, everything.

She sat down beside him. "Quite a view, isn't it? I'm thinking it's a much-better view of life than you had behind bars for all that time."

"Freedom. Finally. Unbelievable. There were so many times I wondered whether I would ever take another breath as a free man." He continued to take it all in. "Of course, if it wasn't for you, I probably never would have. I owe you, in so many ways."

She pulled him close and kissed him. "You owe me nothing, Barrett. I just did what needed to be done. I couldn't live with myself knowing you were convicted of a crime you clearly never committed. Of course, that wasn't all there was to it—I was madly in love with you, and that helped fuel my fire."

She kissed him again, and as she did, he heard a familiar voice behind them say, "Hey, you two. Get a room. That type of activity is not allowed on the courthouse steps."

They both turned to see Chad McNamara, smiling and walking their way. "Can I sit with you a minute or is this only a party for two?"

Barrett said, "Not a party for two... yet. Maybe in a while, but right now we'd invite anyone to join us in our short celebration of freedom."

"Love to." He sat down beside Barrett.

After a few moments of silence, Kris leaned around Barrett and said, "Okay, it's time we know. You need to tell us why you were so interested in this case."

Chad smiled and said, "Well, it really wasn't about the case—it was about John."

"What about him?"

Chad thought for a moment then said, "I've only been married once. Didn't end well as both of you already know. When I could see it wasn't going to work, I employed John to handle the dissolution. I paid him a chunk of money as a retainer."

"That certainly isn't unusual. What's wrong with that? Isn't that normal?"

"He did nothing. He sat on his ass. Weeks, then months went by, and nothing happened, except he would send me monthly bills showing work he said he had done, and then asking for additional funds."

"Did you go see him, discuss it with him? Surely, he had an excuse."

Chad laughed. "He certainly did. Every time I went to see him, he had an excuse and then wanted more money. I finally fired him and retained a different attorney. The second attorney I retained had the marriage dissolved in a month. It wasn't as if custody was an issue. It wasn't as if we'd been married a long time and alimony was an issue. It was a six-month mistake. She got a settlement and no alimony. It wasn't complicated."

"What about John? What happened with him?"

"I told him I wasn't happy and I wanted at least some of my money back. I went to see him three separate times. The last visit did not end well. I told him I would report him to the bar, and he laughed about that. I never ended up with a penny from him."

"Did you report him?"

"No, I've never believed in a system of attorneys policing themselves. That's why I never sued him either. Once again, you have the legal system policing their own."

"So is that how it ended?"

"No. Now, please understand I'm not bragging. I'm just telling you the tale—you asked—I'm explaining, so don't take this wrong. I'm worth millions. I didn't get this way having people stealing from me the way he did. That doesn't sit well with me. I just started keeping track of him figuring at some point I might have an opportunity to even the score. When I saw you two were involved with him, I started following the trial."

"Were you here every day? Barrett and I became somewhat involved after we fired John, and I didn't have much time to look around to see who was and wasn't in the courtroom."

"No. But I was there enough times to notice something wasn't right. You two, by the way, make a hell of a good partnership."

Barrett smiled and said, "Maybe this isn't a good time for this, but since you've mentioned you're worth quite a bit of money, would you consider a little loan? We're going into partnership together, and we've fallen onto some hard times."

"Absolutely. We can talk about that later today, or tomorrow—whenever you wish."

Kris said, "I think we have plans for later today, but I'll give you a call tomorrow, and maybe we can discuss it over a cup of coffee."

As Kris and Chad continued to discuss her plans for the future, Barrett watched the people as they walked up and down the courthouse steps. They were all so busy, so much to do. Thank God he would again get to be a part of what he had missed so much. He would never complain about his life again—no matter the problem, the issues, the pressure. Nothing could be worse than what he had been through.

As he looked out over the concrete approach beyond the steps, he noticed traveling in their direction, a familiar walk, a familiar figure. He shaded his eyes from the sun to get a better view.

While he still hadn't yet reached the steps, Barrett could clearly determine it was John, and he was headed in their direction.

"Well, this should be an interesting confrontation."

As Kris said, "What are you talking about?" Barrett noticed John pull his hand out of his suit coat pocket. The sunlight reflected off something of a metallic nature. He was pulling out a pistol!

Before he could say a word, he heard John yell, "You're not going to ruin my life, my career, you son of a bitch."

He started firing at them, and Barrett could hear the bullets as they ricocheted off the courthouse steps. *It was clear they were all three in terrible danger.* The first thing he thought of was to try to protect Kris. Barrett leaned toward her to shield her from the bullets, and as he did, he felt an incredible pain in his right shoulder where one of the shots found their mark.

As he fell over, he noticed movement from his right. When he looked up, he saw Chad McNamara, pistol in hand, standing beside him, but starting to walk directly toward John, firing shot after shot. Barrett turned his attention to John, just in time to see him drop his pistol and fall to his knees grabbing his midsection. Chad continued to fire until John fell backward, the result of a carefully placed bullet, which removed a small portion of John's head. Barrett couldn't move.

Kris said, "Hey, you okay?"

"I don't think so. I think I took one for the partnership."

He heard her giggle and say, "Yeah, right." As he moved away from her, she was able to see the blood covering his shirt near his shoulder. "Oh my god, you did. Help!" she screamed. "We need help."

Chad walked back up the steps, saw Barrett's wound, laid his pistol down, and said, "You okay?"

"Yeah, I'm fine. He got me, but it's a hell of a long way from my heart. Thank God you were carrying that thing."

"I carry it everywhere I go."

A guard was running in their direction. "Don't any of you move. Don't touch that pistol, mister."

Barrett said, "Well, I guess that takes care of collecting your money."

"I most likely wasn't going to get it from him anyway. Just one less thing to worry about. Now, let's wrap something around that wound and wait for an ambulance."

Right before Barrett passed out, he couldn't help but smile. *First day out of jail and someone* shoots *me,* he thought. *Whatever—better shot while I'm free, then live one more minute in that...*

52

One month later
The Offices of Armstrong and Thompson, Private Investigations

"Well, again, Gary, thanks for all your help. I'll think about what you said, but I really like what I do. I'm not sure I'm ready to throw it all out the window and take that much time out of my life to follow a new and extremely uncertain pathway. But I'll give it some thought." He terminated the call just as Kris walked in his office.

She leaned down and kissed him as she said, "How's the shoulder this morning? You left so early I never even heard the door open."

"I know. You were sawin' logs pretty good when I walked out the door. It's better. Still sore. I'll be glad to get this sling off next week. It's damn difficult to do much of anything physical with it hangin' round my neck."

Kris sat down, smiled, and said, "Yeah, I can tell it's affecting your style. But as active as you were with me last night, I'm about half afraid of how active you might become once you regain the use of that other arm."

"Whatever. You really acted afraid. You almost killed me. I can see right now we're gonna have to set some boundaries in bed. You're way more woman than I'm used to."

She laughed. "I figure over the next fifty years, we'll get it all figured out. I'm not in the least bit worried. So who was on the phone?"

"Gary Comstock—you know—that guy from the public defender's office. He told me how good a job I did during the trial.

He told me I should go to law school. He said I have a knack for the courtroom."

"You're kidding. That was certainly nice of him, but would you even consider doing that? You know, I can run this place while you go, if it's what you wanna do."

"I think I'll maybe get a little further down the road before I make that decision. It was because of a lawyer that I ended up in jail. It was because of another lawyer I wasn't given a fair trial, and *then* a lawyer shot me. I think I'll get that bad taste out of my mouth first before I try to make an objective, unbiased decision as to whether to become one of them."

Kris said, "Probably a good idea. By the way, one of my friends called and said she had heard Charles Whitmore might be disbarred. She knows the family, and I guess there are all kinds of rumors going around about him. You heard his son committed suicide, didn't you?"

"Yes. Charles shouldn't be in the practice at all in my opinion."

"Sounds like the bar association agrees. By the way, I think I'll get that Donaldson case ready. They're, going to have me testify and the trail is next Monday. Today I'm going to take time to review everything I have on it. What are you working on?"

Barrett said, "Until the arm heals, as you know, there's not a lot of physical work I can do, so I think I'll just stick around today and take care of appointments either you or I need to handle. If you're working on Donaldson, I'll handle the appointments. It's way too soon to have Tom handle any of them. We need to let him get his feet on the ground around here before he starts seeing people."

"I hear someone mention my name?" Tom Williams walked in Barrett's office door.

"Morning, Tom. Yes, we were just discussing you. Everything going okay? Your new office going to work all right for you?"

"Absolutely. I just wanted to thank both of you again for giving me a chance here. I'll try and do a good job for you."

"You're going to work out just fine, Let me know if you need anything. I'll be here all day."

As he left the room, Kris said, "Have you ever seen so much business? Are we gonna need to hire someone else to help us?"

"No, at least not now. I like it just the way it is, and I think once I'm able to get going again, we'll have enough time. If we don't, we'll just start turning people away. I like it with only the two of us and a couple of office staff. I like it just the way it is."

"You know, we're going to have to work the marriage into all this to—find time to plan it and get ready. You're going to need to help me with that, Barrett Armstrong. I am *not* going to do it all on my own."

"Oh, I will, but just keep in mind, I got this bum arm. It could affect—"

"That's bullshit and you know it."

Barrett smiled. "I'll do whatever you need me to do. You sure we need to do a church wedding? Be a lot easier just to go to a Justice of the Peace. Cheaper, simpler, less people involved."

"Listen, I don't plan on getting married again. This is it for me, buddy, and I'm going the religious route. I figure I'm going to need all the help I can get to keep you in line."

"You know, if John hadn't tried to get me convicted and sentenced to prison for the rest of my life, and hadn't killed who knows how many people, and hadn't shot me, and then got himself shot to death, he would have been my best man."

"Obviously, you made a huge mistake in character assessment when it came to him. Who are you thinking you might ask?"

"I've been thinkin about asking Chad. Since the trial, we've all become pretty close. Whatta you think?"

"Good idea. I really like him, and he did save our lives."

"Where're we at concerning that loan with him?"

"We just need to sign the paperwork. Whoa, is he ever giving us a good deal. Low interest rate and plenty of time to get ourselves on our feet financially before we need to start paying it back. He's a good guy. Now, there's one instance where you correctly assessed character. See. It's not that hard."

Barrett smiled. "By the way, have you reached everyone that testified for us to tell them thanks for what they did?"

"Yes. I was able to reach Jack yesterday. He was the last one. He told us to stop in for a drink when we had time, and he would give us one on the house."

"Did you get a chance to talk to Maggie?"

"Yes. She said to tell you thank you. She said you helped resolve a problem that most likely would have haunted her for the rest of her life. She said John would have never quit being that same asshole for as long as he was alive."

"She was probably correct about that. What about Bertha? You talked to her, didn't you?"

"C'mon, Barrett, you know I did. You didn't forget we're taking her out for dinner tonight, did you?"

"No, of course not. Well, maybe for just a few minutes I did. Okay, I did. What time do we pick her up?"

"About six. And she said she wanted to show us a number of pictures of her family once we take her home."

"You're kidding me!"

"Barrett, Barrett, just relax. And when you do, you think about how much you owe her. It won't hurt you to spend a little time with her. If she hadn't taken the time to view the security videos for that night, you and I wouldn't be sitting here talking right now. You'd be in prison, and I'd be alone. We owe her big-time."

She stood. "I need to get to work. I'll see you later this morning."

He said, "Come here."

She smiled and walked behind his desk, leaned down and kissed him.

"I owe you… everything."

"You owe me nothing. I just did what I thought was the right thing to do."

"I don't know what I would have ever done without you."

She walked away, and as she did, she said, "By the way, while I'm thinking about it, be sure and contact Chad. We need to make sure he's available the day of our wedding."

Epilogue

He took a quick look at the clock—2:15 a.m. He had plenty of time before sunrise. He sat naked, in the only chair she had in her bedroom.

Chad McNamara looked around the room, surveying his accomplishments. He had done quite a lot in a short time and had done it well, if he did say so himself. He stood and started humming a verse of one of his favorite oldies—"You Are My Sunshine"—as he danced around the two sides of the bed that weren't pushed up against a wall.

As he softly hummed, he would take three steps and turn, take three steps and turn. After he had finished the verse, he stood at the bottom of the bed to survey the evening's "project."

Carol, he was just pretty sure that was her name, had been so easy to seduce. His charm, his good looks, and plenty of money was all it took, and they were off to her small home in Hendersonville at the stroke of midnight.

She was so… wait. Something wasn't quite right. He folded his arms. Nope, something wasn't the same. What was it? Oh hell yes, he thought, it's the hands. She was completely naked. He had propped her up against the headboard, spread her legs, and had reintroduced the knife into the same wound, shoving it in as far as it would go. But he hadn't placed her hands on the knife, as if she had done it to herself, nor was her face looking downward at those same hands.

With his hands encased in latex gloves, he gently reached over and tilted her head so she was looking directly at the knife. He then reached for both hands, one at a time, and molded her fingers around the handle of the knife. Once finished, Chad stood back, hands on hips, to survey his new work of art. It was perfect. It needed to be. She needed to be exactly like the others that had gone before her.

Again, he sat down in the chair he had previously covered with a thin plastic sheet, to consider what he had learned tonight. He had all the money he ever needed. Excitement, after all he had done in his life, didn't come easy. Chad thought perhaps doing this, having sex with a dead body, might generate that extra thrill he still craved. But clearly, after tonight, he concluded he sure as hell wasn't a necrophiliac. The issue of control just wasn't all it was kicked up to be. He could buy control. He would need to seek his thrills in some other manner from now on. This just didn't do it for him.

Certainly, law enforcement would be confused. They all figured John Weatherly had murdered Layla, and of course, *he had*. But with another crime consisting of an identical set of facts, and with John dead, no one, including law enforcement, would have any idea what the hell was going on.

Kris had told him earlier in the week they were taking Bertha Phillips out for supper tonight and expected it to be a long evening— she was taking them to her home to look through old pictures. He figured that would provide enough of an alibi for both of them to remain out of consideration concerning tonight's murder. He certainly didn't want to endanger his newfound friends, which is why he picked tonight for this new endeavor.

Chad started to put his clothes on. It was time to move on. He had already wrapped all the bedsheets and comforter in plastic, and the bundle waited for him in the living room. Once he finished dressing, he again wiped everything down, making sure there was nothing left in the room that would tie him to tonight's project.

As he started to walk out the bedroom door, he smiled and took one last look at Carol as he said, "Thanks. You served your purpose well. Your life wasn't in vain. Just remember that. You have definitely convinced me I'm not a necrophiliac, and that's certainly worth something, at least to me. Now I can move on."

He turned off all the lights and walked out the front door. As he did, he whispered, "I need to remember to call Barrett today. He left a message about me being his best man. I need to tell him I'd be glad to. I've never done that before. Should be fun." Chad smiled. "Another first for me."

He softly hummed a few bars of "You Are My Sunshine" as he slowly walked off into the darkness.

About the Author

J. B. Millhollin has published a number of mystery/legal thrillers, with *Redirect* his most recent. He currently resides near Nashville and continues to use the city as a background for many of his stories. If you enjoy his novels, you should remain in touch through Facebook, Twitter, and his website. JB has many new tales to tell, and his plans are to continue publishing as long as his fans continue buying his books.

Novels written by J. B. Millhollin

Brakus (Volume 1 of a three-volume series)
Everything He Touched (Volume 2 of a three-volume series)
With Nothing To Lose (Volume 3 of a three-volume series)
An Absence of Ethics
Out of Reach
Forever Bound
Coming soon: *Plausible Deception*
For further information concerning any of his novels,
visit www.jbmillhollin.com.

CPSIA information can be obtained
at www.ICGtesting.com
Printed in the USA
LVHW111908210119
604681LV00003B/309/P